BOBBY DOES DALLAS
Hill Country Heart 3

BY

SABLE HUNTER

This is a work of fiction. Names, characters, places and incidents are either the product of the author's imagination or used fictitiously, and any resemblance to actual persons, living or dead, business establishments, events or locales is entirely coincidental.

Bobby Does Dallas
All rights reserved.
Copyright 2012 © SABLE HUNTER

Published by Sable Hunter
www.sablehunter.com

Cover by JRA Stevens

ALL RIGHTS RESERVED. This book contains material protected under International and Federal Copyright Laws and Treaties. Any unauthorized reprint or use of this material is prohibited. No part of this book may be reproduced or transmitted in any form or by any means, electronic or mechanical, including photocopying, recording, or by any information storage and retrieval system without express written permission from the author / publisher.

Dear Reader,

BOBBY DOES DALLAS ties together the entire Hill Country Heart Series. It goes back to the beginning, even before Unchained Melody takes places and goes through the same time frame as Unchained Melody and Scarlet Fever. You will get a second look, from a different angle, at Ethan and Alex's story and find out some details that you did not know. So bear that in mind—Bobby's story takes us from before the weddings all the way to Dallas. As you read about how Bobby Does Dallas—if you're like me—you'd just wish Bobby would do you.

Ha! That belongs on a T-Shirt!
Sable Hunter

Sable Hunter

Chapter One

"Next up is Bobby Stewart," the announcer's voice came booming over the loud speaker. The raucous rodeo crowd immediately grew silent. Most of them had come just to see this particular cowboy ride. He was a favorite on the circuit. "Stewart's in first place, ladies and gentleman. This young man is a senior at the University of Texas where he plays football for the Longhorns. Bobby is a big man to be a bull rider. At six-foot-four inches and two-hundred-fifty pounds, Bobby makes the bulls work for their living."

The women in the audience were on their feet, all of them wanted to catch a glimpse of the handsome cowboy. The unseen man in the booth continued his introduction of Bobby's ride. "We've got a record crowd tonight, folks. Everyone is eager to see if young Stewart can be the rider to master the brutal Rock Star. No cowboy has managed to successfully stay on this monster bull for the full eight seconds. He's put seven men in the hospital, the rest of them on their keister. Rock Star hasn't been conquered in eight years."

Bobby sat on the hulking, gray Brahman bull listening to the broadcaster build up the crowd's interest in his ride. Everyone knew this was for big money. Many people wanted him to succeed and there were a few that would love to watch him fall flat on his ass. He, for one, voted for coming out of this alive. Squeezing his legs around the heaving sides of the bull, he knew that the moment the chute opened, the angry animal would become a tornado of deadly hooves and horns.

The crowd was holding their breath. Bobby did his normal ritual, whispering the familiar scripture from memory. "Fear not, for I am with you, be not dismayed, for I am your God, I will strengthen you, I will help you, I will uphold you with my righteous right hand." As the last word left his lips, the chute opened and Bobby's world went into overdrive. Rock Star was two thousand pounds of explosive energy. With vicious, violent twists the huge bull launched himself into the air and slung his entire body weight first to the left and then to the right. Bobby instinctively moved with the bull, knowing that the only way he would stay on this perfect storm would be if he didn't fight the formidable force of nature. Letting his mind become perfectly still, Bobby became an extension of the bull's body. He didn't fight the pitch and roll of the vicious animal, but anticipated the direction that Rock Star would lunge and went with it. It was wild—eight seconds of soul-jarring, body-wrenching, mind-blowing adrenaline rush. One of the reasons that he did this death-defying, dangerous sport was simple. After riding a demon like Rock Star, Big 12 football was a cakewalk.

No matter what anyone said, eight seconds was an eternity. Eight seconds could mean the difference between a winning ride and a harsh collision with the hard ground of the arena. For some, eight seconds could be the difference between life and death. A good friend of Bobby's had been stomped to death by a bull in July. Tonight, he rode for Shaun.

When the loud air horn sounded, Bobby could hear the screams of the fans. Not one who chose to wear a helmet, he waved his trade-mark black Stetson in the air. Mixed in with the roar of the crowd, he could hear the squeals of the buckle bunnies. As he bailed off Rock Star and dodged the razor sharp set of horns that swiped out at him, he thanked the good Lord for the bull fighters that put their lives on the line distracting the enraged beast.

As Rock Star danced off to one side, Bobby jumped up on the fence and shook hands, receiving numerous pats on the back from a dozen other riders who knew the true value of his accomplishment. It wasn't just a big pay-off, it was the matter of conquering your demons—being able to *cowboy up* and do what very few men could do, face his fear and live his dream.

A cloud of loud perfume announced that he was about to be awarded a whole different kind of prize. "Hey there, cowboy!" Mary Alice Solice threw her arms around his neck and plastered her ample breasts to his chest. "It's my turn to take a ride. Are you up for it?" She boldly rubbed his crotch with her flat little belly getting exactly the kind of reaction she craved. Bobby hardened instantly. After all, he was twenty-two years old. He could get an erection at the drop of a hat, not to mention the aggressive groping of a former Miss Texas who had no qualms about going after exactly what she wanted. And right now, Mary Alice wanted Bobby Stewart.

"I'm always up for it, Miss Mary," Bobby drawled as he threw an arm around the cute little doll with tight jeans, big tits and sex on her mind. "Just exactly where would you like to go to take this ride?" He was teasing her, he knew exactly what she wanted.

Running her hand into the tight back pocket of his jeans, she pinched his ass. "I'm not interested in going anywhere, Cowboy. You know what I want. I want to cum…over and over again," she whispered as she nipped him on the shoulder. Mary Alice was a wild cat. It didn't take much to set Bobby off. He was a young, healthy male with an unrivaled sexual appetite. Bobby Stewart had a reputation on the circuit and on campus. All of the ladies knew that he could be relied upon to provide sexual satisfaction on a grand scale.

The rodeo had been held in Mesquite, Texas—about three hours north of Austin and about four and half hours from the Bed and Breakfast resort that he owned with his brothers. To prevent driving back in the wee hours, Bobby had rented a hotel room at the nearest Holiday Inn Express. Mary Alice faithfully followed the rodeo circuit, but she was a local and had an apartment a few minutes from the exhibition hall and, like most women, preferred to have sex in her own bed. That suited Bobby, he liked to get his business taken care of and be able to leave when he got ready. Cum and Run. He knew it wasn't very romantic, but this hook-up wasn't about romance—it was about pleasure. And Bobby Stewart was a master at giving pleasure.

After a minimum amount of discussion, Bobby followed Mary Alice to her apartment and in a few minutes she had him right where she wanted him—naked and in her bed. "That's it baby, let me at him." She pushed him back on the bed and knelt between his legs. "God, I love to kiss your cock." Without preamble, she fitted her hungry lips over the large mushroom head and began to suck voraciously. Mary Alice was good at giving head. In a few seconds, she had Bobby's hips lifting rhythmically off the bed, seeking to push further into the hot recesses of her throat.

"That's good, Mary, so good," he praised her. Bobby would have been just as happy to shoot his load in her mouth, but Mary Alice had other ideas. Her pussy was hungry for cock and Bobby had a big one. She took him to the edge of climax, but pulled back just before he reached the point of no return.

"My turn," she sat up, big breasts heaving. Turning over, she presented her cute little ass for his delectation. "Ride me, cowboy." With an inviting wiggle, she didn't have to ask twice. Bobby rose up, sheathed himself with a condom, and mounted her from the rear. If there had been a mirror, he would have thrown up his arm in the typical rodeo rider pose—the girl's loved that image. But, there wasn't, so he set to pumping and thrusting until he had her moaning with ecstasy. Oh it was good, and Bobby was grateful, but Mary Alice's response was so staged. She moaned and carried on as if she was starring in a porn flick.

Bobby didn't doubt that he was making her feel good, but he almost felt like he was watching their sexual antics from a distance. There was no emotion, there was no feeling—it was just sex. *Crap!* At that unexpected thought, Bobby almost lost his erection. He had to fight to stay focused and finish out the erotic romp. Closing his eyes, he tried to imagine a different scenario. Instead of the woman he was pleasuring, the girl was sweet and unjaded. His dream girl was so excited to be with him that she trembled with delight at his touch. Her moans of pleasure would be unrehearsed and honest, she would be his for the long haul, not just for a few moments of fleeting passion.

Bobby held Mary Alice's stingy, white hips and rammed his turgid rod deep into her clutching pussy. Once—twice—three times was the charm. She screamed and he yelled, and he had to fight every instinct he had to keep from grabbing his gear and high-tailing it out of her apartment as naked as a jaybird.

"That was incredible, Bobby." Mary Alice fell to one side, completely sated and satisfied. "I'm glad I ran into you today. You know how to make a girl feel good."

"Happy to oblige, ma'am," Pulling on his clothes, all Bobby wanted to do was get home and see his brothers. Maybe, he wouldn't linger in Mesquite till morning. Ethan and Alex were waiting on him. He had promised he would help them paint. Their Bed and Breakfast was nestled in the beautiful hill country near the Lost Maples State Park south of Austin. "Look Mary Alice, I had a good time, sweetie, but I gotta run." It was a damn shame when painting a house was more appealing than after-sex snuggling.

"Sure, babe, no problem." Bobby was sure that if Mary Alice were a smoker, she would be puffing away by now. "We'll hook up again, sometime. I'll keep an eye out for you."

Not if I see you first, Bobby thought, then immediately regretted it. It wasn't like him to be ugly. After all, Mary Alice had done just exactly what he had wanted and expected. The only thing different in this equation was him.

Maybe it was time for a change. Bobby Stewart smiled as he let himself out of the cookie cutter apartment. Everything was beginning to look the same to him—the scenery, the women. Hell, maybe he was growing up. Snorting at the thought, he climbed into his pick-up and headed south.

* * *

"Do you know how humiliating it is when your husband won't make love to you?" Cecile asked in a desperate whisper.

Annalise almost ran her car off the road. "What do you mean he won't make love to you?"

Cecile looked out the window. She should never have brought it up. It was just too embarrassing. Carl had been her husband for seven years and he hadn't touched her for the last three—except when he had to, or if someone else happened to be watching. Glancing back over at her best friend and client, she found Annalise nailing her with a stare, demanding an answer. "Watch the road, Lise. Or they'll find two sex starved females in a crumpled up Jag."

"Hey! Not fair!" Annalise Ramsey protested. "You know my situation. I've had my one great love affair. There's no one else for me, but Ethan. Since I can't have him, I'm not in the market for another lover." Annalise shifted in the car seat. "You know I have issues. The rape changed everything for me. Even if I were able to get back together with Ethan, there is no way he would ever be able to make love with me again. I just can't stand the thought of his rejection. I'm too ashamed."

Cecile listened, sympathetically. She knew part of Annalise's story, but not all of it. It wasn't something that Annalise enjoyed talking about.

"Besides, we're talking about you, Cecile—not me. Now, explain yourself, please. Carl comes across as such a stud. When the two of you are out in public together, he can't keep his hands off of you." Annalise looked at Cecile. "You're beautiful. Never in a million years would I have suspected your marriage was a sham. You, my editor and agent, exude sexuality. After all, that's what you do for a living."

"Don't remind me. I wish I could live up to the hype of my job. Face it, I'm a phony." Cecile represented the biggest publisher of erotic romances in North America. Her whole career was built around sex. Lying back against the car seat, she thought how nice it would be to just drift off to sleep and ignore the curious glances of her dear traveling companion. The quiet engine of the Jaguar was no competition for her racing thoughts. Fine. She'd confess. After all, she really did need someone to talk to. "How Carl treats me when we are around others is all for show. At home, he avoids me like the plague." When Annalise gave her a bug-eyed stare, Cecile laughed. "It's true. Our sex life has never been what it should be." Letting down the passenger side mirror, Cecile played like she was checking her mascara. What she was actually doing was avoiding Annalise's sharp gaze. "It's all my fault, or at least that's what Carl says. I'm not woman enough for my husband. He says that I'm unexciting and getting old fast."

"That's totally ridiculous." Annalise fumed. "You're absolutely beautiful." Annalise looked at her friend. "You're adorable. I don't know how old you are, and I don't care. You could easily pass for a college coed." Her friend whacked the steering wheel and then winced at the pain. "That makes me so mad! Your husband should have his wiener cut off and flown on a flagpole. Why, just look at you! I love your hair. It's a beautiful color of dark brown. I wish mine was as pretty." Before Cecile knew what was happening, Annalise had reached over and picked up a strand of her hair. "With your shoulder length cut and that mass of soft curls, it just begs for a man to run his fingers through it." When Cecile rolled her eyes at her friend, she moved on to a different facial characteristic. "And your eyes are big and the color of vibrant emeralds. I would literally kill for your eyelashes. They're so dark it makes your eyes look like jewels lying on black velvet. I'm sitting over here totally jealous of how you look. Your body, your face, your hair—it's all perfect. Is the man blind or gay?"

Letting out an exasperated giggle, Cecile stated flatly. "Neither, but you sound like a frustrated lesbian." When Annalise swatted at her, she dodged. "Sorry. I know you're straight, don't get your panties in a wad. To hear Carl tell it, the only problem he has is me. He says I just don't do it for him. The last time we tried to have sex, he couldn't get hard enough to penetrate me."

"Bullshit! There has to be something wrong with him." They were heading back to East Texas from a writer's convention in Houston. Stopping at a red light, Annalise aimed the air vent at Cecile. "You're all red, let me cool you off."

"I'm red because I'm mortified to be telling you all of this," Cecile squeaked through clenched teeth. After another pregnant pause she started talking fast, as if she were on a game show with only a certain amount of time allowed to give an answer. "The sex between us has never been good. Even though Carl…is…uh…built small down there, it has always hurt. I've never had an orgasm during sex with him. He won't go down on me, although he used to demand that I give him blow jobs. For years, he has told me that I'm frigid, but since I've been reading and editing these books, I know that's not true. I get hot and bothered all the time from the explicit sex that you write."

Annalise didn't say anything, she looked totally flabbergasted. She kept moving her mouth, as if she was going to start a sentence and then she would stop. Finally, she huffed out a little breath of defiance. "You deserve a better life than you have with him, Cecile. Do you love him?"

What a simple question. It was so simple, that it stunned Cecile for a few moments. It was as if a haze had been lifted and she was able to see the horizon clearly for the first time in a long, long while. "Well, I don't know." Undoing the seatbelt, she turned in the seat looking at Annalise head on. "No, I don't love him. I can't even remember what loving him felt like." She completely ignored the ding-ding-ding of the seat belt alarm.

Annalise whipped into a Sonic. "It's time for a Java Chiller." She rolled down her window and pressed the button, telling the remote bell-hop what they wanted. Once she was assured that their caffeine/sugar fix was on its way, she unhooked her seat belt and sat nose to nose with Cecile. "Divorce the asshole. You can live with me until you decide what to do about your house."

* * *

A Few Weeks Later

Tamara lay on the bed, trembling with anticipation. Opening her legs wide, she offered herself to her lover. Derrick knelt on the floor, never taking his eyes away from the beautiful sight spread before him for his pleasure. She was wet and swollen for him. "I can't wait to taste you, precious. May I kiss you? Here?" He ran one gentle finger down the center of her pussy.

Tamara lifted her hips. "Please, Derrick. I can't wait. No one has ever done this for me, before." She watched in fascination as he bent his head, drawing ever nearer to her eager sex. At the first touch of his lips and tongue, her body almost bent double with delight. "Oh, sweet Lord," she whispered. "That feels so good!"

Derrick held her fast with strong hands as he ate his fill of her sweet cream. "Steady, baby. I've got you."

Tamara arched her back in absolute ecstasy. This was better than she had ever imagined. How had she lived without this pleasure? He cupped her breast with one hand and began to massage the nipple in time with his thrusting tongue. "Sweetheart, I love this. I could kiss you like this forever."

At his words of praise, Tamara pushed herself into his face, wordlessly begging for more. He met her need, circling his tongue around her clitoris—driving her absolutely mad with bliss.

Cecile read the words Annalise had written as erotic romance author Ann Pace. Her hand trembled as she hit the down arrow button to advance the page. Closing her eyes she let the muscles of her sex contract and ease, contract and ease. If she imagined hard enough, she could almost feel a cock moving in and out of her—giving her what she needed, what she longed for. "God! I'm pitiful!" Pushing the laptop away from her, Cecile lay back on the bed and cupped her swollen sex through her clothes. She was so horny that she might expire from sheer sexual frustration! "I've either got to get laid or change jobs," she sighed.

Annalise's writing was so hot! Unable to stand it any longer, Cecile pulled at her own clothing until she was nude. If no one else would make love to her, she would make love to herself. Never having indulged in the purchase of a sex toy, all she had to work with were her own hands, but she was beyond desperate.

Lying back on her beige quilted duvet, she bent her knees and spread her legs open wide. Just the air from the ceiling fan made her engorged clit vibrate. Hungry to be touched, she let her own palms slide up her thighs, over her abdomen and up to cup her aching breasts. Even the touch of her own hands felt good. Tossing her head from side to side, she played with her own tits. Finding that she needed more than a tender caress, Cecile clasped her nipples between her fingers and the base of her thumb and worked the tender nubbins against the hard part of her hand. It felt so good! As she massaged and pinched her nipples, she worked her hips up and down, clenching and unclenching the muscles of her vagina, pretending that a man was pumping into her empty, throbbing sex.

Needing even more, Cecile fingered her own pussy. Sliding the tips of her fingers up and down the lips of her vulva, she inserted one finger into the channel that pulsed with longing and moved it in and out. Finding that to be highly unsatisfying, she moved on up rubbing her clitoris in a circular motion. "Oh, that's better." As she pulled at her nipple and manipulated her clit, Cecile pictured herself as the heroine in one of Annalise's novels, a desirable woman that could attract and please a man. In her mind's eye, she saw him above her. His expression was heated and he had eyes only for her. Lifting her head, she sought his lips—fantasizing about greedy kisses and the mating of fevered tongues. Her hero would want her—*her*—Cecile. His cock would be hard and hungry—*for her*. He would find delight—*in her*. Arching her back she met his thrusts, and parried them with the rhythmic seeking of her hips. Frantically, she ground her clit beneath her own caress until she achieved release, a sad, lonely release. Tears leaked from her eyes and ran down the side of her face to dampen the pillow. Was this the way it was going to be? Would she never know the passionate touch of a lover? How sad, how very sad.

The buzz of her cell phone drew Cecile out of her orgasm induced stupor. As orgasms go, it hadn't been that good, but it was the best she had felt in many a day. Sometimes, Cecile thought that Annalise and the other erotic authors she dealt with on a day-to-day basis made a lot of that *fireworks, the earth moved and volcanic eruption* stuff up. Maybe Carl was right, maybe she was frigid. Her body craved a climax, but the ones she gave herself were weak and short-lived—nothing like what other women boasted of feeling.

Dragging herself off the bed, she retrieved the phone from her desk. For a moment, she hoped it might be Carl calling to check in on her, but it wasn't. It was the gynecologist calling to remind her it was time for her pap smear and mammogram. Yuck! She hated doctor visits! Noting it on the calendar, she was grateful it was over a week away.

For a minute, she stared at the phone wishing she had someone she could call and invite out for a meal. Because Carl was such an asshole, they didn't have many friends and he discouraged her from having girlfriends that she could meet for drinks and go shopping with. She didn't know why. Sometimes she thought that he was afraid that she would talk to them, confide in someone how truly bad their marriage was. So Cecile wasn't close to anyone, other than Annalise, and she lived almost four hours away. Carl didn't have anything to worry about, there was no way she was going to air her dirty laundry in front of her Dallas work acquaintances. They had no idea that she, an erotic romance editor, lay untouched every night in a lonely bed, forced to masturbate for even the smallest of amount of sexual relief.

Climbing back into bed, she opened her emails. There was a message from Annalise, apologizing again for not having the five chapters she had promised Cecile. She confessed that she was experiencing major writer's block. Typing in a quick response, Cecile joked with her, doing her best to inspire Annalise out of her funk. "Maybe, you need to take a laxative." That didn't work.

After talking to her friend coming back from the conference, Cecile had realized she wasn't the only one who was depressed. Annalise Evans was still desperately in love with a man she had met in college. They had a whirlwind romance, but had been torn apart after Annalise suffered a tragic rape. It had happened over spring break during Annalise's freshman year. After that, she had endured several reconstructive surgeries. Annalise and Ethan had never seen one another again, and the only thing that Cecile had managed to get out of Annalise was that she had never told Ethan about the rape.

One thing Cecile did know—Annalise was still deeply in love with Ethan, because every hero in every book she had written was patterned after him. And every dedication in every book had his first name in tribute—to my own hero, Ethan. I will never forget you. At Annalise's insistence, the artwork on the front of every one of her novels carried Ethan's likeness. If he was as good looking as the man on the cover of the books, he was a sight to behold. No wonder Annalise was still in love with him.

If she and Carl got divorced, it would be a long time before she put herself into the dating fray. She was tired of getting hurt, but Lord, she craved sex. Exiting out of her email account, she logged onto a discreet adult site. Yea, they had what she was looking for—pages and pages of them—dildos. Smiling to herself, she clicked through the wide variety of battery powered, vibrating, and thrusting, pink or purple, plastic pleasure toys. Finding one that promised untold delight, she clicked the instant buy button and felt like she had accomplished something.

Feeling like her purchase was a major step toward taking charge of her life, she decided to set the ball rolling with Carl. It was now or never, she told herself. Dialing his cell phone number, she held her breath and waited. "Hello?"

Carl had a deep, sexy voice. It had been one of the things that had first attracted her to him. That and his hair, he had beautiful blonde, thick hair. It was a pity he didn't find anything about her attractive. Taking a deep breath, she jumped in. She knew he had caller ID—he knew exactly who was on the phone. Yet he said nothing personal, waiting for her to make the first move. "Carl, it's Cecile. How are things going?"

She heard him exhale loudly. Lord, was she such a bother? "Not too bad. I'll be able to come home tomorrow, I guess."

He guessed? Where else would he go? Not for the first time, Cecile wondered if he were having an affair. Would it matter? After all, he sure wasn't sleeping with her. "Good. I'm glad you're well." It would have been nice if he had called to check in on her. For the past three days, he had been in San Antonio on business. Nothing had really changed, but at least they had dinner together the night before he left. When she had returned to Dallas from the writer's conference, after her talk with Annalise, Cecile had chickened out about telling Carl she wanted a divorce. Maybe she owed her marriage one last try. So here she was, about to try and execute her plan. Cecile was going to make an attempt to seduce her husband.

"Carl, I would like for us to meet at this beautiful Bed and Breakfast I've found in that southern lifestyle magazine we subscribe to. It's not far from where you are."

With a weary sound voice, he asked. "A Bed and Breakfast? Cecile, you know I don't like that kind of thing."

Quickly, she came up with her pitch. "It's near the Lost Maples State Park. They have eleven miles of hiking trails there. The trails go through some of the most gorgeous scenery in the hill country."

There was a pause. "That sounds like fun. Could you find some shopping to do?"

Actually, she had hoped they could spend the time together. Hopefully, she could work on common interests after they got there. "Sure. I can do that."

"All right," he agreed. "Give me directions. I'll meet you there tomorrow."

* * *

Bobby walked toward the Darrell K. Royal Stadium. It was time for football practice. And there was nothing

Bobby Stewart loved more than football—except women. Jeffrey Johnson and Ladon Mahoney stepped in beside him. "Hey, cowboy. How's it hangin?" Ladon slapped Bobby on the back.

"Can't complain, gentleman." He had come straight from the rodeo arena and was still dressed in full cowboy regalia.

Johnson laughed, taking in the scene. "Hey Stewart, did you know there are four cute little coeds on your tail? I think they like the way you look in those chaps." Bobby swung around and winked at the little ladies, making them giggle as he tipped his hat at them.

"You know it's just not fair," Ladon grumbled. "You've got it all Bobby. Not only are you a football star, you're also a champion bull rider and freakishly good-looking. The only thing I've got going for me is that my people are healthy and live a long time. I've got longevity in my genes."

Bobby laughed and cupped his crotch. "I've got longevity in my jeans, too."

"Heard you rode that killer bull. What was his name, Porn Star? Was he hung like one?"

"I didn't check out the bull's Johnson, Johnson." Bobby shot him the finger.

Jeffrey Johnson laughed. "I like to jack with you, Stewart. You're a good guy—even if you are a lucky son-of-a-bitch who has it all."

"The bull's name is Rock Star," Bobby said with satisfaction. "I stayed on that devil for the full, long eight seconds."

Ladon slung his backpack over his massive shoulders. "Only a bull rider would think eight seconds is a long time. I pity your women, man. They have to learn how to get it in gear and get off fast."

Bobby tipped his Stetson at a beautiful blonde who was walking toward him, and a curvy redhead that crossed their paths and spoke to him sweetly. "Hi, Bobby."

"I always leave my women completely satisfied." Bobby stated matter-of-factly as he opened the double doors to the hall that led to the locker rooms and the player's lounge.

"That's what I hear." Reece Witherspoon heard Bobby's confident declaration. He fell in step with the other three, flinging a towel at the large hamper in the corner. "Word is that Stewart is hung like one of those bulls he rides. Hence, his nickname—Bull Stewart."

"This is a locker room, 'Spoon. We've all seen each other's plumbing." Bobby passed off the good-natured ribbing with his usual smooth return. Looking up, he noticed that one of his coaches was standing at the door motioning him over. "Uh-oh, I'm being sent to the office."

"If it's what I think it is, I believe you'll find it's worth the trip," Reece gave him a knowing smile.

"What's up, Coach?" Bobby didn't think he had done anything wrong, but he had halfway been expecting them to complain about his bull-riding. Some athletic programs frowned on their players doing anything off the field that could be construed as risk-taking behavior, and mounting one ton of pissed off bull was definitely a risk.

"I've got some good news for you." The coach grinned at him. Bobby inwardly let out a breath of relief—this was something else entirely.

"Good news? Do you have a special play that you want me to try?" He loved to be on the receiving end of the quarterback's throwing arm. The younger McCoy could thread a needle with a football, he was just that accurate.

"The deadline for declaring for the NFL draft is

January. Are you planning on pitching your hat in the ring or are you content bouncing around on top of those widow-makers with horns?"

Bobby looked sheepish. He hadn't tried to hide his extracurricular activities, but none of the coaching staff had ever mentioned it to him before.

Trotsky tapped a file folder on his desk. "Look, Stewart, I know extraordinary talent when I see it. It's my business." The balding ex-pro leaned back in his office chair, "Put my mind to rest. You've got that certain something that separates the good players from the great ones. I've always said, give Stewart one shot with the ball, he can make it happen—and make it look easy."

"Thank you, sir. I appreciate it. And the answer is *yes* about the draft. I've already got the paperwork done."

"Good, because Dallas is looking at you. You could be a first round draft pick."

Bobby swallowed hard. Had he heard right? Playing for Dallas was his ultimate dream. "Sir, are you serious?"

"They'll be at the first game. And don't worry about it. We've got a little time to get you ready. Just play like you normally do and try not to get yourself killed by one of those bucking hamburgers-on-the-hoofs, before then." Trotsky stood and put his hand on Bobby's shoulder in a fatherly gesture. "I'm proud of you, boy. I've enjoyed coaching you more than you'll ever know. You're a good kid."

Bobby walked back to the locker room in a daze. The Dallas Cowboys were interested in him—Bobby Stewart! *Hot damn!* He slapped his Stetson against his leg and laughed out loud. Dallas! He couldn't believe it. Hell, this was great news! Dallas wouldn't know what hit it when Bobby Stewart arrived. He was gonna take *Big D* by storm.

Later that afternoon, Bobby set out for home. Class had let out early and all he had to do was run some errands and he was free for two days. The only thing he had to return to Austin for was football practice, which was a pleasure. Grabbing the list from the glove compartment, he checked to see what Alex had mapped out for him. *Crap!* This would take forever. He had to pick up Ethan's liquor order from the beverage store, pick up some samples from one of Alex's environmental conservation clients, fetch Mojo from the vet's office and buy the paint that had been special ordered for the B&B. Glancing out the window, he noticed a storm was brewing. Hopefully, he could get all this done and get home before the bottom fell out.

Turning on the radio to his favorite station, Bobby rolled down the window and started singing Jake Owen's Eight Second Ride at the top of his lungs. He was on top of the world. He couldn't believe he might actually get the chance to play for Dallas. For a moment, he considered that he might tell his brothers the good news while he was home, but he didn't want to jinx the possible outcome. It was tempting, though—anything to nudge Ethan out of the funk he had been in. Since his marriage to that human piranha, Francine, Ethan had been on a steady spiral into depression. He and Alex had told him that divorcing the vicious bitch had been the smartest thing that he had ever done.

Pulling into the paint store, he checked his phone for messages. *Damn!* There were eight messages from assorted girls, and three of them would make a sailor blush. Bobby wondered what was wrong with him, he was fast losing his taste for pushy women. Most men would give their right nut to be in his shoes, but, more and more Bobby Stewart was finding that he wanted a woman who made him feel like a man, not just a piece of meat.

*   *   *

Cecile put on a bit of lip gloss, rearranged her new sexy negligee over her breasts and went to face the music. Cracking open the bathroom door, she could see Carl standing in front of the window. A nature lover, he had been taken by the beautiful grounds of the Bed and Breakfast. Carl had already mentioned that he wanted to check out the rose bed and the picturesque creek which ran behind the main guest house.

He looked good standing there wearing only a pair of light blue pajama pants. Carl wasn't muscled-up like some men, but he had a nice body. On the drive down to Lost Maples, she had tried to remember how it felt when she had first fell in love with Carl, or thought they were in love. There was so much distance between them now it was hard to recall the excitement of his kiss or the warmth of his touch. Moving toward him, she stopped in her tracks when his cell phone rang. He let his gaze rake over her. Without a smile or nod of acknowledgement, he picked up the phone and walked over to the kitchen area leaving her standing there in her skimpy little outfit with a hesitant, expectant look on her face.

From his conversation, she gathered he was talking to his boss. Carl was a very successful pharmaceutical salesman, a glorified pill peddler was what her mother had called him. She went and took his place by the window, waiting for the phone call to end. If she wasn't so nervous about what was about to happen with Carl, she would already have been on the phone with Annalise. She had huge news for her friend, but she couldn't decide exactly how to tell her. Cecile decided she would have to be sneaky.

When she had driven up to check in, the first thing

she had noticed was the Welcome Sign. It had read—Proprietors - Mr. And Mrs. Ethan Stewart. Cecile was jaw-dropping shocked. She knew that name. Ethan Stewart. Could he be Annalise's Ethan? If it was and he was married, she would never breathe a word to Annalise. But, something told her to have a little faith. When she had entered the lobby, there was no doubt in her mind. The man was incredibly good looking—both of them. One was a golden god, and the other was the model for fifteen erotic novels that she had edited for Annalise. To satisfy her curiosity, she had asked to speak to his wife. Cecile told Ethan she wanted to compliment her on the landscaping. The devastatingly, handsome man had gotten a serious look on his face and simply said to her, *there is no Mrs. Ethan Stewart*, which was the best news Cecile had heard in a long time. Maybe, Annalise's dreams were finally about to come true, that is if she could think of a way to convince her friend to visit one picturesque Bed and Breakfast in the Texas Hill Country.

She jumped when Carl snapped his phone closed. Waiting, she held her breath, wondering if he would take the initiative and come to her. It must be obvious by the way she was dressed what she had on her mind. Counting to ten, she stood there like a dunce. Nothing. Very well. She'd be the brave one, or the foolish one, the distinction would be made clear in a moment. Turning, she met Carl's eyes. They were a beautiful shade of gray, she had always thought they were the color of a dove's wing. He wasn't smiling. There was a sad set to his mouth. She couldn't read his expression. "Carl, I appreciate you agreeing to meet me here." Walking slowly toward him, she smoothed her palms down her thighs, nervously.

"I have to go on to Houston tomorrow, it is easier than driving back to Dallas."

His words stabbed her. What would it be like to have

a husband who rushed home to her because he couldn't wait to hold her in his arms? Get a grip, she cautioned herself. She was on a mission. "I'm glad we could have this time together." Walking right up to him, she stood there hoping he would touch her. His muscles tensed up, but he kept his hands to himself. Going for broke, she fell to her knees and tugged on his pajama bottoms. There was no resistance. Maybe, he was too shocked to stop her. He wore a pair of dark green boxer briefs, and it she wasn't mistaken there was movement under them. Taking that small sign as encouragement, she tugged down his underwear to reveal his penis.

Even though she worked with erotic romance, Cecile was not experienced. Carl was the only lover she had ever had. She knew his manhood was average or a little smaller, but if he would have given her half a chance, she would have cherished him and any attention he would give her. She made herself think of a dog that she had once seen. The dog had been tied to a tree and had a small house to get in out of the weather. Every day she walked around in a circle on her short chain and the people who had once petted her as a pup, now walked by her without speaking. That dog would jump up and down in greeting, wag her tail, begging for attention, but no one ever stopped to give her any affection at all. She had felt sorry for the dog. Cecile felt like that animal must have felt. She craved affection, but for the most part, she was ignored.

Time seemed to be dragging—this was so important. She didn't know if Carl realized exactly what was happening, but this was a test—big time—for Cecile. With trembling fingers, she picked up his semi-erect cock. She heard him hiss, interpreting that as excitement, she took him into her mouth and began to massage the shaft with her lips and tongue. Cecile felt a small quiver of excitement. With one hand, she caressed his thigh and with the other she picked up his scrotal sac and rubbed his balls tenderly. She was so intent on her seductive endeavors that she did not notice her tender ministrations were not producing any sort of response. Carl gripped her shoulder. At first, she thought he was going to pull her close, caress her, or encourage her. Instead, he tightened his grip until it was painful. Letting out a gasp, she halted all contact with her hands and her mouth.

"Stop, Cecile!"

Cecile grew very still. Bowing her head, she fought her emotions. "Did I do something wrong?"

Carl stepped back from her. He huffed out a breath and pulled up his underwear. "I'm sorry, Cecile. It's not going to happen. You just don't do it for me. I'm sorry, but I'm not attracted to you."

Stumbling to her feet, Cecile raised a tear streaked face to her husband of seven years, the only man who had ever touched her body. "I can't do this anymore, Carl. There's no use for us to put off the inevitable any longer. I'm sorry that I've been such a disappointment to you. I will be glad to give you a divorce."

Chapter Two

Throwing her suitcase in the back of her Lexus, she wiped her eyes on the sleeve of her blouse and turned over a new leaf. Swearing that this was for the best, Cecile prayed she wouldn't throw up until she got out of sight of the B&B. If the owner was indeed Ethan, she hoped to one day be coming back here for Annalise's wedding. She'd hate for them to retain a memory of some dorky woman upchucking in their front yard.

Wrenching open the door of her car, she stepped in. Just as she shut the door, rain began to fall in thick sheets. Carl hadn't disputed her offer of a divorce, so she had dressed and left the room as quickly as possible. Cecile had no idea if he would return to their home or not. For the time being, that was where she was going, simply because she had no place else to go.

Again, she wondered if Carl had a lover. Or could he be gay? Shaking her head, she tried to clear her mind. Did it really matter? Either way, he didn't want her. Covering her mouth, she stifled a sob. Her husband didn't want her. Although, this wasn't new information, it still hurt like hell. She had made one last ditch effort to make him love her and it had failed. Why didn't really matter.

Driving down Lonely Street, she left Lost Maples and her marriage behind. Cecile made plans in her head. She would let Carl have the apartment and she would find a new place to live—maybe a quaint little house in an older neighborhood, maybe uptown or Victory Park. She would have to change her mail, and her phone number. God, she had so much to do. There were phone calls to make, like the lawyer and Annalise. Lord, she needed to talk to Annalise. Now, wasn't the time to tell her about

Ethan, but she did need to tell her that the divorce was on. Watching the road, she used her car phone located on the steering wheel to speed-dial her friend in East Texas. A faint buzzing sound alerted her that there was no cell service in the area. Belatedly, she realized how far back in the sticks she was. Turning off the phone menu, she tried to concentrate on the road. It was narrow and curvy and in the dark, it all looked alike. Pity she wouldn't be staying longer at Lost Maples—it was a beautiful place.

Narrowing her eyes, she tried to determine what she was seeing. It was some type of reflection. It was eyes! With a squeal, she realized that a little dog was standing directly in the road ahead of her. Applying her brakes, she threw her whole weight into trying to stop the car without throwing herself into a tail spin on the wet pavement. She managed to stop, but the backend of the car swerved, nearly making her scream with fright. Pulling off the road, she jumped out to make sure the little dog was okay. It was a dachshund, her favorite breed. "Come here, fella. I won't hurt you." She called to the little dog who scampered away. Cecile took chase, knowing that as fat as the little dog seemed to be, he was, undoubtedly, somebody's precious baby. She didn't want to think of him smashed in the road come morning.

Carefully, she ran down the highway after the dog. Her shoes were slick on the bottom, so she tried to watch her step. In such a hurry to get away from Carl, she had thrown on a pair of jeans and a thin white blouse. Running through the downpour, she was completely soaked. "Wait, puppy! Wait!" Rounding a curve, Cecile realized that she wasn't alone out on the dark, lonely road. She had run right up on a pickup that had slid off into the ditch. The top was up over the engine and a man stood looking over the side, working on Lord knows what. She wasn't up on the mechanical inner workings of a car.

Seeing the man, the little dog headed straight for him. Apparently, he seemed to be less of a threat than she was. Cecile slowed to a stop. She never considered that the man might be dangerous. Today had been such an ordeal for her that the thought of facing anyone other than Carl seemed easy. "Excuse me, sir. Is this your puppy?" Cecile scooped the little dog up, afraid that another car could come upon them at any time.

* * *

Bobby heard a voice. The rain was coming down so hard, at first he thought it was his imagination. His truck was held together with baling wire and good intentions, and now he had gone and skidded into a damn guard rail. But, that voice…it was soft and husky and decidedly feminine. Immediately, his cock rose to the occasion. Straightening, he couldn't wait to see the face that belonged to such a sexy voice. There was a halogen lantern hanging from the top of his hood, and he was momentarily blinded. Staring into the darkness, he waited for his eyes to adjust. Recognizing the tail-tale whimper, he crooned to the animal. "Mojo! Baby, how did you get out of the truck? Don't you know we couldn't do without you?"

"Good, I'm glad he's yours. I didn't want to leave him on the road." The woman stepped sideways trying to get out of the glare.

"Hello, angel."

"See," she rubbed the dog's head. "Your owner is glad to see you."

"Actually, I was talking to you." He stepped closer to her. "Thanks for rescuing my puppy. A deer ran out of nowhere. I didn't hit it, but my pickup had an unkind run-in with this guardrail. My fuel line looks busted. Not to mention my passenger door got crumpled, that's how this little guy got out, I guess." Moving to one side, Bobby tried to get a good look at Mojo's rescuer. Ah, now he could see her. Bobby feasted his eyes upon one of the most delectable women he had ever seen. She was wet from head to toe. Her hair hung in curly little tendrils around a sweet, heart-shaped face. But what lay below was what took his breath away. Her blouse was utterly transparent from the rain and she didn't have a stitch on underneath it. His hands cupped and his fingers itched to cover those jiggling mounds with his hands and squeeze. The white shirt gleamed in the lantern light and he could see that she had big nipples—and the poor baby was cold. *Damn!*

"Can I take you somewhere? There's no cell phone service here," she offered breathlessly. When he hesitated, she explained. "For some reason, you don't make me nervous. The way you talked to the dog alleviated any misgivings I might have had."

Bobby took Mojo from her grasp. She had been holding him at waist height – thankfully, not covering up those generous, stupendous tits. Hiding those from his sight would have been an absolute crime against nature. "You have nothing to fear from me. My mama raised Southern gentlemen. But I can't leave my truck, it's full of supplies that could be stolen. Besides, I'm not too far from my house, sweet girl." Another car passed by, fairly close. And she reached out for him, pulling him closer to her. Her protective instincts made him smile.

As if realizing what she had done, she apologized. "Sorry. I was afraid they couldn't see you very well." She pulled her hand back, quickly. "Be careful out here. When I get to an area that has a good signal, can I call someone to come help you?"

Bobby was smitten with his would-be rescuer. He

had never been so immediately, completely infatuated. "I've already called my brother on the radio. But, I sure appreciate how sweet it was for you to stop and rescue this big fella. I'm Bobby, what's your name, precious?" He held his hand out in greeting and, after a moment's hesitation, she placed her hand in his.

"My name's Ceelee. That's what my dad always called me."

"A beautiful name for a beautiful girl." His words made her blush, he could see that even in this light. "Are you chilly?" He hated for her to cover up, but he couldn't stand the thought of her being uncomfortable. "I might have a jacket in my truck."

Momentarily confused, she followed the direction of his gaze. Looking down, she let out a small horrified moan. "Good Lord, I might as well be naked." Lifting her arms to cover herself, she apologized profusely. "Good grief! What you must think of me! I'm so sorry. I didn't think."

The look on her face bothered Bobby. Every other woman he knew would have thrust those tits out or rubbed them against him. This one acted like she expected him to berate her for exposing herself. As she moved away, she seemed so distressed that all he wanted to do was draw her close and assure her that seeing her beautiful body was a treat and a privilege, not some hardship to be endured or avoided. "It's okay, sweetie. You don't have to turn away from me. I wouldn't hurt you for the world." His words didn't seem to bring her any comfort. She still looked as if she thought she had committed a crime.

"I'm glad your dog is okay. If there's nothing else I can do for you, I should leave." Desperately, she pulled on the wet material that was plastered to her body. "I'm so sorry," she apologized again. "I'm glad you're both okay. Excuse me, again." She began to walk away from him, as if she wanted to leave the embarrassing situation as fast as she could.

Stopping her with a light touch, he spoke softly. "You have nothing to apologize for. You are absolute heaven to look at." Bobby couldn't take his eyes off of her. Even with wet hair and no make-up, she was the cutest thing he had ever seen. "Would you like to go out with me sometime?" She flashed him an exasperated, disbelieving look. "Are you free—I mean, do you have a boyfriend or husband?"

He watched as desolation rolled over her face. Something was wrong. "There's no one, not anymore."

She seemed to catch herself before she said anything else. Straightening those fragile, yet strong little shoulders, she faced him with arms crossed over her breasts and smiled a tremulous, shy smile. "I can't stay. I'm on my way back to Dallas. But thanks for asking, that was very nice of you. You didn't have to, you know. There's no charge for puppy rescues."

"Don't go. Not yet." He took hold of her arm, noting how she jumped at his touch. Had someone been mean to this little angel? "There has to be some way for us to get together, I want to properly thank you for coming to our aid." Sidling up to her, slowly—so as not to scare her, he rubbed his hand down her arm, letting her feel his heat. "You're like a dream walking up on me out of the dark. You're so beautiful. Can I kiss you, sweetheart? Would you let me taste your lips?" If she had been one of the buckle bunnies, she would have given him a sexy come-on smile and kissed him before he kissed her. Instead, this doll stared at him with a puzzled expression.

"You want to kiss me?" The wonder and disbelief in her voice was unexpected.

"More than you can possibly imagine." Still holding the dog in one arm, he used his other hand to push back a few strands of her soft hair. Cupping the side of her neck, he tugged her forward about halfway, leaving the rest of the journey up to her. "Isn't this romantic? We're going to share our first kiss in a Texas rainstorm. Kinda fittin', baby, because you're certainly taking me by storm." His words seemed to hypnotize her, she leaned forward slowly as if being reeled in by the heat of his gaze. "Oh, yeah. Come to me, love. You're my every fantasy come true, did you know that?"

"I'm not," she protested softly. "I'm quite ordinary, really." Even as she spoke, her focus was on his lips and hers were opening in invitation. "But I would love to taste your kiss, just once," her last words were said as his mouth covered hers. Both of them groaned at the bliss.

"Sweet. Lord, you're sweet." Bobby pulled at her lips, biting them gently. Nibbling. Sucking. Seducing her, teasing with barely-there-kisses, making her respond with caresses of her own as she sought more of the incredible pleasure he was offering. Little whimpers of need escaped her lips and he ate them with relish, upping the ante with an aggressive kiss that devoured her, making her stand on tiptoe and push those firm, feminine tits topped with hard, berry nipples into his chest. "God help me. I'm gonna come in my britches, baby girl."

Sweet baby was hungry. She slid trembling hands up his chest and over the top of his shoulders. Straining to get nearer still, she wrapped her arms around his neck. Coherent thought became an impossibility, all he could do was feel the fire that was blazing between them. Boldly, she let her tongue rub over his. He captured it and sucked it into his mouth, she tasted like honey and he wanted to eat her up like candy. When her hips jerked and she pressed her sex against him, he felt his cock surge within the tight confines of his jeans. Accidentally, she bumped the little dog making it squirm to get down, but Bobby gathered Mojo closer and continued with the mind-blowing kiss that was fast changing all of his preconceived ideas about what loving a woman should be like.

A bright flash of lightning followed by a loud clap of thunder heralded the big drops of rain that began to fall. It was time to hunt shelter. Gentling the kiss, he tried to bring them down from the near orgasmic high that had them clinging to one another with unrestrained passion. "Oh, sweetheart. Thank you, baby." He nuzzled her face, kissing her cheek, under her ear and then down the side of her smooth, soft neck. "Where did you come from, angel? Today was my lucky day. I can't believe you are here in my arms." As he talked, he nuzzled her cheek and neck. Small sighs of pleasure told him that she was enjoying herself as much as he was. "What a gift you are. I don't think I can let you go. Come home with me. I can't wait to get you in my bed."

As if she had awakened from a dream, she pushed back from his chest, searching his face as if trying to remember what had happened. "I must be crazy. What am I doing? I've got to go, Bobby. This was a mistake—a wonderful mistake, but I don't belong here." She pulled away from him and started walking toward her car. She had wrapped her arms around her middle, bowed her head and headed out into the rainy night. There was no way in hell he was going to let her walk out of his life.

"Ceelee! Wait! What do you mean? There was no way that kiss was a mistake, baby. It was a beginning!" He started after her, but before either of them could say another word, the rain started coming down with a vengeance. "Wait! Please!" Bobby called after her. He hadn't meant to do anything that would upset her. He wouldn't have hurt her feelings for the world. "Sweetheart, please don't leave," he begged.

Still holding the dog under his arm like an oversize football, he took off after her. But another crack of thunder, and a powerful bolt of lightning scared Mojo so badly that he swan-dived out of Bobby's arms and took off like a ruptured red bug. Shit! Another car was coming, so he didn't have a choice about it, he took after Ethan's little dog. Scooping him up, he straightened up just in time to see Ceelee's taillights highlight her license plate. Damn! He was only able to make out the last three digits B72. *Well, hell!* She seemed determined to get away from him. Bobby stood and watched her until she disappeared from his sight. He felt like something infinitely precious had slipped from his grasp. What could he do with just three digits of her plate number? Would that be enough to find her? There was one thing for certain, he was gonna give it a good ole' Texas try. The few minutes he had been able to spend with her had been more exciting than any of the encounters he had experienced with the rodeo groupies or the UT coeds. "Ceelee, I'll find you, baby. Dallas ain't that dang big." With that, he crawled into his pickup and waited for Ethan or Alex to come and pick them up.

* * *

Cecile was shaking like a leaf as she drove away from Bobby. She had to drive with one hand because she kept using the other one to touch her lips where he had kissed her. "Oh My God, I can't believe I kissed a strange man on the side of the road!" She laughed out loud at herself. Well, it was better than crying. It was hard to keep her mind on her driving. All she could think about was what it felt like to be in Bobby's arms. How different it had been than anything she had ever experienced with Carl. She had felt wanted, desired—God help her—she had felt like a woman. Even now, she was aching with longing. Her skin was tingling from his touch and her lips were still warm from his kiss. With a ragged sigh, she fought her need to turn around and head back, to find him and beg him to hold her again. Gripping the steering wheel so hard her knuckles were white, she tried to get an equal grip on her emotions.

Almost immediately, she regretted not giving him her name. Now, she had lost him forever. A sick feeling overwhelmed her. It took everything in her to keep herself heading north, she wanted to spin her car around and drive back to him as fast as she could. But most likely, he would already be gone. A sob hiccupped out of her chest. What had she done? Tears were streaming from her eyes.

Think, Cecile, think. Be reasonable. Nothing that had happened between herself and Bobby had been real. Bobby's only impression of her was one gathered under cover of night. If he had seen her in the bright light of day, he probably wouldn't have been quite as eager to spend time with her. If he had gotten a really clear look at her, he probably wouldn't have kissed her at all. What happened had been a mistake—on both of their parts. But, God how the man could kiss! From the moment she saw him, she had been fascinated—a big man like him talking baby-talk to a dog, it was the sexiest thing she had ever heard. The very idea of the six-foot plus, broad shouldered he-man caring for a little animal was a powerful aphrodisiac to her. Carl had been as apathetic toward animals as he had been to her. He wouldn't have stopped to chase down the little dog, he might not even had tried to avoid hitting it.

Reliving how it had felt to be near him, her whole

body flooded with warmth. Never had she felt so aroused. Her nipples were still hard and her clit was throbbing. *Wow!* The guy had been potent! And Cecile couldn't believe that she had told him to call her Ceelee. It had been years since she had used the name that was so dear to her heart. Somehow, it had seemed fitting that this man should use her nickname too.

As the weather went crazy outside the car, she tried to focus on the road. The windows were fogging up and it was almost impossible to see. Fiddling with the controls, she tried to turn on the defrost to angle the air up to try and clear the glass. A blast of cold air against her wet clothes and skin had her twisting knobs and pressing buttons. Shit! Looking down at her still drenched blouse, she was reminded of how she must have looked to Bobby. She couldn't believe she had stood there holding a conversation with him like an idiot, with her huge breasts outlined in see-through nothing. Lord, he must have thought she was coming on to him. Damn! Carl had told her several times that her breasts were too big for her frame. Once, about a month ago he had flat out told her that she needed to wear looser clothing, that her body was no longer that of a teenager. How humiliating!

With a small laugh, Cecile adjusted her rear view mirror catching a glimpse of herself. What had he been thinking? Even if it were possible, there was no way she would put herself in the position of going out with Bobby. He was light years more attractive that Carl—in fact, he had to have a night vision problem, that was the only explanation. After all, not more than an hour ago, her own husband had pulled his dick out of her mouth and calmly explained that she wasn't sexually attractive enough to give him a hard-on.

So why had he kissed her? Even though the distance

between them was growing with every turn of the wheel, Cecile could still feel his lips. They had been firm, but, oh, so yielding and they had caressed her with the gentlest of movements. The memories of his body next to hers made her tremble to her very core. She couldn't remember ever being that aware of a man, before. God, if things could only have been different. But she had just left her husband, who had repeatedly ground her self-esteem into the dirt. Cecile had no faith that another relationship would end up any different. Right now, she had zero sexual self-confidence.

Still, their encounter had been magical. It would be a joy to dream about and to relive. One thing was for certain, the next time she made herself come, the man of her dreams would have a brand new face.

Wiping the tears from her eyes, she started making plans. After about a hundred miles, things were beginning to come together. Tomorrow, she would call a lawyer and initialize divorce proceedings. She would also start looking for another apartment. There was no way she was going to remain in the space she had shared with Carl—too many bad memories. And she had that gynecologist appointment coming up. It would be a good time to ask questions. He might not have the answers to her problem, but it was a good place to start.

Having made that much progress, she felt empowered. The only sad spot was walking away from that incredibly sexy man who had seemed to enjoy her kiss. Why couldn't it be different? Why couldn't she be a different person? Why couldn't her body and the love that she had to offer be enough to make a man happy? Turning the radio on, she found a loud rap station and cranked up the volume, using the driving beat to chase away sad thoughts. Clearing her mind was imperative, because she had something really important to decide—what to do about Annalise.

Cecile was about an hour out of Dallas and there was little traffic on I-35. Her stomach growled and she remembered that it had been hours since she had eaten anything. Pulling into a convenience store, she jumped out to buy a soda and some cheese crackers. Throwing a shirt over her white blouse, she laughed again at how she must have looked to Bobby. A drowned rat came to mind—make that a drowned rat with an overabundant bust-line. As she walked across the parking lot, Cecile tried to straighten her hair, but the dampness and no hair dryer had turned her curly top into an unkempt mop. By the expression on the night clerk's face, she was a scary sight, indeed. Oh well, that only confirmed what she had known all the time.

Getting back on the road, her thoughts returned to Ethan and Annalise. He was divorced, and she was still in love with him. What a shame it would be if she didn't do something to try and get them together. Annalise was beautiful and a few scars would not be enough to keep her from being cherished by the right man. And Ethan, definitely, looked like the right man. If she came right out and told her friend about Ethan, she would never consent to visiting Lost Maples, but if she went down there for an entirely different reason...*hmmmmm*.

The wheels in Cecile's mind were turning as fast as the wheels on the Lexus. And for that she was grateful. Right now, she was grateful for anything that would take her mind off her own problems. And Bobby.

* * *

A Few Days Later

"I've tried everything, Cecile," Annalise's voice was

weary. "I've rested, relaxed, watched soft porn—I even lay on the bed and stared at that one photograph that I have of Ethan. It's of him and his brothers, Alex and Bobby, but it's the only one I have."

Cecile spat out a mouthful of coffee. *Bobby? Bobby?* Could her Bobby be Bobby Stewart? That would be an impossible coincidence. With thoughts and possibilities swirling through her head, she realized that Annalise was still talking.

"Nothing is working. I have a severe, severe case of writer's block."

Putting aside her own confusion, Cecile smiled as she listened to her friend. Okay. Here goes. "You know what you need?" Not waiting for an answer, she plunged in. "You need a vacation."

"I'm not in the mood for a trip," Annalise whined pitifully. She was as cute as a button.

"You'll like this place. It has everything." Cecile smiled to herself. Big, hunky everything. "It's where my fiasco with Carl happened, but I can't say enough about how beautiful it is there." She went on to tell Annalise about the amenities, the surrounding area, the shopping—everything she could to convince her friend that spending a few days at this restful Bed and Breakfast was exactly what she needed to get her creative juices flowing.

"Okay! Okay! You talked me into it." Annalise laughed. "You want those chapters really bad, don't you?"

Crossing her fingers, Cecile lied like a dog. "Yea, the important thing is to meet that deadline. The publishing house has been on my back about this, Annalise. But, I know you can do it. You haven't let me down, yet."

"All right. Enough said. I'm packing as we speak."

Hanging up, Cecile smiled at the thought of her friend finding happiness. Her good mood faded quickly when she thought about the upcoming court hearing for her own divorce. She hated to face Carl again. He wasn't contesting the divorce, but she dreaded having to look him in the eye after all of the humiliation he had put her through. What if he had told his lawyer and his friends of their problems? She had often suspected he made fun of her to his friends. Many times she had seen him whisper to them in front of her, and they would all look at her and sneer.

Hell, there was no use worrying about the divorce proceedings today. That was tomorrow's problem. What she needed to do was relax. As she got ready for bed, all she could think about was Bobby. He haunted her dreams. She remembered how broad his shoulders were and how kind his eyes had been. His arms and chest had been strong and muscular and he looked like he could have picked her up and toted her forever. When she closed her eyes, she could still feel his lips and the touch of his hands. Flopping over on the bed, she moaned at the futility of her dreams. Giving into temptation, she opened the drawer in her bedside table and removed the pink, vibrating dildo she had bought. It now had a name. Battery-operated-boyfriend—Bob—was no longer a joke, for Cecile's sex toy was named after the man who fueled her fantasies. Its name was Bobby.

Shedding her clothes, Cecile examined the fake penis. It was way bigger than Carl's dick, quite a bit longer and much thicker. She knew it would hurt if she pushed it all the way in. There was something wrong with her, sex always hurt. Soon maybe, she would have some answers about her problem, after her doctor's appointment. Picking up the box, she read that the insertable portion was five and half inches long. This morning, she had slipped into the local CVS and bought some lube. She longed to experience penetration without pain. Squeezing out a dollop into her palm, she dipped two fingers into the gel and applied it to the shaft of the dildo and more to the opening of her vagina. With one forefinger, she inserted some of the lubricant into her pussy.

Cecile wasn't naïve, she realized that the most likely reason for her pain was that Carl had never made the effort to properly arouse her. Over time, after he had begun to ridicule and reject her—her body would anticipate the mental anguish and react by tightening and refusing to produce enough natural moisture to make intercourse enjoyable. The problem would escalate and multiply because Carl would accuse her of frigidity and being less than feminine, which in turn, caused her nerves to tense and all of the symptoms would get worse. It became a vicious circle and, she supposed, it cost them their marriage.

As all of these thoughts tunneled through her mind, she rimmed the opening of her womanhood, wondering if she would be able to enjoy the sex toy. Maybe if she just put it in the very edge of her pussy and let the clitoral stimulator make up the difference. Arranging herself on the bed, she placed a pillow under her hips and inserted the remote control device, resting the soft rabbit ears on her clit. Tentatively, she turned it on and she was pleasantly surprised by the pleasurable sensations that warmed her sex.

Lifting her hips, Cecile increased the speed and gasped at how good it felt. As the soft thrusts of the plastic shaft teased her opening she let her mind wander and imagined that it was Bobby who was making her feel this way. She could see his massive shoulders blocking out the light and feel his warm breath as he leaned in to capture her lips. Hungrily, her vagina held on to the soft plastic. It wasn't deep, and it didn't hurt. Lord, it felt amazing! She wanted to thrust it deeper but, right now, there was no pain, so she thought she ought to be satisfied.

Cecile could almost imagine that it was Bobby bringing her to climax. For the first time, she managed to relax as something other than her own finger penetrated her vagina. Closing her eyes, she felt Bobby's weight press her into the mattress, she felt his lips kiss her neck, and it was his name she whispered when her orgasm hit. "Bobby! Oh yes, Bobby!"

* * *

Bobby leaned back and surveyed the section of wall he had finished painting. Not bad. A noise behind him caused him to jerk and the ladder waved precariously.

"Watch out, Bobby. You don't want to fall off that ladder, what would the women of Texas do?"

Bobby steadied himself and climbed down. This was as good an opportunity as any to get the information he needed from Ethan. And he was desperate. Memories of that one shared kiss with his little water sprite haunted him night and day. No other woman would do, it was as simple as that. "You and Alex have some friends that are PI's. Do you think you could give me their names and numbers?"

With a contemplative look, Ethan crossed his arms over his chest. "Sure. Lately, I've noticed something different about you. You seem more serious." When Bobby didn't comment, but began pouring the excess paint back into the can, Ethan answered his question. "Of course, I'll give you their number. Their names are Bo Roscoe, Chase Trahan and Dominic Vance. We've know them for years—they're good guys. They'll find whatever or whoever you're looking for."

"I'm thinking about asking them to help me find

Ceelee. I can't get her out of my mind, Ethan. What would you do?" Bobby expected him to make a couple of wisecracks, but he didn't.

"Go for it. I'd give everything I had for a chance to find Lise Evans."

"Why don't you?" Bobby couldn't believe his ears.

"It's been too long, Bob. Too much water has run under the bridge. Even if I were able to find her, it wouldn't be the same. I'm just not the man I used to be." Sadness colored every word that Ethan spoke.

"Bullshit!" Bobby said flatly. "You're more man than any of those pansy-ass cowboys that I ride with. I love my Longhorns, but you've got all of them beat, too. Ethan, you've been my rock for years. Don't tell me that you're going to let that ice cube of an ex-wife steal the rest of your life. Do something. If you're still hung up on Lise Evans find her. She may still be in love with you."

"I doubt that, Bobby. Lise was perfection. She was loving, gentle—and her body responded to mine like she was created just for me." Ethan helped Bobby fold the ladder and clean the brushes. "Not a night goes by that I don't have memories of making love with Annalise flooding my mind and heart. She always wanted me. She never turned me away." Bobby's heart broke for his brother. Living in the same house as his brother and *the bitch* had made it impossible for him to miss Francine's rants. The voice of the pit viper as she ripped into Ethan grated in his memory, *You're lousy in bed, Ethan. I'm never able to come with you inside me. I can get a better orgasm with a dildo and a romance book that I can with you.* "Don't give up on finding Annalise, Ethan." Bobby lowered his voice, noticing a couple of guests walking by. "Please."

Ethan stooped and sealed the paint can while Bobby cleaned the last brush in some paint thinner. "What are your plans for the rest of the day?" Bobby knew this was Ethan's way of taking the focus of the conversation off him.

"I'm gonna take the bull by the horns." Bobby was adamant. "If you'll give me that number for Roscoe, I'm gonna call him as soon as I get through here. Then, I've got to run over to San Marcos and register for the charity rodeo. I'm riding in memory of Shaun."

Both of them grew silent for a moment—remembering the vibrant young man whose life was snuffed out in an instant by crushing hooves and cruel horns. Standing, Ethan squeezed Bobby's shoulder. "Be safe and come back hungry, I'm gonna fix a big pot of spaghetti sauce."

"All right, I'll be back before supper." Bobby headed to the truck. "And tell Alex that I know he short-sheeted my bed last night. He tried to make me believe that it was little Mrs. Osborn who stays with us all the time, but I know it was him." Bobby couldn't help but grin, revenge was sweet.

Ethan shook his head. "What did you do?"

"If he wants to play like we're at summer camp, I have my ways to get even. Go look at the flagpole." As Bobby pulled away and waved, Ethan walked to the front and chuckled as he saw the burnt orange pair of Longhorn boxer briefs with Alex's name wrote in big letters across the crotch. They were waving merrily in the breeze from the very top of the flagpole.

"I live in a looney-bin," Ethan sighed.

Bobby made the phone call and gave Roscoe all the information he had on Ceelee. The PI assured him that he would do his best. As he drove, he planned what he would do when he found her again. It amazed him, they had only spent a few minutes together, but holding her had seemed so right. There was no way in hell he was giving up on this. Something in his gut told him that they were meant to find one another again, and he was going to do his dead level best to make it happen.

Making his way into the complex, the sun glinted off the steel roof and almost blinded him. Pickups and rigs were pulled into the parking lot, haphazardly. Some of the cowboys who followed the circuit lived in their trailers. Bobby had been lucky enough to live at home for the most part. Living in central Texas had its advantages. It put him within driving distance of the majority of the rodeos. Parking and climbing out, he saw Trace and they went into the office together to get registered for their events. After paying their fees, they decided to put their plan in motion. "Have you seen him?"

"Yea, he's out back. Let's go." Trace had enlisted them some help, including one big bull who had been fed a double measure of corn just for the occasion.

"Hey, Tad! We could use your help over here." Bobby wasn't a cruel person, but he did have a keen sense of right and wrong. And he was just about to piss off an arrogant, urban cowboy-wannabe who had overstepped his bounds with a woman. There were plenty of buckle bunnies for the choosing. Bobby was just as guilty as the next rodeo cowboy of accepting what they offered—be it right or wrong—but he drew the line at demanding what wasn't offered. Even in their macho world of bucking broncs, sweaty men, and big-eyed eager girls, *no* still meant *no*. Bobby and Trace had happened on Tad as he was pinning a young woman to the wall and fumbling with her breasts, while she had been begging for him to let her go. Bobby had pulled him off and they had drug him away and hauled him to the woodshed for a serious talking to. But Tad had persisted, and other women were complaining about his rough hand and asshole attitude.

So, Bobby and the boys had decided to take him down a notch.

"What's up, Bobby?" There was reluctant respect in Tad's voice. Bobby knew he had a reputation. He was big, well-liked and could whup ass at the drop of a hat. No brag, just fact.

"This bull's sick. We need you to help us take his temperature." Three other cowboys helped Bobby hold the pissed off bull tight in the loading chute. Sixteen hundred pounds of tense, mad bull strained to break free.

"I don't know what you mean," Obviously, Tad was reluctant to get too close to the bull. He rode broncs and did some bull-dogging. Only the toughest cowboys mixed it with the bulls.

"We've tried to take his temp the regular way, but he keeps biting down on the thermometers and breaking them," Bobby said with a straight face. One of the other cowboys nearly choked on the out-and-out insane claim that Bobby was making.

"What do you want me to do…feel his forehead?" Tad eased closer, trying to keep as much distance as possible between him and the dangerous creature.

"No," Bobby spoke evenly and reasonably. "I need you to stick a couple of fingers up his rump and tell me how it feels—I mean, how hot it feels." Another cowboy coughed, trying to hold in his mirth. "If it feels as warm as…say…a fresh Dairy Queen hamburger, then old Cupcake here is gonna have to get a visit from the vet." Like a child, at the mention of a doctor visit, old Cupcake reared backwards almost dislodging all four of his captors.

Trace grabbed a new hold on the bull and laughed. "This old bull's acting like he understands every word you're saying."

Tad eased up and lifted the bull's tail. "Don't I get a pair of gloves or something?"

Bobby swallowed. This was just too good. "The gloves would dull your sense of touch," Bobby said evenly. "It's best if you just dive right in." They all held their breath as Tad Smith stuck his hand up the bull's rectum. It was a symphony of movement. As Tad pushed in, Cupcake pushed back. He bucked once, twice, and Tad was hanging on tight with his interior grip. There was a whoosh of noise and Tad got more than he bargained for.

"Shit!" Tad yelled.

Literally.

"Hell yeah!" Bobby exclaimed. As Tad ran off to clean up, Bobby slipped old Cupcake an apple. "Good boy," he praised the bull. Justice had been served.

* * *

"I'm almost there," Annalise told Cecile in a happy-go-lucky voice. "Ah, gee…I just turned down Lonely Street. I hope this isn't going to be the Heartbreak Hotel."

"Just keep going, I think you'll be pleasantly surprised." She prayed with everything in her that she wasn't setting Annalise up for more hurt. A couple of days ago, Annalise's mother had answered the phone when Cecile had been returning her friend's call. It was their first, and Cecile hoped their last, conversation. Mrs. Evans didn't approve of Annalise's writing, therefore she did not approve of Cecile. She even had something to say about the artwork on the covers and the dedications.

What did come out of the conversation was the whole truth about the day that had stolen her friend's dreams. She had been in Houston on Spring Break with her family. After spilling some cocktail sauce on herself, she had walked back to the hotel to change clothes before they went on the rest of their outing. Annalise hadn't made it. A gang of young men had attacked her and one of them, who had been trying to gain membership into the gang, had tried to rape her. He had been too drunk to have intercourse, so to save face he had broken the top off of a glass whiskey bottle and raped her with the jagged weapon.

Annalise had almost died from blood loss and while in the hospital, her mother had said that she cried out Ethan's name over and over, begging him to come to her. When she was finally able to talk on the phone, an unknown female had answered Ethan's cell and informed her that he didn't have time to come to the phone, and that he had decided to see other people. It had broken her heart. She had not returned to UT until the next semester, and by then Ethan had graduated and moved on. Mrs. Evans did not approve of Annalise's continuing *obsession*, she called it, with Ethan Stewart. Frankly, Cecile suspected there was more to the story than Annalise knew.

"Who knows, Annalise? Romance might be waiting for you at Heartbreak Hotel." Cecile couldn't resist a tiny hint.

"You know I'm not in the market for a man." Her voice didn't break, but her tone grew serious. "Believe me, there are worse things than being alone. I haven't told you all the pitiful details of my rape and my injuries. But trust me, it's a blessing that Ethan and I didn't get back together. I won't gross you out, but seeing me naked wouldn't be a treat for any man. You remember that my parent's pushed me until I married the youth pastor at their church. It was a whirlwind deal, but on our wedding night, he took one look between my legs and promptly threw up off the side of the bed. The idea of Ethan reacting like that would be the absolute worst thing that I could ever imagine. So I cherish my memories, and visit him every night in my dreams."

"Honey, I'm so sorry that happened to you. Know this, and it's the gospel truth. You, Annalise, are beautiful and any man would be lucky to have you." She wanted to say more, but it was her sincere hope that after this weekend she and Ethan would be making their dreams come true.

"Okay, I'll call you in a couple of days and let you know how I'm doing," Annalise promised her. Cecile had to bite her tongue to keep from asking Annalise to keep an eye out for a raven-haired hunk with a darling, little dog named Mojo.

* * *

It was him! Annalise didn't know whether to laugh or cry. She had recognized his voice even before she had seen his face. When he had walked into the lobby area and their eyes had met, he had rushed across the room and swept her up in his arms, holding her like she was his lifeline to the world. "Lise! God, Lise! Is it really you?"

She couldn't help it, she wrapped her arms around him and clung to him, knowing that it was wrong. He was married. The sign said so. The one called Alex had watched the whole episode with a stunned look on his face. Ethan's body felt so good against hers, she just wanted to melt into his arms and hold him forever.

In spite of her best intentions to hold herself back, her hands began moving over his back and shoulders—caressing, rubbing—soothing out their heartache. The other man cleared his throat and Ethan let her body slide slowly down the length of his. That movement, like no other, highlighted the fact that he was fully engorged and erect. There was no way her mind, body, or heart missed the fact that he was as glad to see her as she was to see him.

    Annalise literally shook with desire. She wanted his lips on hers more than she had ever wanted anything. Unable to stop herself, she lifted her face, wordlessly, begging for his kiss. It was if the clock had been turned back six years, to a time before they had been forced apart and she had been damaged beyond repair.

That thought sobered her up. What was she doing? Stepping backward, she was desperate to put distance between them. Holding out her hand, she tried to restore sanity. "Ethan, it's so good to see you. I've thought of you, often."

Chapter Three

This time it was Toby Keith's Gimme Eight Seconds that he was singing at the top of his lungs. That he couldn't remember the words correctly didn't bother him a bit. He had the gist of it, so he just made up his own. "Gimme eight seconds, that's all I need. I may be insane, riding this bull is like taming a hurricane." Bobby was making so much noise, he didn't pay any attention to the grinding racket his truck was making. By the time it was audible over his caterwauling, it was too late. There were knocks, rattles, scrapes and squeals, Bobby pulled over just before he heard the crack. Damn! His truck had it in for him.

As he opened the door to check out the damage, he was hit by a memory, a wave of longing for a sweet little doll named Ceelee. He would give his last dime to hold her again. Bo had called him this morning with an update, and even though the PI had assured him he would pull every string he could to find her. Unfortunately, the info Bobby had given him just wasn't enough to make any concrete promises.

Lifting the hood, he groaned. It was a busted U-Joint. "Crap." Knowing he had no other choice, he called Ethan and sat back to wait, knowing this time his angel wouldn't come walking out of the night to rescue him.

Lying back to rest, he had dozed off when the slamming of a vehicle door announced that one of his brothers had arrived. "Bobby, Bobby—son, didn't you renew your Triple A? We've had to rescue you and this piece of shit twice in the last month." Ethan teased his little brother, who was younger, not necessarily smaller.

Bobby appeared contrite. "I guess not. Sorry, bro." Bobby stepped out of the vehicle and stood with his brother while they looked under the hood. Both of them were fairly decent mechanics, but Ethan agreed with Bobby that a u-joint had broken, leaving one end of the drive shaft on the pavement. And that wasn't something they could fix by the side of the road.

"We're getting you a new ride, pronto." He flipped on his cell phone and called a tow truck.

"With that purse from the last win at the Mesquite Rodeo, combined with what I've already got saved up, I can buy the truck for myself. I can even pay cash for the most of it." Bobby expected Ethan to argue with him, tell him that he needed to save his money, but Ethan was strangely quiet. It was obvious he had something on his mind besides a new truck.

Bobby stood by and let his big brother have his down time. In a few minutes, a friend of Ethan's appeared. In no time, they had the truck hoisted and ready to be moved. Ethan made arrangements to have it delivered to an area mechanic and soon they were ready to head back to Lost Maples. Ethan handed his keys to Bobby, "Here you drive, I need to think."

Bobby looked at him curiously. "What's going on?"

"Lise Evans is at the B&B." Ethan said the words evenly, but Bobby knew instantly that this was huge.

"Lise? The Lise? The girl that disappeared on you so long ago?"

"Yeah, she's back and I don't know which end is up."

"What are you going to do?"

"I know what I want to do. I want to make love to her so badly I ache with it."

"What's stopping you?"

"Well, I am here with you…" Ethan smiled. Bobby knew he was joking. "No. Bobby, so much has happened.

There's so much I need to ask her. I don't even know why Lise left me in the first place."

"I'd say it's high time you found out."

Ethan dry scrubbed his face. "I kissed her a bit ago. A damn hot kiss. She still responds to me, of that I have no doubt. It feels like things are the same between us, but we haven't said the words. And the words have to be said."

"Sounds like you've got some work to do."

Bobby concentrated on the driving, giving Ethan time to think of Lise. He had his own doll-baby to dream about. As Bobby parked the truck, Ethan spied Annalise walking down by the creek. He was out of the door and halfway across the lawn before Bobby could put two words together. "Have a good time!" he called after his brother. Hope speared him in the chest, he hadn't seen a smile like that on Ethan's face in many a day. Keeping his eye on them until they walked out of sight, he headed into the house—his stomach rumbling. "Alex!" Bobby called out for his brother.

"I'm in the kitchen."

"You're such a homebody," Bobby teased his broad, strapping brother. Alex lunged at him teasingly, but Bobby stood his ground. "Whatever you're cooking smells heavenly, dear."

"Watch it, stud," Alex flipped a chocolate chip cookie at him and he caught it in mid air

"Ethan tells me that Lise Evans is here. What do you think about that?"

Alex pulled a chair out and joined Bobby, handing him the whole cookie jar. "Here, I know you can't eat just one. Just don't spoil your supper." He slowly stirred the cup of coffee he had poured himself and seemed to weigh his words. "I think it could be the best thing that ever happened to Ethan," he looked up at his brother with a wistful smile on his face. "You should have seen them. I have never seen Ethan react to a woman like that. It was like one of those romantic chick flicks, he swept her up in his embrace and she wrapped her arms around him and they clung to one another for dear life." Alex paused and then snorted. "It was the most damned romantic thing I've ever seen."

Looking up, Alex laughed out loud at his brother's expression. "I expected you to have some smartass thing to say about my sentimentality, instead you look like you're up for a Lifetime movie marathon. We're pitiful, do you know that? Soon, we'll be watching Dr. Phil."

Bobby agreed, he knew his outlook on life was changing. "I don't tell you this often enough, but I appreciate being part of this family. When I think back to those days when I was abused and then abandoned..." Bobby stopped talking, giving himself a minute to pull it together. Alex laid a big, comforting hand on his shoulder.

"Bobby, you're not just a part of this family—son, you're the best part," Alex was big of body and soft of heart. "Mom and Dad loved you, and as far as Ethan and I are concerned, you're closer than blood, you're a part of us."

"Thanks, it's been so hard watching Ethan be unhappy. I hope this woman doesn't hurt him any more than he's already been hurt," Bobby pulled another cookie out of the jar and began munching on it.

"I don't think she will," Alex spoke slowly and thoughtfully. "If you could have seen her face, it literally lit up when she saw Ethan. You could tell she was overjoyed to be with him again."

"You remember that girl I met the other night?" Bobby said between bites.

"You meet a girl every night, don't you? I mean you've brought home—at last count—forty two different girls from UT, not to mention all of those little groupies that follow you around at the rodeos."

Alex wasn't jealous, Bobby knew he never lacked for female companionship. "I know," Bobby smiled, aware that he was blessed with that hunk quality that drew women to him like bears to honey. "But, this girl was different—special."

"Which girl are you talking about?"

"I'm talking about the one from the side of the road."

Bobby spoke so flatly and seriously that Alex exploded in a belly-shaking laugh. "That's just like you, bud, you can find a woman anywhere." Seeing that Bobby was as serious as a heart attack, he stopped chuckling and inquired. "What was so special about her?"

"She stopped to help me in that rain storm when I broke down, she even rescued Mojo. I didn't realize the little shit had gotten out of the truck after I plowed into that guard rail."

"I've told you about driving too fast on wet roads." Ever the older brother, Alex couldn't resist lecturing a little.

Bobby pushed his Stetson up off of his forehead. "I told you that a deer ran out in front of me." Bobby knew Alex remembered his habit of braking for animals. He had almost obliterated a set of new tires dodging squirrels. "Anyway, she came running up to me soaking wet." He started to tell Alex about her wet shirt and those magnificent tits, but that memory was too precious to share. "She wasn't worrying about her looks or trying to come on to me, she was genuinely trying to help."

Alex laughed again. "Wow. I never thought I'd see the day when a woman not coming on to you would peak your interest." Waving his cookie at him, Alex made his point. "That's a sure sign you've gotten entirely too popular with the ladies. It's that bull-riding you've been doing. Did you know I took twelve messages for you last week? And they were all from women with more sugar in their shorts than brains in their head?"

"How old are you?" Bobby looked at his brother. "You're acting like you're seventy-two. You need to get laid, Alex. You've been baking too many cookies."

Alex grumbled under his breath. "You like my cookies."

"There was just something about this woman, Alex. She had the most beautiful face, and there was this innocent, unspoiled quality about her." He leaned back in his chair and stretched his mile long legs out in front of him. "I just wanted to pick her up, cuddle her and bring her home."

"So, where is she now? In your room?" Bobby knew Alex wouldn't put it past him, he had found more than one woman in Bobby's bed when he went in to collect his laundry.

"No, I can't find her."

"It's not like you to lose a woman, Bobby. How did you misplace her?"

Bobby didn't crack a smile. "It all happened so fast, I kissed her and it was the *best* kiss of my life. And she kissed me back, but then she acted like something was wrong. I didn't get a chance to find out her last name or her number. She just drove off into the night."

Alex straightened his face and leaned forward. "Do you think she was in some kind of trouble?" All of the Stewart boys were hero material. None of them could stand to see a woman, old person, or an animal mistreated in any way.

"I don't know," Bobby shook his head. "When I

reached out my hand to touch her, she was pretty skittish. It seemed like she wasn't used to a man's touch or something." Getting out of his chair he ran a weary hand over his face and sighed. "I'm gonna go grab a shower."

Alex studied his brother for a moment. "She didn't know you from Adam, Bobby. Any woman is going to be wary of an unknown man they meet at night on a deserted road. I'm just surprised she stopped to aid you at all." Bobby nodded his head and put the cookie jar back where it belonged. Alex drained his coffee cup and got up to put it in the sink. "Great, now I've got two more things to worry about—Ethan and his old flame, and you and your mysterious storm siren. Hell, my business is enough to give me a headache. Rick LeBeau is driving me nuts. I swear to God, he's more trouble than he's worth."

"Austin is next door, Alex. Environmental engineers are everywhere. Your consulting firm is top notch. You can get another employee, easy."

"Thanks, bud. I just believe in giving everybody a fair shake. I hope I don't live to regret it. But, know this, I'll help you in any way I can. I've made light of your roadside romance, but if you need something, just ask."

"Thanks, Alex. I'll be back in a little while."

Alex watched Bobby saunter off, *too handsome for his own good*. Walking to the window, he saw Ethan standing with Annalise on the front porch of her cabin. "Well, well—love is in the air. Looks like everybody had somebody in their sights, but me. Damn! I'm lonely."

Bobby soaped himself in the shower. The warm water felt good against his skin. Leaning one arm on the tile of the shower wall, he rubbed the shower gel on his dick and balls. As he had for the last few weeks, his thoughts turned to Ceelee. Lord, how he wished she were here with him. It had been dark, but the light of the lantern had revealed she had big eyes. Big green eyes that looked like beautiful jewels, and they had been so sad.

Shit! Lord, when he thought about how it felt to hold her close, he moaned at the memory. Why hadn't he made her understand how much their brief meeting had meant to him? She had the sweetest face. He smiled just thinking about the cute little dimple that had appeared when she had laughed at Mojo. If she were here with him, he would kiss that sweet dimple. He would dip his tongue in the little indention, and lick his way to her plump little lips.

Fisting his cock, he thought about what he would like to do to her tits. God, he loved a woman's breasts. He could love on them for hours. There was nothing sweeter than holding one with both hands, lifting it up to your lips and filling your mouth with a luscious, fat areola and a hard little nipple. He dreamed of nursing on Ceelee's perfect breasts. He would fall on his knees and hold her close, and suck and kiss and massage her breasts until she was weak in the knees. While his mind and heart was making love to Ceelee, his own hand was stroking and pumping his cock. He leaned his head against his forearm, picturing her face as she came, purring from his loving. "Ceelee!" he shouted as his own climax roared through his body, streams of white cum jetted out from his cock and splashed against the shower wall. His hips pumped sympathetically, longing to be pushing their payload against willing, eager female flesh.

What in the hell was he going to do? He hadn't slept with a girl since he had kissed Ceelee next to the highway. He didn't want anyone else, he wanted the little sprite that made his heart burn with desire and his cock stiff as a board. For the first time, Bobby Stewart wondered if love at first sight was more than just a myth.

After he had dried off and dressed, he went to the kitchen, and found Ethan and Alex putting the finishing touches on dinner. "Annalise is coming to eat with us," Ethan announced, sounding as proud as if he had managed to bring peace to the Middle East.

"Good. So, what's going on with you and Lise?" Bobby asked as he got four plates down from the cabinet.

Ethan cleared his throat, as if he were making sure he said the right words. "Having the chance to be with her again is a dream come true. A lot has happened to both of us, and I'm being very careful to take it slow with her. But that's okay, she's more than worth it." A knock at the front door had Ethan sprinting to answer it. In a few moments he returned, leading a breathtakingly beautiful woman who smiled at them shyly. Bobby noticed that Ethan held on to her hand as if he was afraid she would bolt. Bobby was so glad for him, he only wished that one day he could look that content to just hold a woman's hand. Maybe…Someday…

Ethan made the formal introductions. "Alex, Bobby, this is Lise Evans, uh, Ramsey. Lise these are my brothers." Both men came over and solemnly shook the hand that she had to pry from Ethan's grip. "It's wonderful to meet you both." Annalise spoke sincerely.

As the evening progressed, it became clear to Bobby that Annalise was one special woman. They shared stories about Austin and their college days at the University of Texas and she was very interested in Longhorn football. Annalise had something in common with them, she was the owner of a miniature dachshund that looked almost like Mojo.

"He's so much company for me. I know he's not a person, but I swear I can understand most of what he says. When he wants something to eat, he goes and stands near to where I keep whatever he wants. I know he wants a treat when he stands by the cabinet, and if he wants some of what I had for dinner, he goes and stands by the stove.

And when he stands by the frig—I know he wants a butter sandwich."

Alex roared with laughter. "A butter sandwich? Annalise, no wonder he's a butterball. You're overfeeding that dog."

Annalise looked a bit guilty. "I know, but I can't seem to say no to him. It was just a bit cool the other night and he stood by the fireplace until I lit a fire for him."

"Mojo is spoiled, too. You have a soft heart, I'm counting on that."

Bobby was so taken with Annalise and the change that had come over his normally sad, older brother that he spoke up without thinking. "This is great! We haven't laughed this much since before Ethan married Francine." All grew quite.

"You married Francine?" Annalise sounded so shocked and stricken that if Bobby could have pulled the words back, he would have. From the look on her face, it was clear she was shocked.

Ethan looked miserable. "Not the smartest thing I've ever done. I'll admit that.

"You can say that again," Bobby chimed in. Alex punched his brother, who grunted from the blow.

Ethan continued his explanation to Annalise and his brothers. "Annalise knew Francine. Her personality didn't improve with time, she was a bitch in school like she was here. It was also Francine who cast the rod and reel carelessly at me and Annalise stepped in the way to keep it from hooking me in the eye. She had no idea that her petty act backfired on her—because, that was the moment I found out how truly amazing this woman is."

Annalise attempted to place everyone at ease. "Francine is a beautiful woman."

"She's not as pretty as you are," Bobby was having

trouble keeping his mouth closed.

"There are many kinds of pretty, Bobby." Annalise explained. "There is sophisticated, elegant beauty, and then there is pleasant attractiveness."

"More correctly, there is the cool beauty of a marble statue and then there is the warm, giving, sexy, beauty of a real woman." Ethan's soft words seemed to affect Annalise, for she shivered in the comfortable room.

Bobby knew exactly what Ethan meant. All of the other women he knew, or that had come on to him since that night on the road, seemed plastic and shallow. He wanted a woman like Annalise—like Ceelee.

Alex got up, "Bobby, let's take the dog for a walk, and run a check on the cabins."

"We already did that," Bobby protested.

"Let's do it again." Alex pulled his brother to his feet and Ethan and Annalise were left alone.

When they got outside, Bobby observed dryly. "I thought we were going to walk the dog." He walked by Alex as they made a round by each cabin.

"They needed to be alone." Alex said simply.

"Do you miss being married?"

Alex didn't answer for a moment. Then he let out a long breath, "Bonnie and I weren't meant to be. The passion just wasn't there."

"Would you ever consider remarrying?"

Alex snorted, "The chances of that happening are less than me getting struck by a bolt of lightning, bud."

"I'll remember you said that." Bobby laughed.

* * *

"I've been your gynecologist for years, Cecile," Dr. Lambert looked at her oddly. "Why is today the first I've heard of sex being painful for you?"

As she lay there spread open like a filleted fish,

Cecile smiled weakly at the man who was way too good-looking to be gazing at her questionably functioning lady-parts. "I was embarrassed."

"Our relationship is supposed to be above that sort of thing." He lectured her in a sincere voice. "Now, tell me the kind of pain you're experiencing." He turned on that odd little coalminer looking light he wore on his forehead, took his cold tools and started peering up her pussy like he was looking in a kaleidoscope tube.

"When Carl would try and penetrate me, it would hurt." She winced in anticipation that what the doctor was going to do would hurt, also.

"Maybe you were dry because you were not aroused." She could feel his breath on her groin and she trembled in embarrassment.

"I wasn't aroused at all, but this was more than discomfort from dryness, it was a sharp jabbing pain and it wasn't constant—it was like when he was at his deepest he would touch something that was very sore." She didn't know if what she was saying was making any sense at all.

Cecile heard him making little studious noises, like he was finding something extremely interesting. Finally, he set up and gave her a funny look. "Cecile, I'm a man, and for a man this is a humiliating question. But since your husband isn't here, I'm going to ask it, anyway. Was your husband well endowed?"

How far off could he be? But Carl wasn't friends with Dr. Lambert, as far as she knew. And right now, she didn't owe Carl a lot of loyalty, anyway. "I was a virgin when I married, Dr. Lambert. But, even I know that Carl is much smaller than average."

"How long would you say he is when fully erect?"

Let's see. Could she remember back that far? It had been years since she had seen him fully erect. "Maybe, four inches—I never really measured." Cecile wasn't handling this conversation well, and it wasn't even her penis!

"That is below average." Dr. Lambert laughed an odd, halfway sheepish laugh. "I know you've had sex, Cecile. Maybe not the best sex, but sex, nevertheless. So, what I'm about to tell you is going to sound very odd."

"Okay." He didn't sound ominous. She had actually considered that she might have a tumor or even cancer.

"Cecile, Carl's penis was short and your hymen is thicker than normal and located a little further back in the canal than most women's."

"My hymen?" Cecile didn't understand what the doctor was trying to tell her.

"That jabbing pain you felt was when Carl's penis would hit your hymen. He just wasn't long enough to pierce it."

"What are you saying?" Cecile wanted him to spell it out.

"As unusual as this may sound, my dear. You are still a virgin. Would you like me to pierce your hymen for you? It's a simple procedure, I assure you it would be clinical and proper with very little discomfort."

"No, thank you." The idea of losing her virginity to a cold, metal, medical instrument just made her sad. The rest of the doctor visit passed quickly and Cecile went home in a daze. Every once in a while she would laugh out loud. If she wasn't a fool she didn't know what one was. A virgin. She was a thirty-one year old virgin, who had been married for seven years! What a joke. She thought of all the cruel jibes and criticisms that Carl had taken great pleasure in flinging her way. She seriously considered calling him and telling him that his dick was so small he couldn't even take her virginity. But she wasn't by nature a cruel person, so she did nothing but wallow in her confusion and self-pity.

How would she ever face a man like Bobby? She felt like such a freak. God, she just wanted to go get in the bed and pull the covers over her head and try to think of something else besides this unbelievable fiasco. So when her cell phone rang, Cecile started to ignore it. But thinking it might be her friend, curiosity got the better of her. "Hello?"

She was right. "I love you, I love you, I love you!" Annalise sounded overjoyed.

"I love you, too." Instantly, Cecile knew exactly where the source of her friend's happiness lay and she couldn't help but smile. "So, you found Ethan, didn't you?"

"Yes, I did. You are one sneaky matchmaker, aren't you? I couldn't believe it when I saw him, Cecile. I love him so much!" Her voice lowered as if she were conveying secret, sacred information. "He asked me to marry him."

"Well, of course he did." Cecile had never doubted it. "When's the wedding?"

"In a month, but I need you here in three weeks. You're going to be my bridesmaid." Cecile got a notebook and began writing down all the information she would need to help Annalise plan her dream wedding. They had a lot of work to do.

"I would be honored to stand up with you. So, everything's okay?" This was Cecile's way of asking about Annalise's greatest fear, that Ethan would see her scars and not want her.

Annalise's voice shook with emotion. "He wanted to make love to me from the moment we were reunited. I wanted it, too. But as you know, I was positive he would be repulsed by my scarring." Letting loose a little nervous giggle, she poured her heart out to Cecile. "He was almost impossible to resist, Cecile. He let me know without a doubt, that he wanted to pick up right where we left off. He even made me confess that I was still hopelessly attracted to him."

"How did he wear you down?" Cecile was sitting on the edge of her seat. Annalise's joy had become her own.

"God, he was so sexy. He followed me to my cabin and kissed me. He kissed my breasts, he was incredible." The sex talk between them wasn't unusual, the difference was that this time it wasn't the plot of a novel they were discussing, it was Annalise's own love life. "Then, something happened."

"What?" Cecile couldn't stand the suspense.

"He told me how his ex-wife had belittled him and told him he wasn't a good lover." Annalise lowered her voice. "Which was the most ridiculous thing anyone has ever said," she reiterated emphatically. "Anyway, somehow she had discovered my books and it made her furious to find out that I had made Ethan the focus. She decided to get her revenge by tearing down his sexual confidence. She told him that a dildo and one of my books brought her more pleasure than he could. Of course, Ethan didn't realize that I was Ann Pace."

"Good grief!" Cecile was completely caught up in Annalise's tale. "What happened next?"

"I was recognized by one of the other guests and Ethan was upset to learn that I was the very author whose books Francine had rubbed in his face."

"But, Ethan was the hero of the books."

"He didn't know that at the time. He walked off and left me, I thought he was never going to speak to me again."

"What happened? How did you get it straightened out?"

"Alex, Ethan's brother had figured it out. He talked to Ethan, gave him my books and told him to read them. Then, he came to me and explained what Ethan had been going through."

"Wow." This was an amazing story—as good as one of their books.

"Oh, this is where the story takes a wild turn," she laughed at herself. Annalise was so happy she just couldn't hold it in. "Alex asked me to prove to Ethan that he was still the man he once was—Alex asked me to seduce Ethan."

"What?" Cecile screamed into Annalise's ear.

"Hey!" Annalise fussed. "I am on the other end of that contraption. Don't yell in my ear."

"Sorry," Cecile couldn't help it—she was shocked. "Did you do it?"

"First, I explained to Alex why I couldn't do it. I told him about the attack and the scars. But after he told me how Ethan had suffered, and the doubts he had about himself, I couldn't stand it. I arranged with Alex to leave the door of the B&B unlocked and I went in under cover of darkness. I convinced myself that I could make love to Ethan if there was no chance he could see my scars."

"How was it?" Cecile asked before she thought.

Annalise groaned at the memory. "It was heavenly. We made love all night. He is the best lover in the whole world."

"That's right, make poor love-starved Cecile jealous."

"You don't have to be love-starved, you're gorgeous." She didn't give Cecile time to refute her unlikely claim. "That one night didn't solve all of our problems, but it sure did open the lines of communication." She giggled at her own joke. "Every time we made love, Ethan proved to me that we were perfect for one another. Finally, I told him about the rape and he convinced me that the only important thing was that we had found one another again."

"I'm so happy for you, Lise." And she meant it.

"I had a couple of close calls, too." Annalise's voice grew serious. "My ex-husband, Jeff, decided that he could extort money from me. He threatened me and even attacked me, twice. Ethan and his brothers made short work of him."

"My God! Are you okay?" She had wanted to play cupid, but had never intended for Annalise be in any danger.

"I'm fine, and before you start questioning your role in this, remember—if I had been alone, not here at Lost Maples, I would have been helpless. Jeff might have killed me."

"I'm just happy that Ethan and his brothers were close by to help you."

"Yea, me too. Alex and Bobby are wonderful. Alex has become one of my best friends and Bobby is a charmer."

When Annalise mentioned the brother named Bobby, her heart jumped. It probably wasn't the same man she'd met on the road, but his truck had broken down so close to the B&B that she couldn't help but wonder. And her Bobby had even referred to the fact he had a brother. There was no denying it, Cecile was dying for any little bit of information on her dream guy she could find. So, she went fishing. "Tell me, are the brothers younger or older than Ethan?" Yea, that question sounded pretty harmless. Perhaps, she would learn something useful.

"They're both younger. Alex is an environmental consultant and Bobby is in his last year at the University of Texas. He plays football for the Longhorns."

Bobby Stewart was still in college! Well, he wasn't her Bobby, then. Her Bobby was a fully grown, mature hunk of a sexy man, not a college kid. So much for that possibility.

"Marrying Ethan is the culmination of an impossible dream. Life is good." Letting out a relieved, happy sigh, Annalise made Cecile feel much better about the whole situation. "Everything worked out perfectly, thanks to you. You are my guardian angel."

Cecile didn't feel like an angel. Even though she was thrilled to death for Annalise, she couldn't help but be a tiny bit jealous. Would her dreams ever come true? Before she went to bed, Cecile knelt by her bed and prayed to find someone to love.

* * *

The wedding draws closer—

"Who's the cutie?" Bobby asked Ethan. He had just returned from football practice and arrived to find a mild form of chaos in his home.

"That's Scarlet, Annalise's sister," explained Ethan. "Watch your brother." Bobby turned his attention to Alex who looked like he had lost his best friend and somebody had kicked his puppy at the same time.

"What's wrong with him? He looks sick." Bobby, on the other hand, was feeling hope for the first time in months. He had received a call from Roscoe that he might have found Ceelee. Bobby was waiting on pins and needles, ready to leave at a moment's notice. All he needed was an address or a telephone number and Miss Ceelee wouldn't know what had hit her. Meanwhile, Alex looked in dire need of cheering up.

"He has a terminal case of foot-in-mouth disease. It

seems he was having a pissy day and inadvertently took it out on little Scarlet. She walked up behind him as he was explaining to me that he resented the fact she was coming so early. He said that he was afraid she would expect to be entertained, and that she would develop a crush on you or him. In the same breath he also managed to refer to her as a plain spinster and a homely church mouse." Bobby's eyes widened at the uncharacteristic behavior of his normally courteous and gentle brother.

"Good God!" Bobby whistled. "She's gorgeous. Why would he do that?"

"He has employee problems. Apparently Rick LeBeau knows Scarlet and was filling Alex's head with complete nonsense about her. Oh, and to top it off, the bakery burned that is supposed to be baking the wedding cakes and the caterer is being uncooperative. All of it together had your brother in a tail-spin. Hell, I don't know." Ethan chuckled. "I do know that he took one look at Scarlet and fell for her like a ton of bricks. Look at his face. I've never seen him like this. He's worrying himself to death, trying to make it up to her. " Ethan and Bobby crossed their arms over their chest and leaned against the wall, watching Alex try to get Scarlet to talk to him. "You know what you ought to do?"

"What?" Bobby was game for anything that could pick at his brother—he had years of paybacks to implement.

"Go over there and greet Scarlet with a hug and a kiss. And say something to Alex that will make him think you're attracted to her—and just watch him. This will be hilarious."

Bobby laughed at Ethan's plan, "Remember, I would like to live to see tomorrow. I've had a hint of good news from Bo Roscoe on Ceelee."

"He won't hurt you…much." Ethan egged Bobby on.

"When do you expect to hear back from Roscoe?"

"He said he'd call me tomorrow or for sure the next day."

"Good, now go flirt with Scarlet and watch your brother swell up like a toad-frog."

Taking his own life in his hands, Bobby eased over to the woman who had caught his brother's eye. Annalise saw him and did the honors. "Hey, Bobby! Scarlet this is Bobby, the younger Stewart. Scarlet, this is our sweet Bobby."

Bobby didn't even hesitate. He waltzed up to Scarlet and swung her up in his arms, giving her a big-ole Texas welcome. "Hey, sweetheart. It's wonderful to meet you. We're so glad to have you with us." Was that growling he heard behind him? Giving Scarlet one more hug—yes, that was definitely growling. Now for the clincher. He set Scarlet down, kissed her cheek and turned to Alex and winked. "I'm in love," he whispered.

Ethan busted out laughing as Alex's countenance darkened like a thundercloud. "Back off, little brother." Alex ground out under his breath.

Scarlet was passing out gifts that she had made everyone. "Bobby, congratulations on your winning career with the Longhorns. Annalise sent me a photograph of you to use as a pattern. I hope you like it." In awe, Bobby took a tapestry from Scarlet that showed him catching a football.

"Wow! This has everything on it—I see Bevo, the band, and the cannon. There's even Big Mack! Thank you so much, Scarlet." He hugged her again. She had made something for everybody, and Bobby was amazed to see how Alex reacted when she gave him a tapestry with an endangered whooping crane on it, one of Alex's pet environmental projects. Alex was touched, and head over heels for the sweet Scarlet. Sadly he felt exactly the same, but for now, he was alone.

* * *

The Next Day

"I found her, Bobby." Roscoe's words were music to his ears.

"Where?" This was the message he had been waiting on, and Bobby was ready. All he needed was an address or a telephone number and he would be on Miss Ceelee like white on rice.

"I'm on her tail right now," Roscoe sounded funny, like he found the situation humorous.

"What highway are you on?"

"It's not a highway." Roscoe explained mysteriously.

"Well, whatever it is, just tell me. Give me your twenty and I'll head that way." Bobby gathered his billfold and his keys, ready to roll.

"That won't be necessary."

Bobby was fast losing patience with Ethan's friend. Just because they were more than client and investigator did not mean that Roscoe could get away with jerking him around. "Dammit, Roscoe!" Bobby couldn't stand the suspense. He needed to know where Ceelee was, now!

"She's slowing down. She's parking,"

Bobby froze, waiting for what Roscoe would say next. He seemed to be alone in the house. Where was everybody? "Where are you, Roscoe? Talk to me," Bobby demanded, tired of the bullshit.

A soft knock sounded at the front door. At first, Bobby resented the intrusion. Next came suspicion. "Aren't you going to answer the door?" Roscoe drawled. "And don't ever say that Bo Roscoe doesn't deliver." A dry laugh came over the phone, then a drier, "You will get my bill." Disconnect.

Too afraid to hope, he opened the door and there she was. Her small, sexy gasp told him clearly that she was as shocked to see him as he was to see her. "Bobby? My God, you *are* my Bobby!"

One moment she was standing on the outside looking in, the next he lifted her up in his arms and cradled her close. "Ceelee! Thank God!" He buried his head in her neck and inhaled her fresh, sweet scent. "I'm so glad to see you. You'll never know how much I've thought about you." Bobby wasn't trying to hide his joy at her arrival and when her little arms crept around his neck to hold him close, he thought he'd died and gone to heaven.

"I've thought about you, too," she confessed softly. "I shouldn't have. But I did. You'll never know how much."

Bobby couldn't help it, his lips found the soft skin of her neck and he rained kisses on the silky smoothness. His mind was so fogged with relief that it took him a few seconds to realize she was trembling. "Baby, what's wrong?"

"There's a man outside. He was following me. I was afraid I wouldn't make it safely inside." She clasped his shoulders and Bobby felt like a heel.

"Oh, baby, that was Roscoe, he's harmless. He's been doing his best to track you down for me." He rubbed his nose against her cheek. He couldn't believe it! She was here! He had her in his arms and she was not only letting him hold her, she was clinging to him like a sweet little honeysuckle vine. Part of it was nerves, and that was his fault. "I thought I had lost you forever, Ceelee. All I had was a first name and the last three digits of your car plates—" Before he could say anything else, Ceelee was pushing back, trying to look him in the face.

"You were trying to find me?"

They were still standing in the door, but he didn't care if the whole world saw them. "I couldn't forget your kiss, sugar. I couldn't forget your beautiful face." She had on a sleeveless red sundress and he took advantage of all of that exposed creamy skin by running his hungry hands up and down her arms. "Roscoe is a family friend, he has a PI firm." Then, it dawned on him what was going on. Roscoe didn't bring her to him, he had just followed her here. "I can't believe it. You came looking for me, didn't you?"

A little frown marred her features. "No, not exactly." He didn't understand what she meant, but his attention was more on what she was doing with her hands than what she was saying. It was as if she couldn't stop touching him. To Bobby's delight, she caressed his chest and shoulders through his cotton shirt. A groan slipped from his mouth, and he clasped one hand and brought it to his lips. "Actually, I came…" She didn't get to finish her sentence due to a squeal that came from the porch directly behind her.

"Cecile, you're here!"

Bobby was confused. Annalise had scrunched in between them, pushed him away, and had Ceelee in a girl hug that clearly indicated they were friends. "Cecile?" What the hell? He backed up out of the door-way to let the whole crew in. As Alex, Ethan and Scarlet made their way into the house, Cecile was lost in the excitement of introductions and greetings. For a moment, Bobby thought he had been forgotten. But when Ceelee's eyes met his over Annalise's shoulder, he saw she was still aware he was there, and that was all that mattered. "Bobby, I'd like for you to meet Cecile Fairchild. She's my editor at Passion Publishing, my best friend and my bridesmaid. Cecile, this is Bobby, Ethan's brother."

The group parted and left them facing one another. Bobby was about to announce they had met before and how, but that decision was taken out of his hands. His water sprite stepped forward, extended her hand and pretended they had never met before.

"Hello, Bobby. It's so nice to meet you,"

He took her hand in his and played along, determined to get to the bottom of this mystery as soon as he could get her behind closed doors. "Cecile, I've been looking forward to seeing you. It seems like I already know you."

Her beautiful green eyes shot him little darts of warning. Well, tough! He had been yearning to be with her for weeks. If she didn't look so sad and unsure, he would have demanded answers and to hell with hiding the fact that he knew the taste of her kiss.

Chapter Four

"Girl, I am so glad to see you!" Annalise hugged Cecile's neck. "Just leave your luggage there and we'll get you settled in a bit. The men won't mind being left to their own devices for a few minutes. We need some girl time. I can't wait for you and Scarlet to get better acquainted. Let's make a pot of coffee and gossip."

She allowed herself to be led away, carefully avoiding Bobby's probing eyes. To say she was shocked to see him was an understatement. Oh, she had entertained a hope that Bobby Stewart was her Bobby, but she had never really expected it to be true. How was she going to handle this? And why was she hiding it? They hadn't done anything wrong. Just because she had let a strange man kiss her on the side of the road wasn't a crime. God, he was good looking.

"I wouldn't have missed this for the world," Cecile assured her friend, trying to sound normal as thoughts clamored around in her head. "I'm so happy for you and I'm glad of the chance to get to know Scarlet." She was intrigued by Annalise's sister. There was something about her that she just couldn't put her finger on. Scarlet resembled Annalise, but she appeared more fragile, somehow. And there had been no missing the way Alex had looked at her. If she wasn't mistaken, there would soon be another wedding to plan.

"So the two older brothers have been claimed." Cecile sighed, attempting to sound nonchalant and teasing. "That's a shame." It wasn't the two older brothers that interested her. Lord, help her, she had melted into his arms like warm honey on a biscuit. But the fact remained that he was way too young for her. Any hope she had harbored of reconnecting with her dream lover was gone.

The Bobby she had built up in her mind didn't really exist. Oh, this Bobby was just as sexy and just as appealing, but knowing he might be ten years her junior changed everything. To say she was disappointed was the understatement of the century. And that was why she hadn't wanted Annalise and the rest to know about how she and Bobby had met—it was just too embarrassing.

Still—he seemed attracted to her. What if? Cecile let impossible thoughts run through her head. Face it, if she was secure in her sexuality she'd be all over that college boy. Other women did it. What were they called? Oh, yeah—cougars. Yeah, right. She almost got tickled at herself. Who was she kidding? She was a virgin for God's sake—a frigid, thirty-one year old freak of a virgin. Being with Bobby was just an entertaining fantasy.

Scarlet protested Cecile's statement, a little too loudly, "I have no claim on Alex."

"I think he's claimed you, sis." Her sister winked. "Cecile, there *is* another brother." Annalise smiled wickedly. "One that's tall, dark, and handsome. He has a body to die for and he plays football. Sound interesting to you?"

"Bobby. Sweet, gentle Bobby." Scarlet summed up.

"Sounds dreamy, all right." Cecile agreed, trying to sound normal. "The only problem is that he's what, twenty-one?"

"Twenty-two, he's a senior at UT."

"Yeah, a senior." Cecile laughed, wryly. "And I, comparatively speaking, am a senior citizen."

"Nonsense." Annalise waved her hand. "You're gorgeous and so is he, a perfect match."

"We'll see." She wanted to lead Annalise off that subject and fast. "Now, where is that dress I've been hearing so much about?" Cecile and Scarlet followed

Annalise to her room where Scarlet worked for a half hour, pinning and perfecting. After she was satisfied, Scarlet left Annalise and Cecile alone to catch up. They talked books, the wedding, Carl—everything but the one topic Cecile wanted to hear more about, but was afraid to ask, Bobby.

When the bride-to-be was satisfied that Cecile knew everything she needed to know about the wedding, and they were sufficiently caught up on the gossip, Annalise offered to get one of the guys to help her to her room. When they stepped just past the bedroom door, Cecile was surprised to find Bobby standing there like he was waiting for someone. Thank God, she hadn't asked a lot of questions about him.

"Oh, there you are. Bobby, would you help Cecile with her bags? Put them in the room next to yours." Automatically Cecile's eyes locked with Bobby's, and it was if they were connected by a live wire. She could feel her whole body tingle. Oh boy, this could be interesting. Annalise gave Cecile one more hug. "I can't tell you how much I love you. You mean the world to me." Cecile whispered her thanks and love in her friend's ear, more touched than she could say.

Bobby did an *after you* gesture. "It's the fourth door on the right, Ceelee," Cecile noticed he used her nickname. That was his way of reminding her of their previous association, and it made her smile. "We'll get you all tucked in, snug as a bug in a rug." As soon as they were out of earshot of the others, he seemed to change his mind about their destination. "No, excuse me, third door on the right—I get confused." He watched her follow his directions. "Go on in, sweetheart."

The seductive tone in his voice made her think of the spider and the fly. She needed to get a handle on this situation, and fast. "Bobby, we need to talk. I can't believe we're meeting like this. When Annalise told me that Ethan had a brother named Bobby, it crossed my mind that it might be you. But I never really considered the possibility..." She turned toward him just as he was closing the door. Now they were alone in a room, with a big bed and her words just faded into nothingness. God, give me strength, she prayed. She was so aware of him. He casually placed her luggage on a low chest and then faced her. Again, she was overwhelmed by his size and masculinity. Bobby Stewart was a gorgeous man—a man, not a boy. He wore a pair of athletic shorts and a tight t-shirt that let every muscle stand out like it was sculpted from bronze. His biceps were as big as her thighs and the thin cotton did nothing to hide the breadth of his chest and shoulders. Lord, his body was made for sin. He made Carl look like a stick figure. And he thought he wanted her? He was mistaken.

"Do you like what you see, sweetheart? You don't have to stand way over there and just look, you can come close and touch." He lowered his voice and his words were slow and smooth. As far as Cecile could tell, Bobby had gone into full seduction mode. Lord, how was she going to resist him? And did she want to? Closing her eyes, she reminded herself how vulnerable she was and how foolish it would be to get into a situation to be hurt, yet again. Not to mention the age difference—who could forget that? But, when she looked up, he was on the move. Like a huge, graceful tiger, he stalked her. Cecile backed up, it was an instinctive move of self-preservation. When her knees hit the back of the bed, she swayed, momentarily losing her balance. And when she did—he pounced.

The bed creaked and groaned as it protested the sudden drop of solid man onto the mattress. God, did he know what he was doing! He was on top of her, over her, surrounding her, but she lay there completely safe and unharmed. He bore his weight on his arms and one knee. "You've done this before," she managed to croak.

"A time or two," he chuckled. Their faces were so close she could feel his breath against her cheek. "I don't care why you came, Cecile. I'm just thankful you're here." Without waiting for permission, he covered her lips with his and drank deeply from her mouth. Without preamble, he made himself at home in her kiss, letting their tongues soothe one another and reacquaint themselves in the age old dance of seduction. Weeks of fantasizing and longing coalesced into a devouring kiss that surpassed expectation.

Panting and with her heart pounding, Cecile could do nothing but tell the truth. "I'm glad, too," she admitted between kisses. Despite her reservations, her hand found its way up to cup his head. She fisted her hand in his hair, holding him fast—taking her pleasure—making little grunts of delight that made him chuckle as they paused to draw in another ounce or two of necessary oxygen.

"Damn! You've made this bullrider happy! You're back in my arms and that's all that matters."

Part of her wanted to say screw the consequences! The erogenous zones of her body were making their case that she was right where she needed to be. For just a second she gave in and wrapped her arms around him, squeezing him hard. This was paradise, to be held and kissed by a man who seemed to want her as much as she wanted him. But in the midst of her elation, Carl's words came back to haunt her—*I can't even get an erection with you. You're not sexy enough to make a man want you. You're a plain, frigid excuse for a woman.* Forcing herself to calm down and face reality, Cecile placed her hand on his cheek and rubbed her thumb over the lips that gave her so much pleasure. "Oh Bobby, it's so wonderful to be here with you. I have to confess that I fantasized we'd meet one day. I just wish—" He didn't let her finish. When he kissed her finger, drawing the end of it into his mouth and giving it a little suck, she lost her train of thought.

"Doll, my fantasies about you were off the charts. Now that you're here in my home and we have this time together, we can get to know one another and make all those fantasies come true." He leaned over to join their lips once more, but she stopped him.

"We can't. It wouldn't be a good idea."

"Are you teasing? What do you mean, *we can't*? We're two consenting adults—why, can't we enjoy one another? I thought you said there was no other man in your life." He lowered his hips just enough so she knew without a doubt that he desired her. "I want you, desperately. I feel a connection with you that I want to explore. No other woman has ever made me feel this way. Don't you want me?"

"Don't be mad," she caressed his face, but wouldn't quite look him in the eye. Instead, she focused on his chin and its intriguing cleft and the sexy stubble that made him look like a Hollywood sex god. "What happened the night we met was beautiful and I thank you for it. At that moment, I needed to be kissed and held and made to feel like a desirable woman more than you'll ever know. But, it wasn't real. We were caught up in the romance of the night and the electric atmosphere of the storm." Cecile was about to add that she hoped they could enjoy the wedding and its preparations without anything being awkward between them when Bobby took both hands and pinned them over her head.

"Look me in the eye and say that," he commanded.

"Not a day, hell not even an hour has gone by since you drove off into the darkness that I didn't wonder where you were, or if you were all right or if I would ever see you again."

Feeling completely vulnerable, Cecile tried to turn her head. "You don't understand, Bobby."

"Well, explain it to me. Make me understand how I've misread the want in your eyes or misinterpreted the heat in your kiss."

Cecile's heart ached. There was no mistaking this man's sincerity. She owed him a degree of honesty. So, she closed her eyes and opened her heart. "I'll tell you this, and then you've got to promise to let me walk out of here. Okay?"

"I don't know if I can do that." She heard the pain in his voice and wondered if she was making the biggest mistake of her life. But after all she had been through she just couldn't take the chance. "I may edit erotic romances, but in real life I'm sort of a dud in the sex department." Her words dropped to a whisper. "I'm afraid that I'd only be a disappointment to you."

Of all the reactions she had been expecting, she didn't see this one coming. He lifted himself over her, powerfully, doing a push-up move over her body and looking her square in the face. "Impossible! You don't believe that, do you?" He waited a moment to read her reaction. Cecile felt a wave of shame cross her features and she knew he saw it. "That's the most unbelievable thing I've ever heard. Who told you that you were anything less than perfect?" Cecile shook her head, unable to speak. Kissing her soundly, he placed his forehead against hers and rubbed their noses together. It was the sweetest gesture he could have made. Cecile's heart felt like it was being put through a wringer. "Impossible. You are the sexiest woman I know."

It was surreal to hear a man defend her that way. It was like a dam broke inside of her and her emotions and insecurities came bursting forth. "No, it's true. Bobby, I assure you, you're not missing out on anything. I am not what you need." Just as soon as she verbalized her thoughts, she regretted it. Next, she'd be confessing her advanced age. Averting her eyes from his, she wished she was anywhere but in his arms. "I need to get up," she pushed gently at his shoulders, her whole body awash in a blush that was created by embarrassment as well as sexual tension.

"Hold on there, beautiful. It's all right, I've got you. You're safe with me." He spoke softly, as if he were trying to calm a frightened filly. "You can't make a ridiculous statement like that and just think I'm going to let it pass." He captured her chin in his big hand and gently held her, not letting her get away from him. "Look at me," he demanded. Slowly, Cecile let her gaze meet his once more, and what she saw took her breath away. If a man could put his heart in his eyes he had done it. "Now, where did that come from? Every time we touch, your little body lights up like a Fourth of July fireworks display. Honey, you set me on fire and we haven't even been naked together—yet. A fact I intend to remedy as soon as possible."

A single tear slipped down her face, she had said too much already. Again, she pushed against his shoulders, but it was like trying to move a mountain. He wasn't going anywhere. God, what was he doing? With a tender touch, Bobby kissed away the dampness from her cheek. His lips moved from her cheek to tease her trembling lips. "Now, what in the world do you have to cry about? You're safe in my room, and you're wrapped in the arms of a man who'd do just about anything to make you happy."

Cecile couldn't help it, she laughed. He was so sweet. "I thought this was my room."

"Do I look stupid to you? Do you think I was going to let the chance pass to get you right where I want you?"

"No, you don't look stupid, at all. But, you don't understand." She was just about to try and explain everything one more time when a knock sounded on the door next to Bobby's bedroom. Annalise was looking for her in the room she was supposed to be in. "Cecile! Honey, are you unpacked yet? I've got some goodies to show you."

At the look of dismay that came over her face, Bobby relented. "Don't worry. I'll take care of it. You stay here. I'll go out and get her off your scent and you can come out in a few minutes. Okay?" Before he got up, he kissed her once—long and hard. "And this isn't over, not by a long shot. I'll put your things in the right room. But don't you doubt it—you and I will be right here, in this bed. Together. Soon." With one powerful, graceful move, he was up and off the bed. Slipping out the door, she heard his voice as he talked to Annalise and lured her off into some fabricated mission to give Cecile time to exit gracefully.

Lord, he was a doll! A handsome, sexy, living-doll. How she wished she were brave enough to take him up on what he was offering.

* * *

Bobby couldn't take his eyes off of her. She was absolutely adorable. Watching her laugh and joke with Scarlet and Annalise had his cock armed and ready like a heat-seeking missile.

"I'm watching you watch that sex editor like she's a T-Bone steak and you're a starving dog," drawled Alex who hadn't taken his own eyes off Scarlet for more than a few seconds at a time. "What about that girl you were so hot to find from Dallas, the one that Roscoe's been helping you look for?"

Bobby sipped his long-neck brew, plotting how he was going to get Cecile alone. The girls had tried on dresses, looked at pictures, ooohed and ahhed over wedding plans until he thought he would go stark-raving mad from an erection that was lasting longer than any Viagra commercial had ever warned about. Shifting restlessly and rearranging his bulge, he leveled with his brother. "She is the girl I've been looking for. Cecile and Ceelee are one in the same."

Alex looked over at Bobby in surprise. "Dehelyousaye? Well, if that isn't a major plot twist. What a coinkydink!"

"Coinkydink?" Bobby laughed at his brother's awful sense of humor. But, when he looked at Alex he could tell that the smile and laughter was all for show. "What's wrong?" Alex was looking at Scarlet with the saddest expression in his eyes.

"She's sick, Bobby," Alex revealed in an agonized whisper.

Bobby whirled around to face his brother. "What? Who's sick? Scarlet?"

Alex took Bobby by the shoulder. "Keep your voice down, bro. Scarlet doesn't want Annalise to find out. Come with me." When they were safely outside the house, Alex sat down heavily on a bench and held his head in his hands. "She's got kidney failure, she's been sick for quite a while. Scarlet was born with a club foot. And her fool of a father wouldn't get it fixed for her. He was some type of religious nut, and thought that God must have wanted her to live that way. When she got old enough to have a say in the matter, she got an operation. Dammit!" Alex hit the bench with his fist. "The anesthesia they gave her damaged her kidneys. She was allergic to it. Now, the doctors tell her she only has a few weeks till she'll have to be on dialysis."

He stopped talking and grew terribly silent. Bobby had never seen his brother cry and it wasn't something he ever wanted to see again. "What can we do?"

Alex wiped his face. "Believe me, I'm moving heaven and earth to try and find an answer. I've called doctors and lawyers, Ethan is helping me. I'm trying to find out if I can add her to my insurance policy and if, by some miracle, I might be a good match to donate a kidney myself."

"I'll be glad to be tested," Bobby didn't hesitate, although he knew a sacrifice like that would mean the end of any football career he might ever contemplate. But, seeing his brother in such pain made him want to fight windmills.

"Thanks, buddy. You don't know what that means to me." Alex looked at his brother, "She's so sweet, you wouldn't believe the gift she gave me."

"I saw it. I liked what she made me, too." Bobby was talking about the tapestries she gave them the first night they met, but Alex shook his head.

"Not that, something far more precious." Alex leaned his head back against the trunk of a pecan tree and sighed. "Bobby, when she got here, she had this list. I found it. It was some sort of a bucket list. There were pages of stuff that she wanted to see or do while she still felt well enough to enjoy them. Do you know what was #1?"

Bobby shook his head. He had never seen his brother like this, it hurt Bobby's soul.

"She wanted to make love, at least one time while she still felt good. And she wanted it to be with someone she could trust," Alex whispered.

"Well, I'm sure she—maybe, you could..." Bobby stammered around, not knowing what to say.

"That was the gift, Bobby. She gave me her virginity. Scarlet let me make love to her." Alex looked off into the distance as if trying to see into the future. "It was unlike anything I've ever known. I'll never be the same. I can't keep my hands off of her, and I can't let her go. She belongs to me now."

"What can I do?" Bobby wanted to help in any way he could.

"Would you pray for her?"

"I'll pray harder than I've ever prayed in my life." He was already intending to pray that Ceelee would learn to trust him, a little more time on his knees for Scarlet would be no problem at all.

* * *

"Why don't you help me grill the steaks, Ceelee?" Bobby swatted her on the butt with a dish towel.

She swung around to fuss at him, but his playful expression stopped her short. Annalise and Scarlet were so caught up in planning and visiting that Cecile had quit worrying whether or not they suspected she and Bobby had met before. She'd confess it eventually, when the time was right. Besides, what did it matter? It wasn't like anything was going to happen between them now except some mild flirting. At least that was the plan. Her heart and body didn't agree with her mind, but her dad had always said she was bull-headed. "Sure, I'll be glad to help." They needed to finish their last conversation. He was still looking at her with those hot, hungry eyes and she needed to let him down easy. Hurting him was the last thing she wanted to do.

Bobby escorted her to the cooking pavilion which was about five hundred yards behind the main house. It appeared to be out of sight of the guest houses and the B&B in order to provide privacy for the family. Located next to the bank of a creek that wound through a grove of native pecan trees, it was a tranquil spot. "It's beautiful here, Bobby. You have a lovely home." She held his spices and turning utensils while he put the big slabs of meat on the grill. Heavens, just watching him work turned her on. Cecile couldn't help wishing she were brave enough to have a fling with him. The thought made her smile—that's what she needed, an affair with a good-looking, younger man. What better way to make her feel beautiful and sexy? If only she had the courage.

Once he was finished, he lowered the lid to the cooker, took everything out of her hands, set it down on the side table and picked her up. She didn't have time to put up a protest, all she could do was gasp at the unexpected pleasure. Walking over to a chaise lounge, he sat down and placed her on his lap. "All right, first things first." Reaching a hand under her hair, he cupped the back of her neck and pulled her to him. "You are so sweet, I've been hungry for your kiss for hours."

Cecile couldn't find the motivation to stop him. He was just too potent to resist. In a few meager seconds, her nipples were hard, her clit was swollen and her panties were so damp she was afraid she would leave a spot on his jeans. And all of that from just a kiss. But, oh what a kiss it was. "Mmmm," she moaned. This time there was no tender forays, no nibbles or licks, she opened her mouth and he took total and complete possession. Cecile strained against him, wanting to be closer, wanting to merge herself with him in the most basic way possible.

"Damn, hold on sweetheart," he sat her gently aside. She had never felt so bereft. "Just hold on, I've got to turn those steaks over. I don't want to have to explain why I let them burn."

He jumped up and Cecile felt shy, she couldn't just sit there and wait for him to return. Distance was good. She needed to think. Did she know what she was doing? Getting up, she walked over to the side of the creek and watched the tiny fish swimming in the water. In a minute or two, she felt him join her. The heat of his body was like a magnet. Bobby fitted his big body to her back, wrapping his arms around her middle and laying his head against hers, stealing kisses from her neck and cheek. "Bobby, we shouldn't do this. I tried to explain earlier why this is such a bad idea."

"This is the smartest idea I've ever had. I'm attracted to you, Ceelee. I can't let it go—hell, I can't let you go. I'm sorry, but you're gonna have to tell me you don't want me or that you can't stand my touch before I turn my back on us. Can you do that?" She shrugged her shoulders, so he walked in front of her. "Can you tell me to walk away from you? That's what it's going to take."

He stood in front of her—big, strong, but with his heart on his sleeve, and she couldn't lie about wanting him. She could lie about her age, but not this. "You know I want you. But that doesn't mean I'm being smart. There are things you don't know," she finished lamely. Telling another person, especially someone you're attracted to, all of your shortcomings is never a pleasant task.

Bobby gave her a seriously wicked grin. "I didn't think you could push me away so easy. I'm fairly irresistible, I hear." Taking her by the hands, he pulled her up to him. The very tips of her breasts were touching his chest and she felt like they were on fire. "Now, explain all of this nonsense about you thinking you're a dud in bed." He picked up her hand and looked at her finger. "I see an impression of a wedding band. You've been married. Talk to me, sweet cheeks."

Cecile didn't answer. Instead, she held her breath as his hands settled on her waist and inched up. Her nipples blossomed at the idea that he might touch them. She was so hungry to be wanted. His thumbs teased the underside of her breasts, and she arched her back almost begging for more. "One of these nights, baby, I'm gonna make you come so hard. You know how?"

It didn't hurt to dream. "How?" Cecile asked with a hoarse gasp.

"I'm going to suck on those incredible nipples until you scream. Have you ever come just from having your sweet titties played with?"

Now there were two fingers teasing each breast, making them swell and ache. If he didn't touch her nipples, she thought she would die. "No," she groaned. He would be shocked to know how sexually deprived she actually was. "Remember, I correct the grammar and punctuation in hot sex scenes, I don't actually take part in any." Pulling out of his embrace, she walked to the grill. "The steaks smell good."

Without saying anything else, Bobby removed the steaks from the grill. Cecile started to gather up the tray of items to help him back into the house. "Wait," he spoke softly, but firmly. "We're not through, you haven't answered my questions, yet." Placing the steaks in the warmer, he took the tray from her hands and then led her deeper into the grove of trees. There was one misshapen tree with a sturdy low-hanging branch that was perfect to sit on. Taking both of her hands in his, he pulled her near and lifted her onto the limb. Then he eased between her legs until they were touching—chest to chest—mound to bulge—her thighs cradling his. It was a very intimate position and stole Cecile's breath away. "You told me the night we met that you didn't belong to anyone, not anymore. What did you mean? Are you divorced?"

She soothed her nerves by studying his beautiful face. He had a beauty mark high on his right cheek and his eyes were golden brown. There was that sexy growth of beard she longed to feel on her bare skin, a strong jaw and lips that were damn near the sexiest thing she had ever seen on a man. Releasing a breath, she was relieved that he hadn't pressed her about who had stolen her sexual self-confidence. She's rather not go there. But if he pressed, she felt she owed him an explanation of why she wasn't the best choice of a sex partner. "Yes, I'm divorced. Recently."

Bobby kissed her on the cheek. "I'm sorry, baby. Was he the bastard who made you feel inadequate?"

Shit! Okay, fine. Here goes. It would be better to just get this over and be done with it. Maybe then they could just be a congenial part of the wedding party. "Our marriage wasn't a very happy one. Bowing her head, she confessed as much as she could stand to. "I'm not very inspiring in bed." Bobby said a few explicit curse words, but Cecile kept talking. It seemed that once she started, she couldn't stop. "The night that I stopped to catch your puppy, I had just left him. I had asked him to meet me here at Lost Maples and I tried one last time to seduce him, but I wasn't successful." How humiliating! Her face was flaming hot. She had embarrassed herself. Trying to get Bobby to let her go, she pushed at his solid chest. But he held her fast. So, she summed it up for him. "Now, you know why we should just be friends." Or one of the reasons, anyway.

With a growl, Bobby grasped her by the shoulders, shaking her ever so slightly. "Listen to me. I'm going to speak as clearly as I can. Your husband was a fuckin' idiot." He hugged her close. "Fuckin' bastard! How could any man who had a sweet doll like you steal your self-confidence and treat you so badly? If you belonged to me, I'd worship the ground you walked on. Raise your sweet head and look at me."

It took her a second or two, but she did. Her eyes were brimming with tears.

"Will you give me a gift?"

Cecile looked confused. "Yes," she said slowly. "But what can I give you? What do I have that you would want?"

"I want you." Bobby said simply, moving his hand to clasp her chin, his thumb caressing the soft line of her cheek. "Will you give yourself to me, Ceelee? I don't mean today or tomorrow—just let me court you a little. Let me have a chance to show you how beautiful making love with the right man can be."

Every nerve, every cell in Cecile's body vibrated with need. How could she risk it? "I don't know. I can think of a couple of very good reasons why this would never work. For one, it probably wouldn't be a pleasurable experience for you." Before he could answer, she pressed on. "Let me ask you this. If it wasn't good, you wouldn't tell anyone or tease me about it in front of anybody, would you?"

"Are you serious? What did that bastard do to you? I promise you, if you'll just give me a name and an address, I'll make that idiot sorry he was ever born." His hands weren't still. He touched her like he couldn't get enough of her. Rubbing her arms, kissing her fingers. Cecile was in awe, she had never felt so cherished. "There's no way making love with you wouldn't be good, doll. I've kissed you, I've felt you melt in my arms. Sex with you would be out of this world. And I would never, ever tell anyone anything about what happened between you and me. As far as I'm concerned, if you put your trust in me—I'll treasure it, and I'll treasure you."

Bobby was very persuasive. Closing the miniscule distance between them, she laid her head on his chest and sighed. "Thank you. You make it sound wonderful. I don't know if I'm brave enough to do something like that. But, I know what I'll be dreaming about tonight—you."

* * *

"Can I help you with those?" Bobby had driven up at the same time Cecile was unloading her car and the moment she saw him, her heart began to pound like a drum. He came right over and stood close while she opened her trunk. Mere inches separated them. Her whole body trembled. Cecile had never known her body could react this way.

Last night, she had managed to get through the meal and the after dinner conversation without making a total fool of herself. Every time she had looked up, Bobby had been watching her. If everyone could read his face as well as she thought she could, then everyone already knew the level of attraction that was sizzling between them. All she could think about was his offer to show her how beautiful love-making with the right man could be. But was he the right man? It sure felt like it.

"Sure, thanks." She didn't quite meet his gaze. "You're not shy are you, Bobby?" He might not be, but she was finding out that she was, at least around him. Bobby took the bag of groceries from her arms and another one from the seat of the car. Nervous as a cat in a room full of rocking chairs, she didn't even wait for him to answer her question, she just started chattering away—saying whatever came to mind. "I thought that if Scarlet could cook for us, I could at least go get the supplies. So, you're a senior at UT? I had hoped you were closer to my age." She almost covered her own mouth. God, she was losing it. Where had that come from?

"Yeah, I graduate in May." He smiled at her and that smile was the cutest thing she'd ever seen. "Is that a problem? I can't be much older than you."

Oh, if you only knew. Cecile didn't know what to say, so she didn't say anything. "Are you planning a career in football?" It wouldn't surprise her, he certainly had enough talent. Ethan and Alex had kept them entertained with stories about Longhorn football the night before. Their pride in what their brother had accomplished had been evident.

"Who knows? I don't know if I have what it takes or not." He acted a little evasive as if he wasn't entirely comfortable with the topic. "We'll have to see what happens. If it doesn't come to pass, I have other things I can do. I'm talented…in lots of areas." He gave her a long slow wink. "I can't wait to show you a few of my best moves."

"I bet you are talented." Cecile could feel the heat rising in her face. She was blushing. The more she thought about making love with him, the more she wanted it. If only she could be sure it would be different with Bobby. If he reacted to her like Carl did, she would just die. Dare she risk it? Could she have an affair with Bobby and then just walk away? Should she?

"God, you're cute when you blush."

Cecile knew this was fast getting out of hand. She was going to have to make a decision. They were going to be paired up at the wedding. If the truth be known, she wanted to pair up with him in every way that counted.

"What other things can you do, Bobby?" God, she was flirting! But, it was fun. She hadn't had near enough fun in her life. Perhaps it was time to play catch-up.

He let her walk up the steps of the B&B ahead of him. "Damn, you've got a fine ass."

"Behave."

He didn't apologize, only laughed. "My repertoire is vast." When she gave him an exasperated look, he got serious. "I've got a job offer in Dallas at Raley and Sheridan, if nothing else with football pans out."

"The engineering firm?" She was impressed. Doubly. She lived in Dallas. Lord, what was she thinking?

"Yeah." He held the door for her. "God, you smell good. How would you feel about spending some time with me? I have a surprise for you tonight, and tomorrow we could drive into Austin. I'd like to show you my stomping ground. We could take in the sights and grab a bite to eat. How about it?"

At once she was assailed by emotions—surprise, delight and dread. Carefully, she formed her thoughts into words. "Thank you, but we need to talk about this. I hate to repeat something unpleasant, but you do know I'm several years older than you, don't you?"

"No, I really hadn't thought about it. But whatever age you are, it's the perfect age. Because you're damn hot and I can't wait to make love to you. How's that for honesty?" They stood and faced one another. She swallowed hard, and mumbled something. "So, is that a yes?"

She couldn't help it and she might regret it later, but for now, she couldn't resist him. Cecile smiled and threw caution to the wind. "Okay, you convinced me. It's a yes."

The idea that Bobby had a surprise for her was intriguing. In fact, it was hard to think about anything else. She spent the day helping Annalise and Scarlet fill tiny bags with birdseed for the guests to throw instead of rice. "It isn't true, you know," Scarlet informed them as she tied her umpteenth tiny pink ribbon around one of the miniature net containers.

"What isn't true? Dammit!" Annalise grumbled as she tried to untie a knot in the spool of ribbon. "Arghh! I am so not crafty!"

"You don't have to be crafty, darling." Ethan kissed her on the top of the head. "You're sexy and that trumps crafty any day." He had come into the kitchen for a beer and he quickly exited before he could be coerced into working on the project.

"Rice doesn't make the birds explode. And I'm crafty enough for the both of us," Scarlet patted her sister's knee. "We all have to be good at something."

"I bet Alex would say you had talents other than crafting?" At the teasing, Scarlet's face flushed the same color as her name.

"Stop it." Scarlet tossed a couple of the bags at her sister.

"I want to know more about the exploding birds," Cecile was curious. "That sounds just awful."

"No birds exploded," Scarlet explained. "But it became sort of an urban tale that if you threw rice at weddings, the birds would eat it and it would swell up in their stomachs and make them explode. But that's not true. Birds eat rice in the wild all the time. I think it was a ploy by the bridal shops to sell special heart shaped birdseed. Most of our holidays are driven by card companies, I always say."

"Gee, sis. Aren't you sentimental?" Annalise teased her sister, who looked a bit guilty.

"Sorry, I've directed so many weddings where people spend way more than they can afford. I think the wedding should be about love, not putting on a show. The ceremony you've planned is simple, you're using Ethan's beautiful garden and your family—me—is making your dress and cake. That's how it's supposed to be."

"I agree," Cecile said. "I think your wedding will be perfect."

"Excuse me, ladies," Bobby spoke up from behind Cecile, causing her to whirl around. "I hate to interrupt your female philosophy session, but I want to steal Ceelee away. We're going on a picnic."

A warm thrilling washed over Cecile. "A picnic? Oh that sounds wonderful, Bobby, Can you two handle this complicated mission alone?" She stood up, almost weak in the knees at the thought of going anywhere with Bobby Stewart.

"There's rain in the forecast," Annalise warned looking out the window.

"That's okay, Alex is loaning me the RV. We'll have alternative shelter," he grinned.

Scarlet let out a knowing little giggle. "The RV is a fun place to have a picnic."

"You ought to know, it's yours and Alex own private make-out machine." Bobby took Cecile's hand and they slipped out while Annalise was giving her sister a hard time.

He carried a picnic basket in his other hand and the aromas wafting from it were tantalizing. "Something smell's good. Is that fried chicken?"

"Indeed it is, with potato salad and baked beans. I hope you like it."

Cecile was touched. "I'll love it." She followed him out to Alex's pride and joy – a forty-two foot luxury motor home that the family used for tail-gating at all the Longhorn games. "Wow, I've never been in one of these." They stepped inside and she marveled at how nice it was with the leather couches, granite countertops and cherry wood. "This is so nice. I can't believe we're taking it on a picnic." She helped him put the items away in the refrigerator until they were ready to eat. Knowing that they would be kissing and touching one another, Cecile wasn't surprised to notice that her hands were shaking.

"Sit up here with me," he helped her into one of the captain's chairs. "Where we're going is only a hop and a skip from here. Have you ever been to the park?"

"No," she had planned to go there with Carl, but that hadn't worked out. "I've read about it and seen pictures. I'm sure it's much more impressive up close and personal."

Bobby expertly backed out the huge rig and they set off down the winding, narrow road. "The maples at the park are an anomaly. It's like they were lost in time. There are no other stands of maples like this in the south, only in the north east. Right now, the colors are spectacular. I think you like it—all up close and personal," he swept his gaze down her body. "But you are more breathtaking than anything we'll see today, and I can guarantee I'm going to get as up close and personal with you as you'll let me."

The man did not lie. They ate their food sitting at a table next to a rushing stream. He fed her most of the bites she took, forcing her to lick his fingers for all the extra goodness. And God was he good. She'd never forget walking down the narrow trail with him, holding hands, amazed at the colors that decorated the woods. There was burgundy and orange, she saw crimson and yellow, leaves of every color on nature's palette hung from the tree's proclaiming the glory of the season. "Thank you for bringing me, Bobby. Seeing this with you is a memory I'll always treasure."

"Speaking of memories, let's go make some more."

Returning to the RV, Cecile tried to calm her nerves.

She still didn't know if this was wise. God, she didn't even know if she could go through with it. What would they do? Would he try to make love to her? It was only mid-afternoon, and the idea of playing with Bobby in the clear light of day was intimidating. He let her walk up the steps first, and she could swear she heard him groan. Looking over her shoulder, she saw that he was staring at her bottom. It made her feel a little better—Bobby was really attracted to her, it wasn't put-on. Gradually her eyes adjusted to the dimmer light. The living area was spacious with comfortable couches and a thick rug in front of the fireplace. There were multiple places where they could enjoy one another, but he led her back to the king size bed and turned down the blanket.

Cecile followed, but she stopped at the door. "My heart is pounding and my knees are weak. I haven't been this nervous since I was sent to the office in fifth grade for passing a note to Tommy Walker."

"I'm jealous of Tommy Walker. You'll have to write me a note, too—a racy one." Bobby stepped back and just looked at her. "You have no idea how beautiful you are, do you?" With deliberate movements, he stripped off his shirt, took off his hat, boots and socks and made himself at home on the bed. "Come here, Ceelee. Let me love on you."

Cecile marveled at the broad shoulders and perfect abs of the young Adonis that lay across the quilt. "I want to. I really do. Actually, I'm shivering just thinking about what you might look like under those jeans, but I can't."

"Why?" Bobby rose from the bed and slowly began to stalk her. "I've been hard for you for two days, lady. I don't think I can wait to touch you another minute." She backed up as far as she could go, until she was leaning against the wall.

"You're very aggressive." She smiled, nervously. "I like that." She did, it made her forget their age difference. He moved directly in front of her. His broad, well-developed chest was close enough that her aroused nipples almost brushed against him.

"I know what I want, and I go after it." He bracketed her with his arms, leaning in, perilously close to her lips. "And I want you, Cecile. In my bed. Now."

"I was in elementary school when you were born," she muttered weakly.

"So? I think I've caught up with you, darling." He inhaled her scent, his lips making a foray down the soft skin of her neck.

"I was in college when you were in Junior High." Her voice was even weaker, the argument not even standing up in her own mind. Not anymore. This youngest Stewart brother was sexy as hell.

"You are the cutest, sweetest, softest, sexiest woman that I know. I'm going to kiss you now, if you're through worrying about our school days." Cecile opened her mouth to say something else, but she couldn't think of anything to say. Her eyes were focused on his full, chiseled mouth, the lower lip a little fuller than the top lip. She loved the cleft in his chin and the sexy dimple to the right of his mouth. Bobby took advantage of Cecile's parted lips. He covered her mouth with his, letting his tongue tease hers into submission.

"That's right, doll. Kiss me. Kiss me, hard." With a whimper, Cecile surrendered. She pushed off the wall and into his arms, her hands cupping his head. He cupped her butt and picked her up, her legs parted and made themselves at home around his waist. "Oh, yeah. I can feel how hot you are right through your jeans." His words excited her so, that she pressed herself against him.

"Oh, Bobby," she moaned. "I need you."

"You got me, baby."

"The idea that you want me, it's too wild to comprehend."

He let her slide down his body, but he didn't let her go." "Oh, I want you. Never doubt that."

She spoke as if she hadn't heard him. "I just don't want to make a fool of myself. I'm so nervous. Shall we turn off the lights—or light a few candles?"

"No, I want to be able to see every glorious inch of you. It amazes the hell out of me that you don't have a clue how fuckin' gorgeous you are." He slid the straps of her lace top from her shoulders, took hold of the neckline and began to peel it down. Inch by inch, he unveiled her. "God Almighty!" Her top had a built-in shelf bra, so when he pulled it down, she was fully exposed. Carl's cruel words flashed through her head. Cecile held her breath. Whatever reaction she was expecting, it wasn't the one she got. He went to his knees. "Oh, Ceelee, sweetheart, you are exquisite." Placing a hand on the outside of each breast, he pushed them together—oh, so gently. "I've dreamed about this moment."

Cecile thought she would sink to the ground—melt into a puddle—evaporate into a mist of ecstasy. Her hands came up to cradle his head, backed off, and then finally settled on his soft hair. He had buried his face in her cleavage and he was kissing first the side of one breast and then the other. She shivered with excitement, and when he started rubbing her nipples, a whimper of delight escaped her lips. He seemed to be enjoying himself. Maybe her prayers would be answered. All she had asked for was to be sexy enough for Bobby to be able to make love to her, just once. If he couldn't, she would never ever put herself into a position like this again.

"Sit down here on the bed, baby. Let me make you

happy."

When he palmed her areolas and began massaging them, Cecile felt an unaccustomed wetness grow between her thighs. "That feels incredible, Bobby."

Bobby looked up at her, tenderly. "I've always liked to suck on candy—lemon drops, peppermint, jelly beans—but these little nipples look like they'll become my favorite. Hold on baby, this is going to make you cream." Still holding one nipple between his fingers, he bent his head to take the other in his mouth. First, he swirled his tongue around it, making it distend, seeking solace.

Cecile felt her toes curl, readying herself for untold ecstasy. She was enchanted by the look on his face as he worked at her breast. He was actually enjoying it. Maybe, she wasn't a lost cause. Kneading the back of his head, she watched intently as he opened his mouth wider and engulfed her entire areola in his mouth. "Oh, yes!" she couldn't help but exclaim. The drawing of his lips, and the suction he was applying winged its way from the tip of her nipple all the way to her womb. As he set a mind-blowing rhythm of sucking one nipple and tweaking the other, Cecile moaned in utter abandon. "God, this feels so good!"

Bobby chuckled. "You like that don't you?"

She nodded her head, arched her back and thrust her breasts out—wanting more.

"Let's lie down on the bed and snuggle. We're gonna take things slow. You've been through enough. I intend to take my time with you."

Cecile wasn't ready for him to stop kissing her breasts. She had felt like she was on the verge of something extreme, but she wasn't nearly at the point where she felt confident enough to ask for what she wanted. He sat back on his heels and she scooted back and over, making room for him on the bed. "Look at your beautiful tits, Ceelee. They're swollen and pink from my loving."

"I enjoyed that so much, Bobby." Carl had never been a breast man, so the pleasure she received from Bobby's lips on her nipples had been a rare treat.

"Oh, I'm not finished, I just wanted to appreciate you a little bit, that's all." Damn, she was perfect. Perfect shape. Just enough bounce to make his heart pound. High, round and oh so suckable. As she backed up, he followed; he couldn't stay away. Reclining on a stack of pillows, she looked as seductive as Cleopatra, yet with an innocent naiveté that made him want to cherish her as much as he wanted to ravish her. "You look beautiful all stretched out there, but I've got an idea. Let me lie down and you sit on my chest and dangle those beauties in my face." She looked doubtful, but she complied. And Lord God, what a sight! "Lean over and put your hands on either side of my face on the pillow."

Following his directions, she bent near his face and her eyes were big with wonder. A sigh of delight escaped her lips as his mouth closed over a nipple that was still damp from his previous attention. The feel of her in his mouth was addictive, he knew he would never get his fill. She was soft as velvet, yet undeniably hard. There was no doubt she was aroused. Bobby wanted to put his hand between her legs so bad, but he held back. She had been mistreated and misused and he fully intended to give her the whole experience. More than anything, he wanted Ceelee to realize how desirable she was. "You're luscious," he whispered against her skin as he nuzzled and rooted against her like a hungry calf.

"Thank you." Her voice was small and breathless.

Manners weren't his main concern at the moment, so

he didn't offer any comment. Instead, he suckled at her, gently—molding and kneading her firm flesh. Some men might say that more than a mouthful was wasted, but they were so, so wrong. He loved having two hands full of sweet tit to cup and cuddle to his heart's content. Rolling the hard bud on his tongue, he relished her taste. She was all things sweet, and Bobby couldn't resist watching her face as she enjoyed the ecstasy he was lavishing on her. Euphoria—that's what her expression reflected. Little moans of excitement escaped her lips, and he felt her bottom rock against him. Damn! Could he make her cum like this? Christ! That would be hot as hell. Committed to trying, Bobby flicked his tongue against her nipple over and over. Now for the other one. "If you'll cum for this bullrider, baby, I'll be the happiest man alive." Pushing her tits together, he lavished attention on the neglected twin.

"Cum? But what about you?" Her mind might be questioning the appropriateness of being what she would call selfish, but her body was voting for it wholeheartedly. Bobby could feel the little moves of her body as she sought fulfillment.

"Don't worry about me, baby. Giving you pleasure is as good as getting it myself. I love to touch you and taste you." As he crooned to her, he toyed with her nipples—rubbing them and pulling them. "I love how your eyes are glazed over with passion and your cheeks are flushed with heat." He smiled, he couldn't help it. "You're gonna cum for me, aren't you?"

"Uh-huh," she purred. Slipping backward an inch or two, careful not to dislodge his hands, she lowered her head and kissed him. Bobby kept massaging her nipples, loving how she ate at his mouth. He could feel the muscles of her legs tighten around him as she undulated her mound on his abs. "Bobby!" she moaned as her whole body shuddered.

He let go of her breasts, wrapped his arms around her and pulled her down on him, holding her. "And that, Miss Ceelee, was just the beginning."

Cecile was happier than she could ever remember being. When she and Bobby returned to the B&B from their picnic, they had found the others making small talk and playing board games. At first, she had been hesitant to join in, almost certain they could look at her and tell she had enjoyed an earth shattering climax in the arms of the youngest Stewart. But other than some good-natured ribbing about avoiding work, no one gave them any problems. Maybe, she was worrying for nothing. When bedtime came, it had taken every bit of the control she possessed to keep her from begging him to finish what he had so ably started. But Bobby had walked her to her door, kissed her tenderly on the lips and promised to continue their courtship tomorrow. Now, tomorrow was here and she couldn't wait to see what it held in store.

As soon as Annalise had found out they were headed into Austin, she had thought of a half dozen errands for them to do. Even Scarlet had asked for them to pick up a spool of thread at the sewing shop.

"We'll be glad to do it." Bobby answered before she could say anything, taking the thread from Scarlet with a smile. His eyes raked over Cecile's body, appreciatively. "You look good enough to eat. Are you ready to go?"

"I was just about to get coffee," A little bit embarrassed at his comment, Cecile motioned toward the pot. Not that she needed it, just the idea of spending the day with him had awakened every cell in her body.

Taking her by the hand, he pulled her toward the door. "We'll get you some on the road. We've got a lot of errands to run." He winked at Annalise and Scarlet. "You girls be good and don't wait up for us."

As he led her to a brand new Dodge pickup, Cecile had to make herself walk normally. Like a child, she wanted to skip. "You've got a new truck, this is not the same one you were in that night on the highway."

He didn't take her to the passenger door, but brought her to his side. When he opened the door, she saw bench seats. Nice. Before she could step up, Bobby had her around the waist and lifted her up with ease. "There you go, baby. Yea, I bought this a couple of weeks ago. My old truck was falling apart." She watched him hungrily as he settled in beside her, he was so big and he made her feel small, dainty and precious. It was a heady feeling.

"Sit close." He pulled her next to him, and put her hand on his thigh. "Hold on to me, I need to feel your touch." He leaned over and kissed her on top of the head. "There's so much we need to talk about. I want to know everything about you. And as we go through town, I'm gonna take you on the Bobby Stewart tour. How's that sound?"

Beneath her hand, his thigh was rock hard and she could only lay her palm across the top of it. Without thinking, she began to massage the firm flesh, enjoying the tactile feel of his rough blue jeans and the knowledge that a man enjoyed spending time with her. "Yea, that sounds like fun." She leaned her face on his shoulder, her chin resting against his bicep, sighing with happiness. "Where do we start?"

Bobby turned down a side road and soon they were at a small rodeo arena. "This is where I learned to ride bulls."

Cecile sat up straighter in the seat straining to see everything. There were a few men in hats and boots walking around, and pens of livestock off to the left. One enclosure held some mammoth bulls and a few of them had horns. Cecile shivered. "Bulls! You ride bulls?" She was flabbergasted. "How did I not know this?" Flickers of wonder and fear wiggled up her spine.

"Doll, I mentioned it yesterday, but you were a little too busy to comprehend it—with all that moaning going on." He parked his truck, but continued to tease her. "Should I get bull rider tattooed on my dick?"

As he held his arms out for her, she readily went into them. "No," she whispered. "I don't want some tattoo artist holding you like that." As soon as she voiced her concern, she realized how it sounded. "Sorry, Bobby. I have no say in what you do."

He squeezed her hard as he let her slide down his body. "You have all the say you want to have. I love that you're acting like you care." Putting an arm around her shoulders, he guided her toward one of the men who was running a curry comb over a quarter horse mare. "Hey, Moose! What's going on?"

The big man turned and broke out in a smile that seemed about to crack the leather of his face. "Why, Bobby Stewart! Long time no see, man! Thought you had forgotten about us little guys. I've heard you're climbing in the ranks this year. One of these days you're gonna be World Champion Bull Rider! Who you got here?"

Cecile didn't hesitate to place her hand in the big paw that was extended to her. Bobby's hand tightened at her waist, protectively. "Moose, this is Ceelee Fairchild. Ceelee, this is Tom Lawrence or Moose as we call him. He's one of the best bulldoggers in this part of the state."

"It's nice to meet you, Mr. Moose." Both men laughed at her. All she could think about was that Bobby was a very successful bull rider, which meant he often faced untold danger in the rodeo ring. Cecile didn't know how she felt about that.

"Come on, let's go meet some of the bulls. They're not nearly as mean when they're not in the chute. When they get herded into that contraption, they know they're going to work and all their spunk comes out." Bobby walked Ceelee over to the fence. She loved the feel of his body bumping up against hers. As soon as they approached the bulls one of the bigger black ones came huffing over, anxious to see if the newcomers were any threat.

"Have you ever been hurt? Do you get thrown a lot?" She couldn't help the worried words which tumbled from her lips.

Bobby tapped her on the end of her nose. "I'm a big boy, baby. I've been doing this for years. Don't worry your little head about it."

Cecile flattened her lips into a straight line of discontent. "So, you're telling me that bull riding isn't dangerous?" She knew better. And thinking of him putting his life on the line by crawling up on one of these monsters made her blood run cold. Despite his assurance, she clutched his hand tight to her chest, wanting to hold him closely to her and keep him safe.

"It can be," Bobby answered slowly, thinking about Shaun. "But there's risk in everything, Ceelee. Here, touch his nose." She slowly put her hand through the fence and touched the big animal's soft pink nose. He let her have one touch and he sprang back, as if he didn't want anyone seeing him be nice to the pretty lady.

"It was like velvet!" she marveled. "They're beautiful animals. You're probably right about taking risks, I guess." Let's see how he felt when the shoe was on the other foot. She didn't know why she was teasing him, but it felt good. "Maybe, I'll take up some exciting sport," Cecile mused. Actually, she was half-way serious.

"I'm tired of living life traveling in the slow lane. How about skydiving?" Her insides jumped at the thought. Could she ever do something like that?

"Hell, no! I don't think so, I can't let anything happen to you." At her cheeky little smirk, he swooped in for a kiss. "Okay, I get it. When we care, we worry." Bobby led her around and introduced her to the cowboys, showing her the arena and the announcer's box. "This community exhibition-hall complex is small compared to the ones I ride in now, but it was where rodeo began for me, and I love it here." Periodically, he would tighten his arm around her and kiss her on the temple or her cheek. Cecile had never known what she was missing. Having Bobby in her life made every moment more exciting.

After they made their way around the complex, he escorted her back to the truck. Opening the door, he glanced over his shoulder to make sure they were completely alone. "God, I can't keep my hands off of you." Enveloping her in his arms, he pulled her close. "Can I kiss you?"

Cecile knew he was being careful with her. She had never known a more considerate man. "Please." She gave her permission.

"Oh honey, pleasing you is all I want to do." Fusing his mouth to her lips, he began a quest to tantalize and tease. It worked, delight coursed through her body, Bobby knew exactly what he was doing. One moment his kiss was demanding, the next moment it was pleading and all she could do was hang on and enjoy the ride. God, he was good. She clasped him tight, her fingers digging into the hard muscles of his shoulders. With every lick and nibble, he was driving away every objection she could come up. With every tender kiss, he was stealing both her breath and her heart. "That's right, my baby. Give me more," he praised her as they gulped for air.

She scooted to the edge of her seat and put one foot behind his knee as if she was afraid he would escape. "You are really good at this. I haven't been kissed this way nearly enough in my life." She couldn't help but praise him. Her confession seemed to spur him on, because he framed her face and dove back in. Their tongues tangled in delight at the chance to taste one another.

"I'll kiss you every chance I get, give you all the sugar you can handle. Can I touch you? No one can see." He pulled away and searched her face. She nodded her assent and then lay her head on his shoulder, biting her lip to keep from crying aloud as his hands cupped her breasts, rubbing and shaping, molding them. The rustle of movement in the distance was the only thing that stopped her from spreading her legs and begging for his touch where she was aching the most.

"I guess we need to go," she breathed as she kissed him on his neck, bringing him down, secretly pleased by the thick, steel rod that throbbed in between them.

"Yea, we do," he rasped in her ear, stealing a kiss from a sensitive spot at the base of her neck. "I'd rather be in bed with you."

"I think I would, too," she agreed softly.

"Damn!" he ground out. "Now, you tell me. Come on precious." He picked her up and joined her on the seat. This time he didn't have to tell her where to put her hand, she did it gladly. "Tell me about your childhood." His hand went to her knee, pushing up the yellow sundress. "You look like a ray of sunshine in this dress."

As compliments go, it was pretty tame, but it meant the world to Cecile. Carl had never paid her many compliments. There had been few kind words for her after the first year of their marriage. "I was an only child," she began. "My dad died when I was nine and my mother remarried…three times." She winced as she told him. "Right now she's single, but there's no chance she'll stop looking for another husband. That's just the way she is. Her last husband was several years younger than she was, and he broke her heart." As soon as she said the words, she regretted them. He didn't need any reminders about their age difference.

"Where did you go to college?"

"SMU," she answered. "English major."

"And you work for Passion Publishing with Annalise. Do you enjoy it? Do you stay turned on all the time?" At his question, she blushed. She was remembering the last time she masturbated with *Bobby* after reading one of the manuscripts.

"Damn, baby." Bobby laughed. "You don't have to answer that question. It's written all over your face." He winked at her. "You are so cute."

"Stop it!" She playfully pinched his arm. "I love my job, but it's not as glamorous as you might think. I don't have anything to do with the eroticism of the stories. I only edit and market. Basically—I fact check, format, correct grammar and sentence composition and then make sure the book is promoted effectively." Laying her head over on his shoulder, she rubbed her cheek on his shirt, enjoying the clean, sexy smell that was uniquely Bobby Stewart. "Most people think my job makes me a sex expert, but there's nothing farther from the truth."

"I think you're perfect just the way you are." He squeezed her knee. "Now, tell me about your marriage, I need to understand."

For a moment, Cecile covered her eyes with her hand, as if hiding from the truth. "Are you sure you want to hear this? I've told you more than I ever intended to tell anyone."

"Come on baby," he encouraged her. "I want to know it all. Don't leave out anything"

Letting out a long breath, Cecile plunged in. "I met Carl in college. I guess you could say he swept me off my feet. I didn't date much in high school, a couple of double dates and some chaperoned parties. My parents were super strict and rarely gave me the freedom that other teenage girls enjoyed. So when I finally got away from them, I was anxious for attention and affection." She stopped and looked at him closely, wondering how much he really wanted to hear. He met her eyes, watching her intently, so she continued. "The first year of our marriage wasn't so bad. We were both building our careers and working a lot of overtime, so the amount of time we spent together was limited."

Her voice dropped, as if she were reliving painful memories. "After that, Carl changed. At first, he had seemed to enjoy touching me, sleeping with me, kissing me. When we had sex, it never felt good, but I enjoyed the closeness. Knowing what I know now," she was evasive, "it's clear to me that Carl didn't know much about physical intimacy when we married. He was from a big family, the only boy, and the youngest. His folks practiced the Mennonite religion, but I don't think Carl was ever into it too much."

She felt like she was trying to make excuses for him—maybe she was. "I tried to get him to participate more in our lovemaking. That sounds funny, but he just wanted to dive right in. He didn't do anything to prepare me and when I tried to be affectionate toward him, he pushed me away. I didn't understand." She pulled her hand away from Bobby's leg and began to weave her own fingers together, as if what she had to say was painful. "I asked to go to a therapist or a marriage counselor, but he refused. Carl had told me our sex life was normal, but I read all of these romances and saw movies. I knew I was being cheated. But, Carl insisted that I had unrealistic expectations. All this time, Bobby hadn't said anything. Cecile was afraid to look at him, she didn't know what he would think about all of this.

"When I pushed for us to get some help, he began to tell me it was all my fault. I'm not sure why he didn't ask for a divorce. Maybe he enjoyed ridiculing me, I guess some people get off on doing things like that. Anytime I touched him in the night or asked him to kiss me, he would push me away and tell me that our unsatisfactory sex life was due to my lack of appeal and my inability to orgasm." Cecile let out a shuddering breath. "He told me I was frigid. Gradually, we stopped touching one another. We slept in the same bed, he on his side and me on mine."

Had she disgusted Bobby with the sad story? Had she told too much? Glancing up at him, she saw that his jaw was tense and set. Finally, he ground out, "I'm sorry, Ceelee. I hate you've lived your life doubting yourself, especially since you're as sweet as spun sugar. Carl was a fool and his loss is my gain."

His sympathetic words spurred her to explain further. "I knew I felt things. When I would read the erotic romance novels by Annalise and the other authors, I got turned on. And sometimes, I would touch myself and it felt good. After spending some time with Annalise at a writer's conference in Houston, I knew that my life had to change. I wanted more out of life than what I had. So I asked Carl to meet me here. Our visit here to Lost Maples was a last ditch effort on my part to save a marriage that wasn't worth saving. Carl wouldn't even give me a chance…" She huffed out a cleansing breath. "And I'm glad it's over with."

"Darling," Bobby spoke from the bottom of his heart. "I regret all that happened to you. But, I can't help but be grateful for the way things worked out. There's a simple answer, you know."

Cecile wiped the back of her hand over her eyes, removing the faint trace of tears that was caused by nothing more than nerves. "What's that?"

"The reason it didn't work out for you and Carl was that it wasn't supposed to, you never belonged to Carl." While she tried to comprehend what he was saying, he leaned over and kissed her, giving her that lethal, sexy smile. "You belong to me." After that phrase, Cecile didn't know what to say, so she just held on to his arm and tried to wrap her head around all that had happened. Bobby was talking like he wanted more from her than just this week. But they hadn't made love yet, nor had she been honest with him about their age difference. Both of those bridges would have to be crossed before she would dare to dream about anything more.

They had one more stop before they reached the Austin city limits. Bobby took her by his practice field. It was getting old and rundown. The bleachers were warped and the announcer's box was getting rickety, but it was still an important part of his history. "Look up there, we painted the Dallas Cowboy star over the old mascot." They held hands as they walked across the small field. "This used to be the home of the Bulldogs, but the little school was shut down. They consolidated a lot of the smaller schools in the area into mega-schools, it might be financially smart, but a lot of communities lost their pride—their school spirit."

"So, you've played football all your life?" Cecile tried to imagine him as a young boy, sprinting across the field, making tackles and touchdowns. It wasn't hard, he would be good at anything he set his mind to.

"I've played football since Junior High. Now, tell me what you like to do. What makes Ceelee happy?"

Tugging him over about ten feet, she sat on the grass and brushed at her feet and legs. "Fire ants," she explained. "They were biting me, good."

Bobby knelt with her, knocking off the little pests. "Damn! I'm sorry, doll. With these old shit-kicking boots on, I never notice anything like that. You don't have anything on your little feet but a couple of straps of leather and some sexy pink polish."

She started to get up, satisfied that she was ant free.

"Sit back down, we're in the shade. Talk to me."

Arranging her dress around her, she chose her words carefully. "Well, I enjoy my work and I'm grateful for Annalise, she's my only close friend. I would have to say that I find my happiness in causes. I've never owned a pet, but I volunteer at the local animal shelter, the no-kill one. I'm too much of a crybaby to work at the other kind. And I also spend time at the nursing home a couple of nights a week, I do the ladies fingernails."

Bobby put a finger under her chin. "I knew it. I'm a good judge of character. You're an angel."

With her eyes sparkling, she teased him. "Since I met you, I think my halo's become a little tarnished. I find myself wanting to do really bad things with you."

Pushing her backwards, he pinned her to the ground. "Don't you know you're supposed to save comments like that until we're alone? You're right, you are a little devil!" Bobby stared deep into her eyes. "I'm happy with you—just doing nothing—I'm happy with you." He said it like the revelation surprised him. "Are you happy with me?"

Cecile sensed a need in Bobby for unconditional acceptance. Her talents were small and her possessions were few, but that was one thing in her power to grant him. "You have made me very happy. Remember when you asked me to give you a gift?" When he nodded, she hoped to make his day. "It's yours when you're ready for it, all you have to do is unwrap it."

She wasn't able to talk for a while—her mouth was way too busy.

Chapter Five

Austin was a fun place to visit. Cecile had not spent a great deal of time there, so she was intrigued by the beauty and the uniqueness of the city. "Look over there," Bobby told her pointing to the Congress Street Bridge. "Every day at dusk from March to November, a million and a half bats emerge from under that bridge. It's an amazing sight, I'll bring you back one night to see it after all this wedding business is over." Her heart jumped at the thought that he planned on seeing her after this week was over.

She smiled at his enthusiasm. "I'd like that. Will you drive me downtown? I'd like to see the Capitol and Sixth Street?"

"Sure." He looked at her tenderly. He did better than that. Bobby pulled into a nearby parking garage and they spent the morning prowling the city streets hand in hand. Cecile was fascinated by the shops and restaurants that peppered the downtown area. "I can't wait to bring you back and introduce you to the nightlife." They sat on a bench and ate a cone from Aimee's ice cream an Austin tradition. He straddled the backless bench and she sat between his legs leaning back on him. There were very few moments when he wasn't touching her somewhere, forging their bond, cementing their connection. When she got through with her cone, he wiped her lips tenderly and then kissed them for good measure.

They walked along the banks of Lady Bird Lake, enjoyed Zilker Park and then headed back toward the parking garage. "We've still got to pick up Annalise's gifts, don't forget." Cecile was so happy, she couldn't remember ever being so content, or feeling so protected and cherished. Bobby Stewart made her feel wanted, and there was no better feeling on earth.

"We've got time for one more stop. I need to run by campus and pick up some stuff out of my locker. If you promise not to tell my brothers, I'll tell you a secret. If all goes well, I'm gonna be drafted by the NFL. Hopefully, I'll be playing for the Dallas Cowboys next year."

"Dallas Cowboys! That's wonderful, Bobby!" The chances of him moving to Dallas looked to be very good. And if he played for the Cowboys? He'd be a celebrity. Everybody would know Bobby Stewart and anyone he dated would be in the spotlight. Cecile gulped, wishing that a genie would suddenly appear and grant her three wishes. She'd ask for him to be four years older and her to be four years younger. And—oh yeah—for a third wish, a spine would be nice. Because if he asked her how old she was—she was going to lie like a dog. "I just wish I were a bit younger," she whispered with dread in her voice.

Bobby looked around, backed into an alley and eased up to a wall until he had her back anchored gently against the brick. "Don't even go there, Ceelee. Don't you know I realized you were older than me? You're out of college, you've got a job, I knew you had to be older than me by a little bit. That doesn't mean you aren't the sweetest, cutest, sexiest little thing I've ever had my hands on."

Cecile was quickly losing her ability to think. His lips were everywhere. He was taking little nips, little licks— branding her with hot, sweet kisses that were making her sweat. "Bobby,' she gasped. "Stop. We've got to stop." She didn't know if she were pleading for an end to the kiss or an end to the dreaming. Her body and her heart were telling her that she was crazy to want an end to either one. But her mind was playing havoc with her emotions, because Cecile was afraid to hope that what they had could last longer than just this wonderful week. God, she so desperately wished it could last forever. In just this brief time, she had felt closer to Bobby, more important to him than she had ever felt with her husband. Tears were beginning to form behind her lids, and as he kissed a trail from her throat to her eyes, she valiantly tried to hold them back.

"I would give you anything you asked for—flowers, candy, jewels—hell, anything, but don't ask me to give you up, sugar. Not now. Not after I've had a taste of you. Please."

"It might not work, Bobby."

"Who says?" Bobby demanded, his voice low and husky. "I want you and, by God, I know you want me too. Right now, your nipples are hard and so is my dick. Now, let's just deal with this right now. How old are you?"

Shit! Here it was. The question she didn't want to have to answer had been asked. Cecile wet her lips, biding her time, raking up her courage. Lies. Lies. She was going to go to hell, but she couldn't bring herself to tell him the truth.

He asked again. "How old are you, baby? Twenty-five? Twenty-six? You look so beautiful to me, you don't look a day older than eighteen. None of the women I know can hold a candle to you. I think you're prettier than a speckled pup."

Lies. Lies. "I'm a little older than twenty-six." She was thirty-one. Not even Annalise knew how old she was and she didn't intend to let the cat out of the bag now.

"So? I don't care if you're fifty-seven, you're absolutely perfect for me." He searched her face, sweet uncertainty making his own expression completely endearing to her.

"But, Bobby, I'm too old..." He pushed against her

with his rock-hard erection, while he plundered her lips with his own, refusing to accept the verdict that she had decided to pass on them both.

"Please, please. No—let's work it out. Just give me a chance, baby. I'll make it so good for you that you'll never look at another man again as long as you live."

Cecile didn't say so, but that fate was already in place. He had fulfilled and surpassed every standard and every dream she had ever carried close to her heart of what a man should be, or how she wanted to be treated. Bobby Stewart had forever spoiled her for any other man. And right now as he ground his cock into the most tender part of her, she knew her heart was irrevocably lost to him. "Please, my baby..." The endearment slipped from her tongue before she could stop it.

"Exactly, I'm your baby," he gently placed her on her feet. "I want to make love to you more than anything. If I had my way, I'd belong to you and you'd belong to me and to hell with age." As he towered over her a good foot, outweighing her by more than a hundred pounds, she felt like throwing her arms around his neck and laying all of her burdens on his wide, strong shoulders—because he was more than capable of taking care of her every need. Closing her eyes, she placed her head against his chest and listened to the strong heart that beat in his breast—and she knew. It might not be forever, but for however long it worked, she wanted to belong to Bobby Stewart.

"All right, we won't let it matter." She felt his whole body relax, tension that she hadn't even realized he was feeling, was let go.

He soothed his hands down her hair, holding her head, making her look at him. "Thank you, Ceelee. You won't be sorry. I promise, before God, you'll never be sorry." He rubbed his nose against hers and Cecile felt like it was more intimate than a kiss. "Now, come on. I can't wait to show you the forty acres."

He never turned loose of her hand. Cecile was pleasantly surprised at the beauty of the UT campus. The infamous tower loomed over it all, where a shooter killed sixteen and wounded thirty-two in 1966. It was a place that Cecile had always wanted to see. A memorial had been built nearby to honor those who had died. It was a place of such sadness, yet a place of such pride. "Anytime UT wins a game they light up the whole tower in our signature burnt orange," Bobby explained. As they walked over campus, Cecile was self-conscious about how young everyone looked. She would glance at Bobby every few seconds and wonder at his poise and maturity. She never would have guessed in a million years he was still in college. He was a man, fully grown. There was no doubt about that—one that was comfortable in his sexuality and knew how to please a woman within an inch of her life. And he was nice and kind, to boot, a catch in anybody's estimation.

He led her through the maze of dorms and class buildings. The campus was graced with huge trees and squirrels played and scampered down the sidewalk. "Look!" Bobby pointed. "There's the albino squirrel, if I were on my way to take a test I'd ace it!"

A pale colored squirrel dashed in front of them on its way to a nearby pecan tree. "He's cute."

"He's the most popular guy on campus. If you spy Blondie on your way to take a test, you're assured of an A." As he held her hand, his thumb caressed her palm. "Since, I don't have a test today, this must mean I'm gonna score with you later."

Looking at him, she saw that he was grinning at her, confidently. He knew how sexy he was.

"You think so? You seem to be pretty confident."

He let go of her hand and cupped the back of her neck instead, still guiding her as she walked, keeping her close. "You may not realize it, babe, but you have me completely at your mercy. I'm smitten. Confident is not the word." His fingers tightened slightly. "Desperate is a much better term."

Cecile was saved from having to respond when Bobby opened the doors to the looming Darrell K Royal stadium player's entrance. He was immediately hailed by a chorus of greetings and a few whistles that made Cecile blush. At the attention of the buff young athletes, Bobby pulled her close, staking his claim. A cocky young man came sauntering over, raking his eyes slowly from Cecile's toes up her body—lingering on her breasts—and finally making it up to her eyes. Behind her, she heard a distinctive growl. Bobby was jealous. The next heartbeat, he had wrapped an arm possessively around her waist. "O'Malley, this is my *girlfriend*, Ceelee Fairchild." He slid one hand over her throat and tilted her head back, kissing her on the cheek.

"Baby, this clown is Rourke O'Malley, our tight end. I know you guys aren't doing anything that you haven't done before—you're ogling a pretty girl. The only problem is that this time, it's my woman. And I don't like it one damn bit." He said the words with a joking tone in his voice, but Cecile had a distinct feeling he meant every word.

"Miss Fairchild." A handsome guy with a goatee held out his hand, trying to be the gentleman in the group. "It's a pleasure to meet you." Making a motion that included the other players, he apologized for their behavior. "You'll have to excuse these mannerless morons for staring. It's just that we've never seen Stewart act possessive about a woman before. It's something to see! We kinda enjoy seeing him tied up in knots over a girl, he's been foot-loose and fancy free for too long!"

"Yea, if you lasso Stewart, the rest of us might stand a chance with the fillies around here," O'Malley said.

Cecile didn't know what to think. "It's nice to meet all of you." Her relationship with Bobby was so new and so precarious, nothing she could say in response seemed right, so she didn't say anything. "I can't wait to watch the Cotton Bowl this year, I'll be there rooting for you."

"If you kangaroos will step back, I want to show Ceelee around the stadium." The crowd parted like the Red Sea as Bobby led her on a guided tour. She was duly impressed with the huge complex that could seat over one hundred and ten thousand people.

"I can't believe I didn't make the connection, Bobby. I've watched Longhorn games, faithfully, for years. I've watched you play. The commentators call you The Bull, don't they?"

Laughing, Bobby nudged up against her—letting his groin press into her hips. "That's because of my penchant for rodeo, of course, and the fact that I'm overly endowed," he whispered the rest in her ear. "Hung like a bull. Soon, you'll see for yourself." She blushed as he picked up her hair and kissed her neck. "I could just eat you up, you are the sweetest thing."

Cecile trembled, turning in his arms, she relaxed against him. Determined to enjoy whatever time she had with him, she ran her hands over his chest enjoying how turned on she got just from touching him. Rubbing her cheek on his shirt, she spoke almost in a whisper, for her ears alone. "I can't wait to make love to you." The words were so foreign to her that Cecile was amazed she had managed to enunciate them. She felt his body go still, and she wondered if she had crossed the line. Holding her breath, she prepared to move back.

"What did you say?"

Drawing into herself, Cecile tried to make her whole being as small as possible. "I said...I said," she stammered, afraid she had gone too far. Flashes of Carl appeared in her mind and her mouth went dry.

"Say it again, baby." Bobby held his head down close to hers. "Say those beautiful words again."

"I want to make love with you, Bobby." With renewed confidence, she let her arms settle around his waist, and did something she had never done before—she kissed a man on the neck and then nipped, catching a little of his flesh in her mouth and then sucking on it with a steady, erotic pressure. For now, he was hers, and she wanted everyone to know it.

Bobby made a rumbling, growling noise deep in his chest. Between them, Cecile felt his cock grow as hard as a steel spike. His obvious arousal made her moan. "Damn, I'm about to lose control." Her tongue soothed the place she had bitten and Bobby's heart bucked in his chest like an unridden bronc. "I'll give you everything I've got baby. Let's get outta here. The faster we get everything done, the faster we can be alone."

After picking up the information he needed for the next couple of weeks practices and games, Bobby and Cecile left campus and headed to the mall. "Tell me about your life in Dallas? I want to know every detail."

Cecile held his right hand in her lap between both of hers. It was so strong and capable, she rubbed her thumbs over the prominent veins on the back and raised it to her lips. He was fast becoming dear to her heart. How had that happened so quickly? It wasn't that she was just starved for attention—it was Bobby himself. He was so possessive and attentive, he made her blood pressure shoot sky high. Her eyes scanned his face, memorizing every feature. There was a tiny scar right at the corner of his eye—she would have to kiss that later. She also noticed that even though it was only noon, he already had a shadow of a beard showing. How sexy was that?

"Talk baby, or we're gonna have to pull over and let me ravish you."

Giving him a sweet smile, she cradled his hand to her breast and just held it there like it was the most precious thing in the world.

* * *

Bobby fell in love.

It hit him like a ton of bricks. He ran off the road, momentarily, before righting the truck in his lane. "Sorry, baby."

"Are you okay?" Ceelee was concerned. "You look startled, like you just remembered something that you needed to do. Something important."

Gathering his wits, Bobby winked at her. "Righter than rain, honeybun." He wasn't ready to tell her, because she wasn't ready to hear it. He tried to focus on the traffic and the passing landscape. The skyline of Austin was so familiar and the traffic on I-35 was something he could maneuver in his sleep—but knowing how to handle this incredible woman sitting beside him was unknown territory.

"I'm moving out of the apartment as soon as I get back," Ceelee began slowly. "With everything that's going on here, I had sort of put that out of my mind. Carl has been staying in a motel, but I'm going to let him have the apartment. I don't want it, I was never happy there."

Bobby exited off the interstate and headed toward Barton Creek Mall. Taking advantage of a red light, he looked over at Ceelee. She held his hand so tight to her breast that he could feel every breath she took, every beat of her heart. He savored the moment. "This is a new start for you. Where do you think you'll move?" He wanted to keep tabs on her this time, for sure. Losing track of her again was not an option.

"I've got a real estate agent checking on a couple of places for me. I want to get a house this time, and a dog. That way I won't have to come home to an empty house all the time. Carl and I were both career centered. Looking back, we rarely spent evenings at home together. It's no wonder our marriage was a disaster. Do you have an apartment or do you live in a dorm?"

Hell! He didn't like to think about that idiot. Carl should be strung up by his gonads for mistreating Ceelee. Of course, Bobby knew he was the beneficiary of Carl's stupidity, but he still didn't like it. "I have a condo just off campus, and if we didn't have to get these gifts back to Annalise, we'd go there and I'd have my wicked way with you."

"That sounds heavenly, but we have to be responsible. Oh, that sounded funny didn't it?" Realizing how she had come across, Cecile laughed out loud.

Totally entranced, Bobby watched her be happy. He wanted to see her look that way over and over. "Playing the adult in our relationship?"

"Somebody has to, and since I am the oldest..."

Turning off Capital City Highway, he pulled into the parking lot and found a spot convenient to the boutique where Annalise had purchased her bridal party gifts. As soon as he put the truck in park, he moved in closer and nipped her on the cheek. This set off another round of giggles. "I'll save all of my adult moves for the bedroom."

"Promises, promises," she said in between her bursts of laughter. Bobby was blowing raspberries on her neck, just to prolong her joy.

"That's one promise I plan on keeping."

They walked through the mall, his arm around her waist. Several people spoke to Bobby, apparently he was well known in town. Nobody acted like they thought she shouldn't be with him, so Cecile finally relaxed. Maybe she didn't have a three and a one tattooed on her forehead after all. "I'm going to make a lot of changes when I go back to Dallas."

"Like what?" He pulled her close as a group of junior-high age boys almost ran over her.

"I'm going to get out more and make friends. Except for work, I've been pretty isolated for the past few years."

Due to the level of noise, Bobby leaned in to catch every word. "That's fine, just as long as you leave room in your life for me." He said it lightly, but he meant every word.

* * *

When was the last time a man had taken her out to dinner? It had to have been Carl, but for the life of her the memory seemed too far away to dredge up.

"I'm glad we came. You look beautiful," he rasped as his gaze traveled from her face, to her neck and down to her chest. Everywhere his eyes roved, she felt warmth spread.

Finding her voice, she whispered, "thank you, I appreciate you taking me out like this. Spending time with you is an unexpected pleasure."

"That's right. I keep forgetting. You didn't come back to Lost Maples because you couldn't get me out of your mind." He was teasing, but there seemed to be a hint of vulnerability in his tone.

"Believe me, I considered it," she confessed lowly. "You made me feel so special." Suddenly feeling shy, she retreated to safer ground. "I think my visiting here, initially, was fate. The last time Annalise and I were together, we discussed how much she still loved and longed for Ethan. And then when I walked into the Bed and Breakfast and saw him, I just knew I had to get her over here. Thank God for writer's block."

"You know, I had the same type of conversation with Ethan just the day before Annalise showed up, too. Perhaps you're right about fate." He covered her hand with his. "It sure seemed like destiny the moment I opened the door and saw you standing there."

"I was shocked to see you, I mean I had hoped to see you again." She blushed and glanced down. "But after a while, our chance meeting on the side of the road seemed more like a dream than anything else. I couldn't believe how I acted with you, it was so unlike me. And when I looked down and realized I had practically flashed you— I nearly died."

"Don't be sorry, that image is burned in my memory. You don't have any idea how I dreamed about finding you again. Hell, I even hired a PI to track you down, and some help he was—he just ended up frightening you and didn't locate you until you were practically on my doorsteps."

"Yea, and we pretended we didn't know one another. Do you think they bought it?" God, he was touching her! Bobby had insisted they sit catty-corner to one another and now she knew why. His big hand was caressing her knee. Closing her eyes for a moment, she just let herself enjoy the attention.

"Actually," he continued to rub her, running his fingers an inch or two up her thigh, "I told Alex you were the woman I've been searching for. By now, I'm sure Ethan knows. I didn't exactly try to keep you a secret." He looked like he wanted to say more, but a waitress came to take their order. When their server had gone, Bobby held out his hand. "From the moment I saw you in that Texas rainstorm, looking like a gift from the gods, I knew I wanted you to be mine. Now, come dance with me. I need to hold you."

She couldn't resist, he was the sexiest thing. The way he bit his bottom lip and winked at her made her dampen her panties. Placing her hand in his, she let him lead her out on the dance floor. Cecile placed a hand on his shoulder and stepped close to him, but not touching. The music was sultry and sexy, a slow number with an underlying beat that made you want to gyrate your hips in the age old rhythm of romance. But Bobby had other ideas, he put a hand to the small of her back and pulled her near so there was no space between their bodies from shoulders to thighs. "Now, you're where you belong." He let out a long sigh. "Oh, sweet baby. I'm so glad to get to hold you."

It was as if his words released something in Cecile. She melted into him, pressing closer, needing the contact and comfort only he could give. At that moment, she didn't care who saw them or if they were moving in time to the music, all she wanted was to be held in Bobby's arms and know she was welcome. "Right now, there's nowhere I'd rather be than with you."

Bobby guided them in slow, sensuous movements across the dance floor. They ended up in a quiet corner, and she was glad.

"Ethan's happiness means the world to me, but reuniting with you is priceless." He pushed her hair back and rubbed his lips over the skin of her neck making her shiver with awareness. "I plan on wooing you like nobody's business."

Cecile couldn't help but laugh. "I don't think I've

ever been wooed before."

"High time, I say."

The dress Cecile had on was soft and flowing with an empire waist, a fitted bodice and a flowing skirt. As they danced, he slipped a leg in between hers, and his hard thigh grazed her clit. "Ummm," there was no way she could have stopped the little noise that escaped her lips to save her life.

Bobby clutched her closer. "Hell, baby. You just purred for me. Do you have any idea what that does to me?" Their movements to the music essentially stopped. Instead, he slid a hand down to her lower back and fitted her as close to him as humanly possible. "Move on my leg. Make yourself feel good," he encouraged.

"Will anybody see?" She couldn't believe she was actually considering it, but she was so turned on she couldn't see straight.

In response, Bobby moved them a few steps farther into the shadows. His back was to the crowd and he was big enough to hide anything she would do. "Now, it's like we're in our own little world."

Kissing her neck, he cupped her bottom and gave a little push. That was all she needed. With wonder, Cecile let her hands slip up around his neck and she lifted her body a scant inch so she would have even more contact with his rock hard muscle. And she let herself go. To the beat of the music, she moved—pumping her hips, letting the friction build between her pussy and Bobby's thigh. "Oh God, Bobby! This feels incredible. I can't believe I'm doing this," she whispered.

"I love it. You're killing me, but it's worth it. Come on baby, rub that sweet spot on my leg and sparkle for me." Cecile never considered herself submissive, but she found her body obeying. Dizzy and delirious with pleasure, she rode his leg until her heartbeat drowned out any qualms she had, and with a gasp, she called out his name. "Bobby!" The rush of a hard climax swept away her sanity and all she could do was cling to him as if the winds of passion would carry her away.

"That's my girl," he crooned to her, holding her as she quivered. "That's my Ceelee." Bobby didn't let go, but cradled her until she could stand on her own two feet again. "I like you leaning on me that way. Being responsible for your pleasure is fuckin' unbelievable." To show his appreciation, he picked her up off her feet and squeezed her tight. "Let's go eat and get out of here. I can't wait to get you alone."

They laughed. They talked. It was a perfect date. Bobby was attentive, gentle and made her feel like she was the only woman in the world. Placing her hand over his, she rewarded him. "You are so sexy. Just sitting here with you has me literally quaking with desire." Throwing all caution to the wind, she told him the unvarnished truth. "I still feel hungry and I know the only thing that can satisfy me—you." There was no doubt in her mind, she was ready for him, more eager and turned on than she could ever remember being. Briefly, she considered telling him about her unfortunate virginity, but decided against it. Surely, he wouldn't know. Maybe. Besides, she didn't want to do anything that would break the mood. A man was about to make love to her—*Cecile Fairchild*—and it was going to be glorious!

* * *

"Damn!" Bobby threw down his napkin and motioned for the waiter to bring their check. Without making a scene, Bobby took care of everything and led Cecile to his truck. He opened the door, helped her in and made sure she was comfortable. Then, he pulled out on the highway and broke all speed records getting to his address. Hell, he was excited, his body was almost vibrating at the thought of being intimate with her. Pulling into the small private parking garage, Bobby was out the door in a flash. "I'm going to make you so happy, I promise." Escorting her to his condo, they entered and he closed and locked the door behind them.

"I'll show you around. Let's start with the bedroom." He didn't even bother to turn on a light and Cecile got the giggles as he pulled her through the dark.

"I hope we don't trip and fall," she admonished him.

"If we do, I'll let you land on top of me—that'll give us a head start." Pushing open a door, Bobby stepped back to let her in to the spacious room. A light from the bathroom illuminated the area, but he turned on an additional one. He didn't want to miss a thing. For once, he was glad he had picked up his clothes and not left them strewn about. Impressing this woman was one of his goals. "Now, I've got you where I want you." She stood still, looking a bit shy. That would never do. Pushing in close to her, he breathed in her scent and felt the warmth from her body. "God, I've dreamed about this moment. Do you know how much I want you?" He feathered a touch down her cheek, pushing back soft strands of silky hair.

"About half as much as I want you?" Her words were sassy, but her tone betrayed her uncertainty.

"Impossible, but I do enjoy the thought." Leaning near, he began with a simple kiss. The moment she parted her lips, he took full and complete possession of her mouth. Electric heat cascaded through his body. Tearing his lips from hers, he groaned. "I need you, Ceelee. Desperately."

"Take me, Bobby. I'm ready." Relief made his hands shake. He hadn't realized how tight his gut was knotted up until she gave him permission to love her. With care, he began to undress her. She helped, their fingers bumping together as they loosened the ties on her shoulders.

"Raise your arms for me." Without a moment of hesitation, she held her arms over her head. That simple act almost floored him. It was the sweetest act of surrender he could ever imagine. Ceelee was totally and utterly feminine. Eagerly, he pulled the dress down over her shoulders and held her hand while she stepped out of it. "Lord, look at you." Underneath the dress she wore lacy red panties and a low cut bra that cupped her breasts as lovingly as he longed to do. "You take my breath away." And that was the unvarnished truth. Ceelee was curvy and luscious and he couldn't wait to explore every inch. Slowly, he peeled off her lingerie like it was the wrapping paper she had referred to earlier. "Oh, baby. God, you're beautiful. Hold on—let me get naked." He stood up and shucked off his clothes, tossing them in the general direction of the hamper. All the while, he couldn't take his eyes off of her. She had the most perfect little body anyone could ask for—a tiny waist, flared hips, delectable breasts and legs that he couldn't wait to have wrapped around his hips. "Turn around," he ordered in a hoarse voice.

An uncertain light in her eyes, Cecile faced the other direction. "Damn!" Bobby couldn't help but want to touch. Skating his hands down her back, he brushed his fingers over her perfectly proportioned ass. Kneeling behind her, he placed kisses from the center of her back down the line of her spine. A sharp little nip on her hip made her jump and squeal with surprise.

Ceelee glanced over her shoulder, trying to get a glimpse of him. "Hey! What are you doing? I want you in front so I can join in the fun."

"Patience, baby." He let his touch dance over skin that was created to be caressed. Ceelee gasped at the sensation. "You've got the sweetest little bottom." Bobby cupped her hips and began to knead. "I've got big plans for this gorgeous ass," he promised. Taking his time, he scattered more kisses over her back and hips, and soon he heard a distinct little moan.

"I need something to hold on to," she whimpered. When he didn't move, she begged. "Please, Bobby. I want to touch you so badly."

"How could anyone deny a request like that?" He stood as she turned. His cock was fully engaged and standing up straight—nine inches of proud male flesh.

"Oh, my! Is it okay for me to touch you?" Bobby was amazed she thought it necessary to seek his approval.

"Please," he choked out.

He noticed she avoided looking at his cock, but that was okay. There was plenty more of him that wanted her attention. Gracefully, she slid her palms over his chest. "You're so hard, yet smooth. I've dreamed about touching you like this."

Bobby stood like a statue. He wanted to give her time and let her play, but it was hard to do. "I think you're gorgeous," she whispered. "Look at these muscles. They appear to be carved from marble, yet you're so warm and alive." Closing her eyes, Ceelee smoothed his skin, letting her fingers explore. "I need to feel you against me." Letting her hands slide up his neck, she moved closer, her nipples nesting in his chest hair. They both groaned at the sensation. Her proximity caused his cock to nudge her belly and she stepped back to get a good look. "My God!"

Bobby laughed. "Is that good?"

Now it was Cecile's turn to go to her knees. "Yes, it's

good. Can I—May I..." she stammered, looking up—seeking his permission.

"Oh, baby. Do you think I'd tell you no?" By the look on her face, he could tell that was exactly what she was thinking. Right now, he was too excited to think clearly. But one thing he knew—her bastard husband deserved to be tarred and feathered for making this angel feel inadequate in any way. "I'd give everything I had to feel your lips on me."

His encouragement made her smile. "I can do this, I think. At least, I'd like to try. Tell me if I mess up." Taking his cock in both hands she massaged its length, feeling his hips buck in response. "You are beautifully made," she whispered. Laying her cheek against the throbbing flesh, she caressed it with her face, planting kisses at the base and then up the shaft.

"Shit, baby." He groaned.

Immediately, Cecile sat back and looked up, like she was expecting to be pushed away. "Shall I stop?"

Cupping the back of her head, Bobby crooned to her. "Lord, no baby. Take me in your mouth, suck the head."

As if with renewed confidence, Ceelee focused on the large purple head of his cock with its topping of glistening pre-cum. Bobby shook a little with excitement as she licked the very tip. "Oh, Jesus," he growled. Opening her lips, she slid her mouth over the head and down the shaft. He thought she might not be totally inexperienced at this, but neither was she sure enough to be totally at ease. Seeking to let her know how grateful he was, Bobby cupped the back of her head and bucked his hips gently, pushing and pulling his cock in and out of her mouth. And when she looked up at him, those doe eyes of hers seeking reassurance, he couldn't hold back. "That's my girl. You're making me feel so good." That was all it took. Ceelee joyously went to work sucking, tonguing, kissing, taking him as deep as she could. "Being with you like this is a dream come true. I can't wait to taste you. I'm gonna love you like there's no tomorrow." His praise seemed to make her want to please him more, so she cupped his sac and began caressing and massaging his balls as she sucked and pulled at his swollen cock.

"Stop, baby," Bobby pleaded.

Ceelee stopped, immediately, confusion in her eyes. Bobby pulled out of her mouth, easing her back onto the bed. "I want to come inside you. Now." Grabbing a condom, he sheathed himself. "Are you ready for me?" He felt between her legs and smiled when he discovered her wet and swollen. "Yeah. You want me don't you doll?"

"Yes." He didn't give her a chance to say more.

"I know I'm rushing things, but Lord knows I can't help it. I've fantasized about this moment for months." Slipping a hand between them, he fitted the head of his cock to her tender opening and plunged in.

"Oh!" Her gasp of pain and the barrier he ripped through shocked the hell out of both of them.

"What the fuck?"

* * *

Cecile didn't know what to do. There was enough light in the room that she could see his face. He was not happy. She hadn't meant to make any noise. It had hurt, but the pain was fading. Having Bobby inside of her was so different than Carl, she could feel him stretching her, caressing her inner walls. She knew it would feel good, if he just gave her a chance. "Please don't stop," she begged.

Bobby looked shocked. "You were a virgin! How? Did I hurt you?" She could tell he had lost his focus.

Inside of her, she felt him lose his interest. To sum it up, Bobby Stewart lost his erection. It withered like a cucumber left too long on the vine. Easing up, he moved to one side. "I'm sorry, baby. I wasn't expecting…"

She lay there for a moment, trying to process what had just happened. It had been so fast. Cecile could feel her soul curl up and die inside of her tender spirit. It had happened again. Bobby might not have been expecting it, but she should have. Cecile was shaking with mortification. Carl had been right. "You don't have to say anything." All she wanted to do was get up and get out of the room. If it wasn't for the wedding and breaking Annalise's heart, she would leave just as soon as she could get back to the B&B and gather her things.

Before Bobby could stop her, Ceelee had grabbed her dress and was out of the bed and in the bathroom. "Did I hurt you?" She could hear him moving around, stubbing his toe on the bed, fumbling for his clothes. Cecile even heard him hopping on one foot till he reached the bathroom door. When he tried the knob, she was grateful she had thought to lock it. "Ceelee, baby? Are you all right? I'm so sorry. I wouldn't have hurt you for the world. Please come out and let's talk about this. I need to understand."

Cecile didn't want to talk. She stood looking in the mirror and wondered how she had gotten herself into this mess. Wiping her face with a damp rag, she forced herself to calm down. She could get through this, she just had to put on a front, a false sense of bravado. There was no reason Bobby had to know how much he had hurt her, and she didn't mean physically. "I'll be right out." She forced out a lilting tone that she hoped conveyed the idea that all was well.

Bobby leaned on the door. "I just want to hold you,

sweetheart. Please come out." As if his words were magic, she opened the door for him. "Lord, you're pale. Did I hurt you? I've got to know."

Cecile put on, what she hoped, was a brave and sincere smile. "Of course not. I'm fine. I'm sorry about—you know…"

* * *

Cecile ducked her head and it hit Bobby like a ton of bricks—she thought he had reacted like her husband. *God!* Not only had he not given her an orgasm, he had reinforced her belief she was undesirable. Not happening. "Ceelee, baby, it's not what you think." She wasn't listening, she was moving past him, purposefully, making for the door and a quick escape. Reaching out he caught her by the arm. He managed to stop her, easily, but she wouldn't look at him.

"Let me go, Bobby. Please? I can't take any more of this. All I want to do is go back to Lost Maples so I can crawl under the covers and put a pillow over my head." She smiled sadly. "I appreciate what you did, it felt really good."

"Stop!" he shouted, making her jump a little. "If you think I lost my erection because I wasn't attracted to you, you're as far off base as you could be." He took her hand and placed it over his reawakened dick. "It was the fact that you were a virgin that blew my mind."

Ceelee seemed careful not to move her fingers. He knew she could feel the heat of his penis through his pants. But she made no move to let on. "I understand." Tugging her hand from his, she asked. "Can I go now?"

"No, I need you." Once more she was in his arms, but she remained stiff, unyielding. "Talk to me, treasure. We can work this out. I've made a mess of things. If you had just told me that you were a virgin, I would have warmed you up, been gentle. Give me another chance, please?"

Cecile didn't move, but she began to talk. "It wasn't your fault. That's the way it is with me. I'm defective." Her voice broke, but she quickly regained composure.

"You are not defective. Your husband had to have been gay. And I'm a moron, but there's nothing in God's name wrong with you." Wrapping his arms around her, he picked her up, carrying her to the bed. She tried to get away, but he pinned her down. "Be still, you are safe with me. I'm going to show you just how desirable you are."

"Please don't," she begged. "Sex has always been a nightmare for me, I don't know why I thought this time would be different." He pushed her hair out of her eyes and kissed the tears away. "Please, I don't need your pity."

"Darling, this is as far from pity as it gets." Bobby decided the time for talking was almost through. He framed her face and slowly, sensuously kissed every square inch. When he made it to her lips, they were open and ready for him. He sank inside, letting his tongue mate with hers, grateful for a second chance. Feeling her mellow, he pulled her with him until he was on his back and she was lying square on top of him, full length—no part of her untouched by a part of him. As he continued to feast at her lips, he petted her, rubbing her shoulders, her back, her arms, gentling her, freeing her emotions from the bonds of self-doubt that kept her from letting go and enjoying the gifts of her femininity. "That's it baby. Feel how much I want you." Bobby lifted his hips, pushing his erection up against her. "This time I'll have you so wet and excited there won't be a moment's pain. I'm going to love you like you've never been loved before. It's going to be so good, baby."

Pushing herself up a fraction, Cecile looked Bobby

in the face. "Will you hush and just kiss me, please."

At her adorable desperation, Bobby laughed out loud. "I think I can handle that." He began tugging at her dress once more, skimming it over her head, he tossed it to the end of the bed—grateful to see that she was gloriously naked underneath. "Sit up, I want to play."

Cecile sat up, astraddle of him, her hands moving up and then down—obviously, fighting a desire to cross her arms over her breasts. "I feel excited. I'm gonna mess you up," she said hesitantly as she watched him raise his hands to her breasts and begin to rub them in circular motions.

Too intent on the pleasurable task at hand, he almost missed her anxiety. "What do you mean, sweetness? How are you gonna mess me up?"

Leaning over, dangling those beautiful tits in his face, she whispered, "I'm too wet to sit on you like this. Let me lay on my back." She started to move off of him, but he stopped her.

"Let me see," he slid his hand between her legs, the back of his hand resting on his own abdomen and curled his fingers into her slit. Yes, indeed. She was creamy and slick with excitement and there was a little blood, but just a speck. "Are you sore?"

"No, I'm just needy."

Hallelujah! He hadn't killed her desire for him. "This is your gift to me, sweetheart. I'm so glad you still want me. Now pick up your tits. Offer them to me, feed me, baby. I'm starving for you."

Bless her heart. She looked so sweet, her heart was in her eyes, and he vowed that he wouldn't let her down again. Picking up a breast in each palm, she brought a nipple to his lips. Closing his eyes, he feasted. God, it was good. Holding her close, he felt her body respond to him. She moved in a rocking motion against him, they were both enjoying this. As he sucked he rubbed her back, letting her know by his groans and grunts that this was heaven for him. He let her nipple go with a resounding little pop. "I can't wait. I want my second course, baby. That was just the appetizer. Lay back, I'm gonna return the favor."

"Are you sure?" she asked hesitantly. "I've never..."

Bobby's heart ached for her. Damn her husband! He couldn't believe a man could have a treasure like this in his bed and treat her so badly. But, then she had been a virgin. He couldn't wait to get to the bottom of that mystery. He helped her settle back, covered her with his body and kissed her slowly and thoroughly on the lips. As soon as he had her panting, he kissed a path down her neck to her shoulder and moved his body down the bed. Spreading her legs wide, he stopped for a moment just to appreciate the sight. Her breasts were moving sensuously with every breath, her nipples were hard, red berries that he intended to feast on repeatedly, but the real treasure lay between her legs. She was breathtaking. "God, you're beautiful." She was so soft and vulnerable, pink and glistening in her arousal.

Bobby was humbled. She was aroused, for him. Even after he had selfishly neglected her needs, going from her sweet offering of a blowjob to hastily taking her virginity, she still wanted him. Amazing!

"Really? I'm beautiful? Down there?" She looked sincerely doubtful.

"Exquisite." Bobby eased himself into a comfortable position and got down to business. Kissing the inside of her thighs, he reached up and caressed her breast, tugging on the nipple until he heard her groan. Her breasts were so sensitive. He'd have to remember that. When he took his first lick, from the bottom of her sweet slit to the hard nubbin of her clitoris, she let out a ragged, hungry moan. Bobby vowed to give her more pleasure than she could handle. Any man who wouldn't go down on their woman ought to be shot. To think she had missed out on that kind of joy hurt his heart. On the other hand, he was thrilled that it would be him introducing her to this ecstasy. "Hold on baby, I'm gonna rock your world!"

He knew she was trying to rise up and watch as he ate her out. Without hesitation or qualm he buried his face between her legs, sticking his tongue deep into her channel, sucking on her clitoris, nibbling her labia. "Bobby! God, yes! Bobby! Oh, God, it's so good!" She whimpered as she came hard, her little pussy pulsing against his mouth. Her hips bucked, but he held her steady, keeping up the sensual onslaught. "I don't know if I can take anymore."

He paused only to encourage. "Yes you can, doll. Come for me one more time, then I'm going to fuck you so hard you're going to scream the roof down." Bobby proceeded to show her he knew what he was talking about. Making himself at home between her legs, he licked and sucked until she was tossing her head in orgasmic abandon. Lord, his heart was so full. He couldn't believe how sweet she was. She was begging and praising and her little cries were not rehearsed and fake, they were real. Ceelee was coming so hard, she was literally crying with release. Kissing her one last time right on top of her sweet mons, he raised up to look at her, and she surprised the hell out of him. Launching herself upward, she clasped him around the neck and began to feverishly kiss his neck. "Thank you, Bobby. Thank you. I didn't think I would ever know what that was like. It was wonderful, you were wonderful."

"It was my pleasure sweet doll," he whispered to her. "Now lie back down and let me come inside you. I want to show you what it can really be like between us. Lie down, now," he urged, "and let me come into paradise." Fumbling for a condom from the nightstand, he was soon ready.

She looked up at him so trustingly, so hopefully that he had to kiss her again. "Don't worry, sweetheart. I'll take care of you." Slowly he pushed inside of her. He didn't take her roughly like before. God, he hadn't meant to hurt her. She was infinitely precious and he was the luckiest SOB in the world to be sliding deep inside of her. *Ah!* She was velvet—hot, wet, soft velvet. He began to move in and out in smooth, sure thrusts. Gritting his teeth, he refused to rush, this time was for her. He was going to show her that she was the most desirable woman on earth—even if it killed him. *God!* This was so good! It might just do him in.

"I like this Bobby." She spoke in wonder. "Can I put my legs around you?"

Words—he tried to form words. His mind wasn't working, it was too fogged with pleasure. Sweet Jesus! She was so tight! It was like a vise around his dick. "Yeah, hold me, baby. Wrap those long, pretty legs around me." As soon as he said it was okay she clasped him tight, wrapping her legs around his waist and her arms around his neck, clinging to him so sweetly he thought he'd died and gone to heaven. "Does that feel good, Ceelee?" He pumped into her over and over, pulling all the way out and then sliding back in. God, what he'd give to do her bare-back. Whatever it took, that was one experience that he would move heaven and earth to try.

"Yes, Bobby," she moaned, holding onto him tight. "Yes!" she cried as his penis drug over a sensitive spot. "Harder! Harder! God, it feels good!"

Bobby complied, her little erotic requests were like saying sic 'em to a dog. He was on it. Rising up on his arms, he gave it all he had. Plunging—pumping—he closed his eyes and let the ecstasy wash over him. When she started lifting her hips, meeting him, accepting him, loving him. *God! This is unfuckinbelievable!* "Ceelee, Ceelee, honey, you are perfect, baby!"

It was as if his approval opened the floodgates for her, he felt her tighten around him, incredibly tight. Her orgasm began in little flutters that caressed his dick like butterfly wings. But as her climax strengthened, so did the convulsions that were massaging his cock. They set off an explosion low in his belly that shot outward through his loins, absolute and total bliss. "Ceelee!" A tsunami wave of dizziness washed over him. As he held her, loving her, she quivered and groaned her release as her dainty little body milked his manhood of every last drop of semen. He had never been so thoroughly loved in his life.

Ceelee held him tight, rubbing his back, almost like she was comforting him. Bobby knew he trembled in her arms. She kissed him on the shoulder. "You said my name when you came. I'm normal. I brought you pleasure, didn't I?"

Joy flooded his soul. "More pleasure than you could possibly believe. And you're not just normal—you're perfect." He opened his eyes to find her looking at him, tenderly. "You're so pretty."

"I was thinking the same thing about you," she confessed.

Bobby cuddled this incredible woman closer to him. "Hmmmm, I'm not pretty, doll-face. I'm a macho, bull-riding, cowboy, football player." Her eyes widened at his teasing. "I love how you hold me. You are so soft, so sweet." He turned his head and kissed the upper swell of one breast. "Thank you, love." He kissed his way to her lips. "You devastated me, I've never come that hard, before." When she didn't answer, he sought her gaze, anxious to know that she was all right, that he hadn't hurt her. After all, he had broken through the barrier of her virginity only a little while before. Speaking of, he pulled himself up so they were lying side by side. "Come here, lay your head on my shoulder."

Cecile smiled, "I've always dreamed of cuddling after sex." Bobby began stroking her back and she eased her knee up on to his thigh and snuck an arm around his waist. "This feels so nice."

"Yea, it is." And it was. Bobby was content. For weeks he had thought of little else but getting this woman in his life, and here she was. Now, he had to make sure he kept her there. Permanently. *Whoa! What a thought.* Was he serious? He was a senior in college, on the verge of graduating, possibly getting a chance to play in the NFL, and he was thinking long term with a woman? Bobby tested his feelings. He listened to his heart. Hell Yeah he was!

He tightened his arms around her and heard her contented sigh. Sweet. Now, to get down to business. He had questions, and she had answers. "Sweetheart, explain to me how you were a virgin? I gotta tell you it's worrying me to death. I'm imagining all kind of things." Bobby waited and when her little body started to shake, he was afraid he had made her cry. It took him a second or two to realize she was laughing. "Am I that funny?" Bobby took the opportunity to goose her a little, which led to more laughter and then to squeals.

"Ssshhhh, ssshhhhh," he put his mouth over hers. They had been pretty loud during sex, and the walls were thick, but a happy Ceelee's voice would carry all the way out to the street. Since, he was there he kissed her. And she kissed him back—pure, erotic play time. He felt the strings of his heart being tugged when she moaned in his mouth and began to massage his neck and shoulders with insistent little fingers. "What were you laughing about?"

Looking at his face, she traced the strong line of his jaw. "I like the way your beard feels. It gives your face such a sexy, macho shadow."

"Thank you, ma'am. Now, tell me what is so funny."

Letting out a sigh, she burrowed her face in his chest. "It is funny. I've been married for seven years and I was a virgin until you made, I mean, had sex with me."

"Made love is the correct term, honey." He assured her. "So, enlighten me about how I was lucky enough to be the one to take your…uh…innocence." He smiled at the face she made.

"I'm almost embarrassed to say, but I'm beginning to think it wasn't my fault." He listened patiently, caressing the side of her face, soothing her hair, letting his eyes rove over her face. "Sex always hurt with Carl." The moment she said that, Bobby frowned.

"He hurt you?"

"No," she assured him quickly. "He didn't hit me or anything." She averted her eyes, looking to the side of his face instead of directly at him. "This is just too embarrassing. To use a play on words, foreplay was not his forte. I went to the gynecologist for my regular checkup a few weeks ago and while I was there I mentioned to him about the pain, even though it hadn't been a factor in a while. Until this morning, I hadn't had actual sex in over three years."

Bobby watched a blush creep up over her skin. This was hard for her. "I don't believe—technically that you've ever had sex at all." She stiffened a bit in his arms. He sought to reassure her. "I hate it for you, so much. But,

I can't say that I'm unhappy about being the one to finally bring you pleasure. You belong to me, now." Her eyes widened at his statement. "Don't look at me like that," he chided her. "I know we have a lot of talking to do."

"That sounds so good." She idly ran her hand up and down his arm. "Your muscles feel like stone, so strong and able to defend and protect what belongs to you."

"You'd better believe it. I wouldn't hesitate to take on any dragon for you. Now, explain why Carl wasn't able to take your virginity? Was he dickless?"

"Poor Carl. I always knew he was built small, not his body, mind you." She made the funniest little face. "Until I saw your penis, I didn't realize how small Carl actually was. The doctor said that my hymen was back just far enough that he butted up against it occasionally, hence the knife-like pain, but he wasn't big enough or long enough to break it. Isn't that the craziest, saddest story you've ever heard? And I wasn't experienced enough to know the difference. When Carl and I married, I was a virgin." At that she laughed and so did Bobby.

"No? he said comically, pretending surprise. She slapped him playfully. "I'm glad you can laugh about it. I'll have you know my new life purpose is to make you smile as often as possible" Bobby couldn't help but smirk a little. "But, I have to say, I'm glad the size of my cock meets with your approval. I aim to please."

Her face broke out into a radiant smile. "You pleased me more than you'll ever know. I almost fainted with the pleasure." She kissed the side of his neck, letting her tongue dart around on his skin. "And you are so kind and nice to me, I don't really know how to process it all."

Bobby narrowed his eyes, he was beginning to get the big picture. "That asshole blamed you for his shortcomings, didn't he?" At Bobby's well-worded question, she giggled. It was the absolute sweetest sound he had ever heard, it had bubbled up from deep within and sounded like pure unadulterated happiness. That realization made him feel like a king. He had made her happy. He had made her laugh. And he intended to see that happen over and over again in the future.

"His shortcomings? I don't think I can be blamed that his petey was small." At her terminology, he guffawed.

"Woman, if you ever refer to my huge, manly dick as a *petey,* I will turn you over my lap and spank your beautiful, curvy, little rump." Her giggling stopped, for it had faded into arousal. Bobby was flabbergasted! So? His little doll fancied an erotic spanking. Well, he'd have to put that on his to-do list. He wasn't into BDSM, but he liked to tinker with the idea. There wasn't a bigger turn-on in the world that a woman giving herself over to her man, completely. He filed that little tid-bit of information away for future reference.

"Let's see, what can I call your manhood?" Pretending to contemplate, she made a show of testing out names for his cock. "I know, I can call it Gargantua, or Dickzilla, or Super-size." At his pained expressions, she had started giggling again. "I know…" She sobered and looked him straight in the face. "How about if I call it—mine?"

Mine! Instantly, he was as hard as the pink granite Texas was so famous for, the granite the Capitol building is made from, the granite that forms the dome of Enchanted Rock—hard, pink steel. "Do you want me?" *Mine!* Her possessive statement immediately turned him on. Gliding his hand down her satin skin, he delved between her legs and found her vulva rich with cream.

" Yes, I'm starving for your touch."

"Ye gods!" Bobby groaned. "Every word you say is like an aphrodisiac!" He rose up over her, feeling more of a man than he ever dreamed possible. He ran his hand down his engorged cock, then asked, "Love, I've never been with a woman without a condom. Are you protected? Are you on the pill?" At her nod of affirmation, he almost begged, "Could I?" He watched her sparkling green eyes for any hint of trepidation. There was none, there was only heat.

Ceelee shivered before him. Without words, she answered him, by opening her legs and welcoming him home. "Please." She lifted her hips in supplication. "I can't wait."

Reverently, Bobby guided the head of his cock to the dainty portal of her femininity. *God!* He was so damn excited, he hoped he didn't embarrass himself and cum before he could pleasure his woman. His woman! Lord, that sounded right. She was so damn tight! He pushed in about an inch and the feel of her hot, slick flesh enveloping him like a glove was the closest thing to heaven he had ever felt. There was an overwhelming need for him to plunge inside of her—jackhammer, piston—push his way to nirvana. But, the idea of hurting her was out of the question. Gritting his teeth, he fought for control. "Oh, baby. You are the sweetest thing in the world!" he groaned. In another inch. "Lord God! I had no idea it would be this good!" He stopped to just feel, to just appreciate, to revel in the miracle of two becoming one.

"Bobby?" She held her arms open wide. "Could you lie on top of me? I want to feel you. I need to hold you."

When she opened and shut her hands as if touching him was the most important thing to her, his heart almost burst. Adjusting his angle, Bobby lowered himself on top of her, careful not to put too much weight directly on her body. But, she wouldn't have it. "More," she demanded. "I want to feel you. Press on me."

"I don't want to squish you, baby. And I can't move much this way." He pressed a little more into her, another inch, another step into paradise.

"I'll move for you, I think I know how. I've done Kegel exercises while reading erotica. Push in some more, baby. I want it all."

Bobby laughed. "Demanding little heifer, aren't you?" But, if she wanted it, she was going to get it. Gently but firmly, he pushed in to the hilt and she let out the sweetest, sexiest sigh of satisfaction he had ever heard. "You like that?"

"Oh, yes. I love it, Bobby."

And then she proceeded to blow his mind.

Bobby had slept with herds of women, he wasn't necessarily proud of it, but that was just the way it was. He had pleasured women that considered sex to be an extreme sport and they were out to earn a gold medal. But never in his whole life had he felt like this. Ceelee was hungry for him. Not a warm body, not a star football player, not a bullrider—him. She worked the little muscles of her canal, drawing him, luring him, massaging his cock with luscious contractions of her sex that had him gasping with ecstasy. She was right, he didn't have to move! It was too soon, it was too fast, but his orgasm rushed upon him like a dam bursting. "Oh, baby. God, baby. I can't stop it. Lord, it feels so good. I'm sorry."

Even as he came, he kept moving, undulating his hips, rocking into her vulva. To his immense satisfaction, as the hot jets of his cum flooded her pussy, Ceelee began to shake. Her orgasm felt like electric pulses around his cock. It set his whole body aflame. Her vagina clutched his cock and he swore she was redefining ecstasy for him. "I never hoped for anything this good," she whispered.

Being on top of Ceelee had its advantages. He was too satiated to move, but he didn't have to move far, he kissed her tenderly and then rolled over, taking her with him. "No, don't move, I don't want to pull out. Let me stay in you. Please?" He wrapped both arms around her and then lifted his hips, making sure that he was still lodged, securely, deep within her sweet little pleasure palace. Lord, nothing had ever been better.

"I love him there. He can move in and stay." Ceelee sighed sleepily.

His baby was tired. "I've worn you out, precious. Go to sleep. I've got you, I'll keep you safe." And he did. All night long.

Chapter Six

Oh, it felt so good! This was the best dream she had ever had! Her pussy was full of cock and her clit was rubbing up against the hard, thick shaft that was giving her the best ride of her life! She pushed up as her dream lover pushed down and she licked her lips. Good. It was so good. "Oh, yes. I love this, I love this," she moaned.

"I love it. too. I woke up with a huge piece of morning wood, and my sweet Ceelee was just too tempting to resist." As he pumped into her, he whispered into her ear. "Sometime during the night, I slipped out of you, but I couldn't stay away. All it took was a couple of kisses to your neck and a caress to your soft pussy and you were wet and ready for me. I'd rather be in your sweet pussy than anywhere on earth."

Her heart jumped at his voice. It wasn't a dream, it was better. "More...more...more," she chanted as he plunged into her in a hypnotizing rhythm. Her clit pulsed with the pounding. Oh, the boy was good, he captured a nipple and began sucking. He was driving her mindless with pleasure. She couldn't think, only feel. Ceelee moved with him, accommodating him, giving Bobby all that she was. She mewled with pleasure, her whole body growing tight with the oncoming peak that threatened to toss her off the edge of the world.

"Bobby!" She screamed so loud that Bobby smiled.

"That should wake everybody up. Come on, precious, take your pleasure. You are so wonderful—so beautiful." The friction of his cock deep inside of her was euphoric. Keeping his connection to her secure, he held on to her hips and rose to loom over her, pulling her lower body up on his thighs. She didn't resist, but stared at him in complete and utter trust. "I'm on a mission, angel. I'm going to wake up your little G-spot."

Her eyes never left his, she was with him every step of the way. "Bobby, you fill me so tight, there's no way you're missing anything." Cecile didn't think he could give her more pleasure than he already had. The thrust of his cock inside her grateful body was already mind-boggling in its intensity. She gave in to the desire to stroke him, milk him, so she concentrated on giving him caresses of the most intimate kind.

"Holy Hell, baby!" I love the way you squeeze me. You're a little wildcat. No, you'll know when I hit it just right." Angling his body, he pleasured her with short, hard jabs, finding that elusive erogenous zone located at the front of the vaginal canal. "There that should be it." He ground down, giving several more thrusts that rubbed his dick right over the spongy area that would make her head spin.

"My God!" He smiled as her back arched and she almost stood on her head, thrusting her hips up harder into his groin, seeking the most contact that she could get. "God! Bobby! Fuck me! Harder! Harder!" She started to quake, her whole body jerking in the throes of climax. Her vagina clutched at him over and over again. Ceelee was holding on to him for dear life. She had become so important to him. A long, harsh groan erupted from his throat and he emptied himself inside of her—giving her his essence, his passion—his all.

* * *

"Thanks for picking up the gifts." Annalise sorted through them, giving her best friend furtive glances. "Is there something you want to tell me?"

"About what?" Cecile tried and failed to act innocent.

"Did I hear the two of you sneaking in this morning?" Annalise cornered Cecile by the coffeepot. "Are you boinking the youngest Stewart?"

When Annalise pinned her with a pointed stare she folded like a house of cards. "All right! Yes, we're getting closer." Cecile couldn't help but smile. "Do you mind?" She had thought about trying to hide it, but why should she? Sleeping with Bobby might be the smartest thing she had ever done.

"Are you kidding?" Annalise laughed, glancing over her shoulder at the three brothers who were in the dining room pouring over a sports article in the newspaper. "I'm thrilled to death for you. If Bobby is anything like his brother, he's an incredible lover." She smiled at the blush that rushed up Cecile's face. "You needed this, and I'm glad you're getting some. And from a younger man—all I can say is *Go Girl!*"

She lowered her voice, as if what she was saying was shameful. "I like him a lot. It's just the age difference that bothers me. He's still in school! Has Ethan told you that I met him the night I left Carl?"

"Yes, he mentioned that. I wondered when you were going to tell me. So, this has been building between you for a while?" At Cecile's dismayed look, Annalise hugged her. "Stop it. I'm thrilled. As for his age? Bobby's a senior in college, and no one could ever say that boy's not a full grown man."

At Cecile's bug eyed expression, Annalise laughed. "Can't help but notice. So, he's a little younger than you. So what?"

"Don't you think I'm too old for him? Really?" Cecile pushed her friend to say exactly what she thought.

"Too old? Are you about to start drawing Social Security? What are you—let's see, twenty-six, twenty-seven? You're not much older than I am, and I'm certainly not elderly."

Lies. Lies. "Uh, yeah that's right." God forgive her, another lie.

"I don't blame Bobby for being attracted to you. You're beautiful, sexy and smart as a whip. Are you going to continue seeing him after this week?"

Cecile knew she was weak. "If he wants to, I don't think I'm capable of saying no to him."

"You have my wholehearted approval. I can't think of another woman in the world I'd rather have for a sister-in-law than you—and my own sister, that is. If she doesn't end up with Alex, I'll be shocked." Hugging herself, Annalise smiled. "This is all turning out perfectly. We're all making our dreams come true."

"I hope so." Cecile didn't sound quite as confident.

Annalise picked up one of the gifts." You know, I should've had these wrapped, it's going to take forever."

Cecile took it out of her hand, being glad for a topic change. "I'll be glad to do it. I'm a bridesmaid, it's my job."

Annalise smiled. "You talked me into it. What are your plans for tonight? Ethan is taking me into Austin. He says he's got something to show me."

Cecile flushed hot, remembering what she and Bobby had planned for the next time they got the chance to be alone. "I'm not sure."

"I know you're going to have sex with him. What else do you have planned?" Annalise laughed. "I can read you like a book. Speaking of a book and sex, I finished the cowboy story. Do you want it?"

Knowing there wasn't a chance in hell she would look at the manuscript, she chuckled. "You can send it, but my plate seems to be full right now."

"Yeah, I bet your plate isn't the only thing that's about

to be filled up—by something hot, long and hard." As Annalise left the room, Cecile hit her in the ass with a sofa pillow.

* * *

"Did you get Scarlet's wedding ring?" Ethan asked Alex, keeping his voice low.

"What's going on?" Bobby was confused. This was supposed to be Ethan and Annalise's wedding.

His two older brothers pulled Bobby to one side, managing to shush him. "I'm marrying Scarlet at the wedding rehearsal." Alex whispered—though Alex's voice was not conducive to a low volume.

Bobby stared disbelievingly at him. "What the hell are you talking about?" Had he missed something? He knew he was totally engrossed in Ceelee, but this was news to him.

Ethan put his arm around Bobby. "Alex told you that Scarlet was sick." Bobby nodded. He supposed his own happiness had made him insensitive to what was going on right under his nose. "Yeah, and I am so sorry about that."

Alex ran his hand raggedly through his own hair. "She needs insurance. Hell, she needs dialysis and eventually a transplant. I can't make any of that happen unless I marry her."

Bobby shook his head. "Isn't that a drastic step?"

Alex's face darkened with steely resolve. "No, it's not a drastic step, dammit! It's what I want! I love her, Bobby. Shit! I don't just love her, she's the sweetest, most unspoiled treasure I have ever found, and I do not intend to lose her."

Bobby listened with a mixture of awe and sadness. His brother's love for this woman and his pain at the thought of losing her was so strong it was amazing to see. "How's this going to work?" Bobby asked. "What does

Annalise and Scarlet think about this? Doesn't Scarlet want her own wedding?"

Again, Alex shushed Bobby. "Neither Scarlet nor Annalise can know anything." At Bobby's surprised expression, Alex explained. "Scarlet and I are going to stand in for Lise and Ethan during the rehearsal ceremony. But the preacher is in on it, of course, and he is going to actually marry us. By the time Scarlet realizes what has happened, I'll have a ring on her finger and my arms wrapped so tightly around her that nothing will ever harm her again."

Bobby was still skeptical. "Is this even legal?"

Alex had the good grace to look a tad guilty. "Well, mostly. Ethan got me a special license and I will coerce her into signing it by telling her that as a witness to the wedding she has to sign the marriage license. I'll just neglect to point out that it is our marriage license instead of Lise and Ethan's."

"Incredible," Bobby was indeed taken aback. "If you pull this off, you deserve an Oscar. I can't believe that you'd expect Scarlet to be happy that you tricked her into marrying you."

Ethan couldn't stay silent. "That's not going to be a problem, Bobby." He seemed convinced what he said was fact. "Scarlet loves Alex as much as he loves her. She's going to think it's the most romantic thing in the world."

"I'm doing it not only because I want to—I'm doing it to save her life," Alex said, his voice impassioned. "Will you go with me and Ethan to the doctor tomorrow? I've got to find out exactly what I'm facing."

Bobby shoved both hands in his front pockets and looked over at his woman who was making calligraphy place cards for the wedding guests. She meant so much to him. He couldn't even imagine finding out that there was something wrong with her. Each of their women were uniquely beautiful and precious to the men whose hearts they held in their hands. "Of course, I'll go. I know how you feel about Scarlet, I feel exactly the same way about Ceelee Fairchild."

* * *

At the clinic, Doc Gibbs ran Alex through a battery of tests. They had to be certain Scarlet's body would accept his kidney. Ethan and Bobby were right there with him, knowing how very important and serious this was. "Don't worry, Alex. Everything's going to be all right. You're going to be a perfect match." Bobby tried to reassure his brother.

"I have to believe that, Bobby." Alex sat in the waiting room, his head in his hands. "Your brother and I have pulled a thousand strings. I've put Scarlet on my insurance role at Econ, so I can keep her alive with dialysis and medicine. That is, if she'll let me." Alex's voice cracked. "She has this hard-headed idea that she doesn't want to be a burden to anyone. I don't know how to make her understand that I can't live without her." Both brothers placed their hands on Alex's back. One sat on one side of him and one on the other. "What I really want for her is a normal life. I want my kidney to be a perfect match, so we can make all of our dreams come true. I want to be married to her for fifty years. I want to show her the world, not just the modest requests on her bucket list. I want to give her everything she deserves. I want children with her." Alex stopped talking. He hated to appear weak in front of his brothers.

They didn't look at it that way, however. Ethan leaned over close to his brother. "You will, Alex. You will marry her, and in a few days you'll give her a hell of a wedding gift—a future. I know it. I'm praying for it,

Bobby and I both are." Bobby voiced his agreement.

"The doctor will see you now." The nurse's simple words brought all three of them to their feet. It might not have been normal, but all three brothers filed into the office, anxious to hear what the verdict was.

If the sight seemed strange to Doc Gibbs, he didn't say so. "Alex," he looked at the middle Stewart brother straight on. "You and Scarlet have a match on only three out of six antigens." At Alex's stricken look, the doctor held up his hand. "No, wait. There's still one more thing to check. We have performed a cross-match test that will tell us the likelihood of Scarlet's body rejecting your kidney. We're hoping for a negative result."

"Negative, how could that be good news?" Alex didn't understand.

"A negative result would mean that the probability of rejection of your kidney would be small. Don't lose hope, in fact, be positive. To not be related, the two of you seem to chemically and physiologically have much in common."

"Well, I could have told you that," Bobby said. "You two were created for each other." Bobby's words seemed to give Alex a tremendous sense of peace.

"You're right, Bobby. Scarlet was created just for me. And I intend to use those words on Scarlet as I make my case about all of this. I'm not naive enough to think that she's going to fall in easily with my plans. She's just too stubborn and too protective of me. Scarlet is going to have to be convinced."

Doc Gibbs wasn't finished, however. "I sent Scarlet's blood off to the premier research laboratory at the University of California. The results should be here this afternoon or in the morning. This will tell us exactly what we're dealing with, how much time we have, and the best way to proceed. Due to malpractice law, I can only call *her* with the results. So stick close to her, just in case she decides not to share with you what I've told her. I'll call as soon as I have the results of the cross-match. "

"Thanks, Doc." Alex assured him. "Now, how much will the transplant cost?" he asked taking out his checkbook.

"She doesn't have insurance, I gather?" The doctor didn't act surprised.

"No, I'll be taking care of everything."

"Why don't we wait and see, there's no use you paying for something that's just a maybe at this point."

"No," Alex said. "I believe in the law of attraction. I'm going to act as if this transplant is a done deal. Now, how much?"

"I can't be completely sure, but approximately $375,000, give or take a dollar or two." Alex never hesitated. He wrote the check, tore it out and handed it to the doctor. "We'll divide it up between you and your hospital later. Okay?"

Doc Gibbs smiled at the trio. "I'm just going to place it in my safe and we'll all pray that I have reason to cash it."

* * *

"I wish the wedding were weeks away. Our time together has just flown by."

"I've enjoyed every moment we shared, Bobby."

"I think we ought to make use of every one of those moments. Lean back on the bed," he directed in a tight, gruff voice. Cecile obeyed, recognizing the tone of voice for what it was—desperate desire. She trusted him, she'd do anything he said. Bobby threw up her skirt, and when she raised her hips, he pulled her panties down and off, stuffing them in his pocket. "Spread those pretty legs, baby. I'm starving to death." Before she could get herself prepared, he used his big hands to open her thighs, exposing her pink wetness to his gaze. Using his thumbs, he spread her wide and pressed open mouth kisses all up and down her slit. Cecile caught her breath at the absolute decadence of the act as Bobby Stewart buried his head between her legs and began to feast. She writhed at the pleasure. Bobby was voracious—eating her out with absolute abandon. Using lips and teeth and tongue, he licked and sucked her labia lips, until she thought she would die from wanting more.

"Bobby." She moaned. "Please, Bobby," she begged. She didn't know exactly what she was begging for, but she knew she wanted it all—everything he was willing to give her. With firm and deep thrusts, he pierced her pussy with his tongue—driving it in and out of her—lapping up the cream that flowed from her in response to his ravaging. "You taste so good, treasure. So good." While he worked his magic with his mouth, his hands had moved up her body and he was steadily milking her nipples through her thin bra and dress. The combination of the dual sensual assault was overwhelming and Cecile began moaning and crying out at the wild desperation that flowed through her veins.

Her orgasm began to build, so she shamelessly pressed her pussy hard into his face. He seemed to like it, because he chuckled deep in his chest. Bobby was a generous lover, always giving her all the pleasure she could handle. Settling his lips over the hard button of her clitoris, he kissed it, massaging it, swirling his tongue around and around it, using the same motions that he would use if he were sucking on her nipples. Cecile went crazy at the rapturous sensations, arching her back. Bobby had to hold her down, forcing her to accept all the attention he could lavish on her.

"Bobby, I need you so!" she screamed as she bucked in the throes of a climax so intense that she saw explosions of white light in front of her eyes.

Bobby stood, unzipped his pants with trembling hands and unleashed his engorged rod. With a mighty, swift thrust he drove his throbbing cock home and literally yelled at the instantaneous ecstasy. "God, yes, baby!"

With hard, short jabs, Bobby pounded into her soft pussy. Cecile tilted her hips, anticipating and welcoming every thrust. Loving every second, she knew she would never get enough of him. Grasping his cock with her vaginal muscles, she was hungry to hold onto every feeling, every sensation. Mindless with passion, she covered her own breasts and began to pull and rub at her nipples, a move she would never have made earlier. This was a whole new world for her—a world created and sustained by Bobby Stewart.

With simultaneous shouts of release that echoed off the walls, Cecile and Bobby gave themselves over to a pleasure more intense and satisfying than they had ever felt before.

A little while later, Bobby lay next to Cecile on his side. His palm cupped her neck, his thumbs rubbing the soft velvet skin under her ear. "I love being with you like this," he watched her closely, as if he could read every emotion that crossed her face.

She turned to face him, kissing him on the chin and then on the nose. "I love being with you, too. I'm going to miss you." There. She had said it and the roof didn't collapse.

"Baby, you're not going to get a chance to miss me. Instead of coming here, I'll drive to Dallas. It's not that much farther. And you'll come to my games, won't you?"

"I wouldn't miss them." Cecile threaded her fingers through his hair. It was so thick and soft. "You're beautiful. Do you know that?" He didn't answer her, but rather, just kissed the inside of her wrist. "Can I ask you something and you'll tell me the honest to God truth?" Maybe she didn't want to hear this, but she was going to ask it anyway.

"I'm an open book, sweetheart. What do you want to know?"

"You can have any woman you want. I've heard Alex, Ethan and Lise talk about rodeo groupies, the buckle bunnies, and the college girls. You have, literally, hundreds, if not thousands of women to choose from. Why me? What do I have that would turn your eye from all of those young, beautiful women?"

"That's easy." He tapped her on the end of her nose, kissed each eyelid before tracing her lips with the pad of his thumb. "From the moment I saw you, my heart recognized you. You are meant to be mine. It's as if our spirits have been intertwined since time began I know it's too soon, but it has to be said...I love you, Ceelee. You are the most beautiful, sexy woman in the world, and I love you."

Her heart contracted with sheer unadulterated joy.

"I love you, too," she breathed as their lips melded together midst the heat of their longing. Even as she reveled in the declaration of their love, Ceelee was haunted by the truth that Bobby had a greater capacity to hurt her than Carl ever had. Shaking her head, she sought to get her mind off of the scary possibilities. "I want to be on top next time," Cecile announced, seemingly, out of the blue. She knew Bobby knew exactly what she meant, but he was so cute. They had just declared their love for one another and he looked like he was on top of the world.

"On top of what? On top of Old Smoky? On top of spaghetti?"

"You know what I mean." She playfully pinched him on the arm, knowing he was just having fun. Cecile lay cuddled up to Bobby's side. His arm was around her back and her head lay cradled on his shoulder. She couldn't believe she was lying here like this. How wonderful it was to be able to touch him, however and wherever she wanted, just because she could. Cecile ran her hand over his chest, loving the feel of his skin, the soft hair on his chest, the rippled ridges of his abs. He was magnificent. "I know we can't right now, because it takes a while for a man to recover." She took a deep breath and pressed on toward her goal. "But the next time we make love, I want to be on top like before, except I want to ride you this time."

"Hell yeah!" He pulled her over on top of him.

"Now? Are you up for it?"

She didn't mean literally, but he showed her without a doubt that he was. "What does this feel like?" He pushed his sizeable erection into her softness. "All it took was your sexy words. So, you want to ride me, cowgirl?"

"Very much. You'll have to tell me if I do it right, but I would love to try." She knew her repertoire of sexual skills was limited. Carl hadn't given her many opportunities to experiment. Bobby had freed something within her. He had given her sexual self-confidence, and that was a new feeling for Cecile. She could now ask for what she wanted, and not fear rejection. "I loved the way you kissed my breasts when we did it last time. Would you do that again?"

"Sweetheart." Bobby ran a finger down the bridge of her nose. "If I live to be a thousand, I would never get tired of looking at you and touching you. Lean over. Hold on to the headboard. I wanna suck."

Just his words made her sex twitch. Bobby scooted up in the bed, so he'd be at a better angle to play with her. Cecile took hold of the headboard and lowered herself, desperate to feel the tug of his lips on her nipples. She wanted him so much her whole vagina was quivering, swelling—opening like a flower that was ready to receive the gift of the sun. "This is fast becoming one of my favorite things in the whole world."

He took her hips in his hands and pulled her a little further forward. She was spread out over him, her sex felt open and vulnerable, she knew he could feel her excitement. "You're so soft and warm and wet, Ceelee. I can't wait to push my cock as deep inside of you as I can get it. Do you know what you do to me?" He looked up at her face. "I wish you could see yourself the way I do. Your beautiful green eyes are glazed over with passion and you're flushed the prettiest color of pink." Cupping her breasts, he picked them up, flicking the nipples. "Every breath you take—those tight, sexy little pants—they make all this incredible woman flesh quiver. You're exquisite, darlin'."

"No, I don't know what I do to you, exactly. But, I know what you do to me. I've never felt like this before. You make me feel like a desirable woman." As she lowered her breasts to his face, she felt her nipples tighten before his eyes.

"Lord, love, you are a desirable woman. See?" Laughing he nudged her in the back with his erection.

"You are so big—*Ah!*" Her tribute to his manhood was cut short by the delicious rapture of his mouth on her breast. Bobby didn't just lick or kiss—which was good—he opened his mouth wide, and enveloped as much of her breast as he could get in his mouth. Cecile felt her juices begin to flow, for he suckled and chewed, applying exquisite pressure and suction. With both hands he plumped her breasts. Squeezing and molding. He switched breasts, chewing light on the nipple, making groans of bliss rise up in her throat. With a gasp, Cecile felt an orgasm building. The pleasure bombarded her. Bobby was just too much—his mouth on her breast, his strong body between her legs. It felt so good! She was swamped with pleasure. Wanting it all, she released the headboard and wrapped her hands around his head instead, grinding her breast into his mouth and her pussy on to his hard stomach muscles. "God! Baby!" she screamed.

Bobby caressed her back, his touch soothing. With his other hand, he caressed her clit, it was swollen and hot. She had come so hard, so good. "How could you ever have thought you were frigid?" Beneath her, she felt him lift up a fraction, his hips seeking a connection. "Baby, I've got to have you. I can't wait." Taking her by the waist, he lifted her. "Guide me in. I'm dying here."

"Yes, I need you, too." With a shaking hand, she enclosed his cock in her fist and held it steady as she lowered her body down onto it. "Bobby!" Impaled! She was so full! Her tissues were swollen and engorged from her orgasm and now she was stretched and invaded—filled and desperate to be fucked. He held up his hands and she entwined her fingers with his.

"Now ride me, honey. Move anyway you want to. Make us both feel good." She pushed on his hands, using them to gain leverage. Rising up on her knees, she drug her vagina up his stalk till only the tip end remained encased in her warmth. With her eyes closed in ecstasy, she lowered herself once more. Bobby's breath came out harshly. "That's it baby. You make my cock feel like it's being massaged by hot silk. Let me feel your little squeeze-box."

Ceelee smiled. Suddenly, she felt powerful. No more did doubt and shame color her world. She could give a man pleasure. Pulling her hands from his, she moved them to cover his pecs—a palm over each of his nipples. "I've always wanted to do this. Read it in one of my books." As she massaged his nipples, she moved her pelvis back and forth—rocking, rolling. At the same time, she rippled her vagina muscles, giving his cock a workout like she hoped he had never felt before.

"God give me strength!" Bobby ground out the words between his teeth. "There's no way in hell I'm gonna live through this."

Bucking his hips up, Bobby let go with a groan. He held her hips and surged upward, his fingers grazing her clit and sending her over the edge. Cecile felt as if her world was whirling out into space and a glimpse of heaven was in her grasp. But not even that was as precious as the words that came from Bobby Stewart's mouth. "Now, I know the difference between sex and making love. And I'll never be satisfied with just sex again." Cecile took those words straight to her heart.

* * *

"You look beautiful." Bobby's eyes ate her up. She was a vision in a pink sheath dress than showed off every luscious curve. Her sable hair hung in enchanting curls to just below her shoulder and he couldn't resist burying his head in the fragrant tresses and inhaling the fresh scent of sweet woman and some tantalizing hint of jasmine. The combination made him think of sex. But, everything about this woman made him think of sex. He literally could not keep his hands off her.

"Thank you," she looked up at him happily. "I was looking on line and saw the foundation that you and some others had set up in memory of your friend, Shaun. If it is okay with you, I'd like to include it in the causes that our publishing house supports. That is, if you wouldn't mind. Does rodeo and erotic romance mix?"

Whispering in her ear, "I think they go together as well as you and I, and we fit together perfectly."

He watched her melt. She turned to him, took him at his word and fitted herself to him—every part of her was touching a part of him. Lord, he never wanted to let her go! "Don't say things like that, Bobby. Not when we can't do anything about it." She moaned into his neck. "Now, you have me tingling all over. I want you all the time." His whole chest vibrated with amusement. Leaning back, she swept her gaze over him. "I've done it now. You look as proud as a strutting peacock. I've just told you what every man wants to hear. And it's true, but you don't have to look so cocksure about it."

It got worse. Bobby roared with laughter. "Baby, the only thing my cock is sure about is that it wants to be buried inside of you - all the time," he said the last three words slowly and with emphasis. If the music hadn't started to get the rehearsal on the way, he would have drug her to the nearest storage shed and fucked her till she begged for mercy. "Now, go take your place. It's time to get this show on the road." He didn't move as she walked off to find the other girls. God, the woman had a fine ass! Rubbing his eyes, he tried to concentrate on what was happening. Today was more than a rehearsal, Alex was about to marry Scarlet and it should prove to be one hell of a show.

* * *

The music began and Alex, Ethan and Bobby walked from the right side of the rose bed to the front of the arbor. Alex was playing the part of the groom, a role that would be reversed the following day. As the music continued, Cecile stepped out to walk slowly down the aisle. Her attention went straight to Bobby. Instantly, he caught her gaze and it never wavered. As she began to move, slowly, down the aisle—she was walking to him. For a moment, she let herself imagine that this was their wedding day and he would hold out his hand and draw her to him. They would exchange vows and promise to love and cherish one another forever. Just before she reached the front, he winked at her and her heart leapt in her chest like a gazelle. As she stepped up on the dais, they continued to look at each other like they were the only two in the world.

Cecile's insides were fluttering like butterflies were dancing around her heart. The only cloud on the horizon was the reality that this wonderful interlude in her life was about to end and she would soon return to the real world of moving, divesting her life of Carl, and making a new start. Would Bobby be a part of her new life? He had promised her they would see each other often. And God, she was counting on it.

Annalise came down the aisle next and she blushed like a school girl as Ethan let out a low and meaningful whistle. Knowing how much she had longed for this day, Cecile couldn't help but shed a tear for her best friend. If anyone deserved to be happy, it was Lise. In a stolen moment, Annalise had told her that Ethan had kissed her scars, told her that there was no part of her that wasn't beautiful and his tender lovemaking had banished every fear and dread that she had harbored for years.

After she and Cecile were in their places, the music swelled and Alex looked up to see Scarlet. Cecile could read his expression as clear as a bell. As far as he was concerned, she was his angel. And Scarlet was beautiful, her body silhouetted in the golden rays of the evening sun. Slowly, she walked toward him. Cecile knew this was just a rehearsal, but there was no doubt—like her—Scarlet was fantasizing that this was her wedding day to Alex.

When she drew close enough, he held out his hand to help her to stand at his side. "Dearly Beloved, we are gathered here tonight to join this man and this woman in holy matrimony." Alex picked up Scarlet's right hand in his and brought it to his lips. The preacher continued, "A marriage ceremony like this is for one purpose only and that is to make one flesh from two people who love and cherish one another above all things. Today, Alex and Scarlet wish to take this step. They have chosen one another out of all others in this life, and now they stand before us ready to repeat their vows."

It was only a few minutes into the ceremony when Cecile knew for certain there was more going on than a rehearsal. It seemed that Scarlet had figured it out, also. Cecile let her eyes rove from person to person. Whatever it was, the men were in on it. And if she wasn't badly mistaken, Alex and Scarlet were actually getting married.

Scarlet's eyes were darting around nervously. Still, she didn't bolt and run. Alex held on to her hand, looked into her eyes and began speaking.

"I, Phillip Alexander Stewart, take you, Scarlet Rose Evans, to be my lawful wedded wife. I promise to love, honor and cherish you…" He paused almost unable to go on. "Till death do us part. I promise to be true and faithful to you for better or worse, in sickness and in health, for as long as we both shall live." Scarlet's eyes were big and focused on every syllable that was coming from his lips. "All of my worldly goods to thee I endow and with my body I will worship yours. I love you, Scarlet. To marry you is my greatest desire."

"Scarlet." The pastor indicated it was her turn.

Scarlet looked over at her sister, who had tears in her eyes. Then, she turned back to her beloved, who had the most sincere look of love on his face that anyone could ever hope for.

She only hesitated for a moment, before she began to speak in a clear, soft voice. "I, Scarlet Rose Evans, take you, Phillip Alexander Stewart, as my lawfully wedded husband. I promise to love, honor, and cherish you, till death do us part." At this point, her voice cracked just a bit too. "I promise to be true and faithful to you, for better, for worse, for richer or poorer, in sickness and in health, for as long as we both shall live."

Scarlet paused again, her eyes big question marks, and Alex nodded his head, as if telling her she was doing great. "All my worldly goods to you I give, and with my body I will worship yours. Alex, I adore you, and marrying you would make all my dreams come true."

"Is there a ring?"

"Yes, there is." Alex reached into the pocket of his coat. He brought out a glimmering eternity band and slipped it on her finger. "Scarlet, with this ring, I thee wed. With this ring, I offer you my heart, my life, my trust and my eternal devotion."

"I don't have a ring for you," she whispered in his ear, but it was so quiet everyone heard.

In answer, he just kissed the ring on her finger.

"You may kiss the bride."

Slowly, Alex drew her to him. It was a tender kiss, a slow meeting of the lips, a cherished moment of utter devotion.

"By the power invested me by the great state of Texas, I now pronounce you man and wife." Turning them to face the crowd, he announced. "It is my pleasure to be the first to introduce you to Mr. & Mrs. Alex

Stewart." A crescendo of music followed and Alex swept Scarlet down the central passageway, past prying eyes and countless questions.

It was the sweetest thing Cecile had ever seen. Before they said *I do* there wasn't a dry eye in the house. The impromptu bride and groom rushed off for a night in the honeymoon suite in the Driskell Hotel and Ethan drew Annalise aside to mingle among their guests. Cecile couldn't imagine what the circumstances were that would make something so wild and irregular necessary, but she had to admit it was very romantic. But there were guests to entertain, so she and Bobby helped where they could.

"Cecile, is that you?"

Turning to see who had called her, Cecile was shocked to see Erica Uvalde. They had graduated high school together and Cecile hadn't seen her since their ten year reunion.

"Cecile Fairchild, I can't believe it's you."

Erica was one of those people that was palatable only in small doses. "Hello, Erica." They hugged and Erica held her at arm's length to look her up and down. "You look so good. What have you been up to?"

"I live in Dallas, I'm an editor at a publishing house. How about you?"

"My husband owns interest in an oil and gas company. He's friends with Ethan and Alex and serving as one of Ethan's ushers tomorrow. Did I see you making sexy with Bobby Stewart?" At Cecile's blush, her school chum pounced. "Mee-ooow," she made a catty noise. "Isn't he a little young for you? Are you practicing your cougar skills?" If the woman had slapped Cecile, she wouldn't have been more hurt. Humiliated, she looked around to see if anyone else had heard. Bobby was approaching, so she mumbled something unintelligible and was grateful when he took her by the hand and led her away.

He was speaking for a few seconds before Cecile could force herself to understand his words. "I had wanted to tell you before, but Alex swore me to secrecy."

"What did you say?" She honestly had missed the point.

Bobby pushed a strand of her hair back and traced the path a tear had taken down her cheek. "You cried. That's so sweet." He doctored her sorrow with a kiss. "I was trying to tell you that Scarlet needs a kidney. It's very serious, she has to have a transplant or go on dialysis or she will die. Having no insurance, she was fast running out of options. Now, Alex has given her those options— and his heart. Don't tell Annalise though, Scarlet will want to break this news to her sister in her own way."

"I won't tell. You mean he's marrying her to save her life?" Cecile started crying in earnest.

"No, he's marrying her because he can't live without her," Bobby said simply and drew her close. Talking about Scarlet and Alex had pushed Erica's rudeness from her thoughts. "Everybody looks to be happy, come with me. I've got to have you. Now." With determined strides, he pulled her into the house. By the time they were behind closed doors, he had his clothes halfway off. "Undress, Ceelee. Now."

Bobby's forceful, take-control attitude turned Cecile on more than she would ever have suspected. With trembling fingers, she obeyed. Her mouth went dry when she saw how hard and erect he was. His cock was fully aroused and dripping precum. "You want me," she stated simply and with wonder as she began a slow strip tease that she hoped would further enflame Bobby's out-of-control desire. It did. He threw off the last shred of clothing and hauled her up against his big, hard body.

"You're asking for it, Fairchild." He didn't kiss her—not this time—he consumed her. Cecile had never imagined a kiss could be an erotic assault. He ate at her lips and sucked her tongue, holding her head still with both hands. There was no escaping his possession and she wouldn't have it any other way. Pushing her hand between them she found his cock and began to rub it, entranced by the liquid that was leaking from the tip.

"I ache," she begged.

"Turn around, lean on the bed and bend over," he ordered. "Stick that sweet ass in the air. I'm going to drill my way to heaven." His words were like gasoline thrown on a fire. Cecile followed his instructions and presented herself like a mare in heat. And she was—in heat. Bobby was big, so when he leaned over, she was covered. He pulled back her hair and bit her on the shoulder, right next to her neck.

"Oh yes, touch me, please," she whispered. This was going to feel so good. He hadn't entered her. He was rubbing her all over, prepping her, gentling her, rousing her to his level of excitement. With broad sweeps of his hands he soothed her skin, then ran his hands under and cupped her breasts, massaging and pulling at the nipples—tweaking them, milking them—making her writhe with desire. "Are you wet? Are you ready for me? Do you want me to claim you as my own?" His voice was almost a growl.

"Yes, I want you so much, please," she begged. She tilted her ass up in the air, knowing she was pushing him to the limit. He moved one hand down to tease her clit, swirling it with three fingers. Cecile groaned, and as she clutched the sheet so hard her knuckles were white, he rammed home. "I love you!" she screamed, unable to hold back her declaration of love.

He was big, thick, hard as a rock, and all male. She

laid her head on the bed and enjoyed every thrust and every pump. She felt taken, ravished, owned. If only it could be forever.

"Does it feel good, baby? Do you like my lovin'?"

"Yes, God, yes." She spoke into the mattress as he pounded into her from behind. He didn't let up, it was a triple play—he rammed into her pussy, fondled her breasts and stroked her clit until she was screaming. She could feel her cream running down her leg.

"Lord, baby-doll. I'm coming. I can't hold back. Come for me, treasure. Come for me." He pressed hard on her clit, rubbing it, pinching her nipple and grinding so deep into her pussy that he was nudging her very womb. With a cry, her whole body jerked and she flew apart in his arms, quaking with frenzied little movements. Her orgasm seemed to trigger Bobby's climax and as he jettisoned his seed deep into her body, Ceelee knew he belonged to her.

It didn't take long after the loving before the doubts came. Was Erica right? Here she was, thirty-one freakin' years old and she was lying next to a twenty-two year old Greek god who might wake up any day and ask her what the hell she was doing in his bed. But it didn't matter, he had stolen her heart and she didn't want it back. Running her hand through the sexy hair on his chest, she rubbed her face on his shoulder. Lord, he was perfect. Please, God. Let me keep him, she prayed. And prayers are always answered, she knew that. But sometimes the answer is no.

"What's your middle name?" Cecile asked as she traced his small flat nipple with her forefinger.

"Sexy," Bobby grinned at his own joke.

"No, it's not." It could be, she admitted to herself. "Tell me. Your first name is Robert, isn't it?" She laid her hand on his chest and rested her chin on it, enjoying their fleeting time together.

Wrapping a lock of her hair around his finger, he twirled it tight and then let it loose. "Yes, I'm Robert Jaidon Stewart. What's your middle name, Ceeleemine?"

His endearment made her want to sigh in happiness. "Cecile is my middle name." She traced a heart on his chest and then drew an arrow through it. "My first name is Madeline—Madeline Cecile. Isn't than a mouthful?"

"Ooh, provocative word?" He got a gleam in his eye. "How would you like to have a mouthful of." In a stage whisper he gave her raunchy instructions which she followed to the letter.

* * *

"Did you have a good time?" Annalise smiled slyly at Scarlet as she hurried into the powder room with her dress. Cecile was already dressed and was putting hot curlers in Annalise's hair.

"Yes, I did." Miss Scarlet answered primly, unwilling to get down and dirty with her sister and Cecile. Scarlet wasn't as comfortable talking about sex as the other two.

"The Stewart brothers all know their way around the bedroom—or so I've heard." Cecile laughed when she realized what she had said.

"Look at us." Annalise sighed happily. "We've all found happiness at the Heartbreak Hotel." Annalise had shared with all of them what she had thought when she had first turned down Lonely Street in search of the Bed and Breakfast. Looking in the mirror, she saw that Scarlet had an odd look on her face. "What's wrong, sis."

Scarlet walked up to her sister and pulled out a chair and sat down near her. "I've been hiding something from you."

Cecile instantly felt uncomfortable. She knew what was coming. "Do I need to leave?"

Scarlet stopped her. "No, it looks like you'll probably be a member of the family, too. I want you to stay." Cecile sat beside the other two, pleased with the thought of family and sisters, but worried about what was coming. All she could think about was Scarlet's illness and how she hoped it would all work out for her.

Scarlet took Annalise's hand. "I have kidney problems."

Annalise didn't say anything. She only stared at her sister. "What do you mean? A kidney infection? That can't be too serious."

"No, it's more than that. When I had the surgery to fix my foot years ago, there was a complication." Annalise squeezed Scarlet's fingers to the point she gasped. "The anesthesia they gave me damaged my kidneys. I was allergic to it."

Annalise shook her head. "What does this mean? How sick are you?"

Scarlet took a deep breath and smiled. "I came to your wedding thinking that this would be the last time I would see you." At Annalise's horrified expression, Scarlet hurried to explain. "Alex changed all of that. He found out about my problem—it's embarrassing, but he found my bucket list."

"Scarlet! Why didn't you tell me?"

Annalise was about to have a conniption fit, so Scarlet hurried in her explanation. "I didn't have insurance and I refused to be a burden to my family." At her sister's vehement response, Scarlet covered Annalise's mouth. "Listen, it's okay now. Alex is my knight in shining armor. We are hopelessly in love and he has made it his business to save my life." Scarlet's eyes were shining. "He gave me an insurance card for a wedding present. Isn't that the sweetest thing? I'm going to live—because of Alex." By the time she got through talking, Cecile and Annalise were both shedding tears of happiness and relief. Gathering their things, they headed to the pool house to finish the final touches before they got ready to march down the aisle—again.

"Has anyone seen the guestbook?" Annalise fretted as she tossed first one thing off the counter and then the other. Cecile picked stuff up as fast as she threw it down.

"Would you settle down!" She tried to calm her friend. "Everything is perfect. We'll find your guestbook."

Grabbing Cecile and hugging her, she took a deep breath. "I know, I know. I just can't believe this day has finally arrived. And finding out about Scarlet, it's almost too much!"

Scarlet joined them in their huddle and hugged them both. "Today is going to be a wonderful day. I'll go find the guest book. You two eat some chocolate or something."

There were a thousand last minute things to do, so Cecile had her hands full. A few minutes later, however, yelling from the front of the property drew her attention. Good Lord! It was the police. Rushing to the where the rest of the family was standing, Cecile saw a strange man being hauled into the waiting cop car. "Who's that? And what happened?" She laid a hand on Bobby's arm and he turned to envelop her in an embrace.

"That's Alex's ex-employee, Rick LeBeau. He just attacked Scarlet in the house."

"Why? Who would want to hurt Scarlet? And where is she?" Cecile looked all around. "Is she okay?"

"Annalise is taking care of her, I'm sure."

"I'm going to go find them," she kissed Bobby on his cheek and headed for the house.

* * *

The wedding was mere hours away. Bobby, Ethan and Alex were already in their tuxes and waiting outside, out of the way—trying to stay out of trouble. "I can't believe that LeBeau idiot. What was his problem?" Bobby asked his brothers.

Alex shook his head. "I don't really understand it all. Rick grew up in the same town as Scarlet, and he bullied her all through school. And today she found out that he was her half-brother. He had built up a life time of resentment against her and her family because her dad never publicly acknowledged him. But, little Scarlet had nothing to do with her father's decisions. She never deserved his abuse, that's for sure."

"How was the honeymoon?" Bobby asked, trying to lighten the mood. The family had been through enough emotional turmoil, enough to last a lifetime.

"Too short," Alex gave an arrogant smirk that told more than it hid.

"Scarlet have a good time?" Bobby just kept on with the egging. Actually, he was trying to cheer Alex up. He knew the idea of that idiot attacking Scarlet had Alex up in arms and feeling helpless. He understood, and he sure knew Ethan did, too. It had only been a few weeks before when Annalise's first husband had attacked her. It made them all wonder what could possibly be next.

Alex had to smile. "I believe that she did." He sighed. "I know I did. She's the sweetest thing, guys. I love her so much. Being with her is the closest thing to paradise that I'll ever know. Now, if I can just get her some help. I'm gonna count on all of your support."

"You've got it," they both assured him. Bobby's cell phone vibrated against his leg. He started to ignore it, but knowing it might be the coach, he had to check. It wasn't. It was Mary Alice Solice. Shit! He hadn't seen or talked to her since he had slept with her in Mesquite. "I guess I'd better take this." He stepped to one side and answered the phone. "Stewart."

"Bobby?" A tearful voice sounded in his ear.

Crap! Nothing good ever came from a crying woman. "Mary Alice, is that you?"

"Yes," she sobbed. "I need to talk to you, Bobby. It's important." Bobby didn't like the sound of that.

"What kind of problem?" He probably didn't want to hear this.

"I don't want to talk about it over the phone. Can I come over?"

"I'm a little busy right now, Mary. My brother is about to get married in a couple of hours."

"Please, Bobby. I need to talk to you. How about tomorrow?"

Bobby let out a mile-long sigh. "Sure, I'll meet you..." He started to say at his condo, but no. "Meet me at the rodeo arena near my house at four tomorrow." Ceelee was due to leave at noon and he wasn't taking one minute away from his time with her. "Wanna give me a hint as to what this is all about?"

"No, I need to talk to you in person."

Shit! That couldn't be good. "All right. I'll see you then."

"What was that all about?" Alex asked when Bobby rejoined his brothers with a worried look on his face.

"That was Mary Alice Solice—buckle bunny extraordinaire." Bobby said dryly.

"Isn't that the one you..." Ethan dropped his voice.

Bobby answered anyway. "Yes, that's the one."

"What did she want?" Alex asked.

"She wants to talk to me."

Ethan looked at Bobby, man to man, ready to give advice. "What about Cecile?"

* * *

Cecile saw Bobby standing with the other guys. She needed to see him for just a moment. Her pink panties would have been perfect with this bridesmaid dress and she couldn't find them anywhere. She had a sneaky suspicion he had confiscated them. If she could locate them, she'd still have time to change. And if all went as she had planned after the ceremony, Bobby could enjoy taking them off of her. The thought made her smile. If he would let her use them she'd be happy to give them back to him.

They didn't see her and as she got closer. She could tell they were discussing something—seriously.

"This doesn't have anything to do with Cecile." Bobby was emphatic. What didn't have anything to do with her? She stopped.

"Do you plan on seeing her after this weekend?" Alex asked.

Of course he did, they had plans. Cecile started to walk on up to them and then the bottom fell out of her world.

"No, one way or the other, after this weekend it will be over. I may have to let her down easy, but I definitely do not have plans to see her after tomorrow."

No plans to see her? She froze in place, trying to make what she heard mean anything other than what Bobby said. "No, please, no," she whispered. What had happened? She fumbled with her dress, stepped sideways, and almost fell. Tears were blinding her so she couldn't see how to avoid the larger rocks on the drive way in her spike heels. She had thought Bobby loved her! Wasn't that what he had said? Self-doubt and confusion hammered at her soul. How was she going to get through the wedding? This was going to be one of the hardest things she had ever done.

Chapter Seven

"Women like Mary Alice can latch on to you like one of them crabs at the beach that pinch like shit." Alex was in a mood.

"Believe me, I know." Bobby knew what he had. "I don't want anything to come between me and Ceelee. When you've got the best there's no use shopping around."

Slapping Ethan on the shoulder, Bobby announced. "I think it's about time. Should we line up? It's your turn today."

"Couldn't come soon enough for me." Ethan smiled as they made their way to meet the preacher.

The wedding went off without a hitch, technically, but something was wrong. Bobby could feel it in his bones. Alex felt the same way. "Look at them. Neither one of them will even look this way. What did you do?"

Shades of his teenage years washed over him. "What do you mean, what did I do? I've been with you all morning, ever since the fiasco with LeBeau. I haven't had a chance to do anything wrong. What did you do?"

"I don't know, but I'm going to find out." Alex took off after Scarlet, who was headed toward the house.

Bobby looked around for Cecile and she was gone, too. So, he went to find her. Taking the four steps up the verandah in one leap, he met Cecile coming out the door. She had been crying. "Baby, what's wrong?"

* * *

Cecile had packed as quickly as she could. She had hoped to get off Lost Maples property without running into Bobby. But here he was, and her only thought was not to let him see her cry.

Annalise was married and all was well with her. She had slipped in to the bride's room and helped her take off her wedding dress so she could visit with her guests in something more comfortable. They had tickets to go to Hawaii, but Scarlet's looming operation had called a halt to those plans. A couple of nights in Austin would have to do for now. Even that sounded like heaven to Cecile—after all, she had nothing to look forward to. Right now, she was totally numb. In an hour or two, it would hit her and she would feel the true extent of her loss. She loved Bobby Stewart, and she had lost him. Forever.

Careful to make her face blank, she answered his question. "I've got to leave a little early. Something's come up."

"A whole day early? What's wrong? I can come with you. What can I do to help? I have an appointment tomorrow, but I can cancel it. They'll just have to wait. You're more important." When she didn't respond to him, he took her in his arms. And fool that she was, she let him. Cecile couldn't resist being near him just one more time. "When will I see you again?"

"It's not that far to Dallas, Bobby. We'll see each other, I'm sure."

"When?" He seemed determined to tie down specifics. "How about next weekend?"

Cecile refused to meet his direct gaze. Pulling out of his arms, she backed away from him. "I don't know, Bobby. But, I want you to know something." She stopped and cleared her throat. "I want to straighten something out with you. I never told you how old I am. You came up with a number and I led you to believe it was true. I lied. I'm not twenty-five or twenty-six or even twenty-seven. I'm thirty-one." To give him credit, he didn't blink an eye. But, why would he care? He had no plans to see her after this weekend anyway. "And, I also want to thank you before I go, for everything."

"Everything? Are you thanking me for loving you or are you thanking me for letting you go? And your damn age is not an issue!"

"Don't make this so hard, Bobby," she pleaded. Why was he fighting it? After all, this was what he wanted. Wasn't it? "We had a good time. Let's just enjoy the memories and not try to make more out of it than it was."

"Make more out of it than it was? I guess we have different ideas about what we've being doing here, don't we? I guess I'm young and stupid, aren't I? Cause you're giving me the brush-off, aren't you, Ms. Fairchild?" Bobby's tone was light, but his face betrayed something else—something she didn't dare try and put a name to.

"We both had a good time. Let's leave it at that."

"I don't understand any of this. Won't you tell me what's going on? Please?"

"Bobby...It's time for me to go."

He loosened his embrace and let her back up a couple of feet. "Fine." His voice was flat. "You go back to Dallas. See your friends. But when you turn out the light at night and lay down in your bed, remember what it felt like when I pushed deep inside of you. Remember what it felt like when I made you come apart in my arms." Bobby jerked her suitcase up and strode off to her car. "If you want to get away from me that bad, I'll help you."

Tears clamored in Cecile's throat. She would have no trouble remembering how it felt to love Bobby. No trouble at all.

Cecile cried all the way to Dallas. This was the second time she had made this journey with her heart broken, only this trip was a million times worse. Carl had only done what she had expected, but Bobby had devastated her. What made it worse was how he had tried to pretend that he still wanted to see her and talk to her. She went back over the conversation she had overheard. No, there was no doubt about it. He had made it plain as day, he had said that he didn't want to see her anymore after this weekend. And he wouldn't. She'd make sure of that.

The only thing that bothered her was how sad he had looked as she drove away. It just didn't make sense.

When she finally dragged herself into her apartment, Cecile, surveyed everything she had to do. There wasn't any use to unpack, she didn't intend to stay in the apartment any longer than she had to. The buzz of the phone made her groan. If it was Bobby she didn't think she could handle it. But, it wasn't. It was Annalise. She didn't even get hello out of her mouth.

"Where did you go?"

"I thought you were on your honeymoon? Or at least a shortened version of it?" Just knowing she was talking to someone who was, perhaps, in the same house as the man she loved made her heart ache.

"Everything went to hell after you left."

"What are you talking about? Is something wrong with Bobby?" She couldn't have kept from voicing the question to save her life.

"Ah-ha!" Annalise yelled in her ear. "I knew it! You care about him, I told him so." Annalise was mumbling and grumbling so fast that Cecile couldn't keep up.

"Annalise. Stop!" Cecile tried to be forceful. "You don't understand what's happened." Thinking about everything going to hell, she had to ask. "What's going on at Lost Maples?"

"LeBeau broke out of jail and came back to the B&B. He held Alex at gunpoint and Bobby had to tackle him." Annalise paused. "He could have been shot—even killed."

Cecile bit her tongue, controlling her response. "But, he's okay?"

"Yes, and Scarlet and Alex worked everything out. Come to find out, Lebeau had been calling Scarlet and feeding her lies about Alex's love for her." Some noise in the background made Annalise put her hand over the receiver. "Anyway, Scarlet's operation will be soon, and..." another pause and some noise. "Cecile, Bobby wants to talk to you. And, I can't fight him off."

Cecile covered her mouth trying to stall the tears.

"Ceelee? Baby? I'm coming to Dallas. I'm leaving in just a few minutes."

God! His voice sounded so sweet. But, she couldn't. She just couldn't. "No. No." She grabbed her heart. "I heard what you said Bobby, and I don't want to see you. Please don't call again." She slammed the phone down before she could change her mind and she turned off the ringer.

Walking through her apartment in a daze, she tried to focus on something besides Bobby and what had happened. Going to the computer, she checked her email. Thank God for work. There were dozens of emails that needed attention. She skimmed through them and logged on to her social media account to see if anything was in dire need of attention there. Nothing caught her interest.

Shaking her head, she realized it would take a long time to get back to any semblance of normal. Cecile missed Bobby. It had only been a few hours, but she missed him more than she ever thought possible. With a shaking hand, she wiped tears from her face. When she brought her hand down, it was smeared with mascara. Lord, she needed a bath.

Logging off the computer, she went to her bedroom

and stripped. The closet was so empty now that Carl's stuff was gone. The bed where they had slept, chastely, on their separate sides seemed huge in the near empty room. Her soon to be ex-husband had taken his recliner and the armoire and his stereo system. Good riddance! She wanted new furniture, anyway.

Her underwear drawer was pitiful. She let out a giggle as she surveyed her drab selection. Before going to the wedding, she had bought several new sets. And boy, had she enjoyed them. Flashes of memory assailed he— she and Bobby kissing, him pulling down her bra and latching onto a nipple, the way he would look at her as he peeled her panties down her hips. Shivers of misery almost stole her breath. Her arms felt so empty and her heart felt like it had been run over by a truck.

Cecile stood in front of the bathroom mirror and washed her face. She was a wreck. Her skin was splotchy, her eyes were red, and her nose was swollen from the crying jags. Reaching into the medicine cabinet, she took out her birth control tablets. Opening the round container, she started to take out a caplet. And froze. What was the deal? The pill from last month was still there. How could that be? Unease washed over her. Crap! The turmoil with Carl must have gotten her completely off-balance. She had never taken it! Damn!

She stood there for a moment and stared at herself. She could be pregnant. With Bobby's child. They had had unprotected sex over and over again. She counted to ten and waited for the dread and remorse to come. When it didn't, she put both hands over her heart and bent double. Bobby's child. And hers. He would be beautiful.

* * *

Bobby hadn't known what a broken heart felt like, until now. What had gone wrong? He had stood in his yard for a good ten minutes after her car had disappeared. Every instinct he had told him to follow her, make her talk and find out what had gone wrong. But, he hadn't, things had gone crazy here at the B&B. Not that it mattered, Ceelee couldn't have made it any clearer—then and now. She didn't want to see him again.

It was his age. That was it. She had decided she couldn't be serious about someone so young. After all, he didn't have a job. He didn't have a way to support her in the manner she deserved. But he would, one day. *Hell!* He walked around in a circle, his whole body shaking. It wasn't over. How could it be over? He just refused to believe it. *Damn!* He'd give her a day or two to calm down and then he would launch his campaign to win her back.

When things had calmed down with Alex and Scarlet, Bobby had tried calling her back. Over and over again—hour after hour—but she wouldn't answer. He knew she had called Annalise and the only thing his new sister-in-law would tell him was that she wouldn't see him and wouldn't take his calls. What the hell happened? He replayed their short conversation repeatedly in his head. What had she meant—*I heard what you said, Bobby.* What had he said?

He had to force himself to take care of his business. Sleep was impossible. Walking around like a zombie, he spoke when he had to and kept dialing and redialing Ceelee's number, leaving message after message. But she never picked up or called him back. Standing in his room, drying off after his shower, he stared at the bed where they had made love. Unable to help himself, he lay down on the bed and buried his head in her pillow. God, it still smelled like her. Groaning, he remembered how her skin had felt under his fingers and how soft her lips had been when they kissed. How was he supposed to deal with this?

Dragging himself up, he dressed. As bad as he hated to, he had promised to meet Mary Alice at the rodeo arena. He'd rather go to the dentist—and he hated the dentist. When he sat down to put on his boots, he found Ceelee's little pink lace panties under the edge of the bed. Picking them up, he buried his face in them. The scent made him crazy—aroused and sad all at the same time. He sat there for as long as he could, but soon it was time for him to go. He stood up, folded the scrap of pink lace and placed it reverently under his pillow—it was all he had left.

When he got to the arena, Mary Alice was waiting for him. She looked horrible. When he opened his door, she was in his face before he could say a word. "I'm pregnant."

Bobby felt like he had been knocked in the head with a two-by-four. "What?"

"I'm pregnant, and I don't know what to do." She burst into tears and fell into his arms and he couldn't do anything but hold her up. It wouldn't have been polite to let her slide down to the ground in a heap.

"How far along are you?" Could he be the father. *Hell!* This was all he needed.

"Two months," she sobbed.

God, it fit. But, he knew Mary Alice. And it didn't speak well for him, but he knew good and well that he wasn't the only one she'd had sex with during that same time frame. But, he didn't want to be a jerk and point that out. Maybe she would own up to it. "Have you been to the doctor to be sure?"

"Yes, and I don't want to have an abortion." Her voice trembled with despair.

Bobby didn't hesitate. "I don't think you should have an abortion, either." Flashes of his future bombarded his brain. What if it were his? What about Ceelee? What about Dallas? What would Ethan and Alex say?

"I'm not saying it's your baby, Bobby. But it could be, and..." her voice broke. "To tell you the truth, I hope it is yours."

Ah, shit. "Let's not get the cart before the horse, Mary Alice. We'll have to talk about this and have some tests run. But if it's my baby, I won't turn my back on it, I can promise you that." He didn't know what he was promising. Not forever with Mary Alice, that was for sure. Because of Ceelee. My God, how could he tell her? For the first time, he was relieved that Ceelee was in Dallas and not here with him. He wouldn't want her to see him this way.

As soon as he got home, Bobby went to his family. They had stood by him through thick and thin, so he had no doubt they would stand by him through this. Now, that wasn't to say they might not take a strip out of his hide, but he knew Ethan and Alex loved him and that was all that mattered.

So, when he broke the news to his brother, the reaction he got was no surprise.

"She's what?" Ethan bellowed. "Bobby! Dammit! I can't believe you've gotten yourself into such a mess!"

"It's not certain that I'm the father." Bobby tried to maintain his cool. He was doing a pretty good job of it, until he looked up and saw Annalise pinning him with a disappointed stare. God, what if she told Ceelee? "Lise, don't—" he began.

"Don't what, Bobby?" Annalise walked into the room with them. Even though she was obviously put out with him, she still hugged him.

"I was going to say, don't tell Ceelee about Mary Alice, but she probably wouldn't care anyway." Bobby bent over, holding his Stetson between his legs. "What am I going to do?"

Ethan stretched his long legs out in front of him and accepted the cup of coffee that Annalise handed to him. He patted his knee and she settled herself down to snuggle. "You're going to find out if that baby is yours. And if it is, we'll deal with it. The baby will be a Stewart and we don't turn our back on family. But, that doesn't mean you have to throw your whole future away because of one poor choice. You're going to go ahead with your plans. If you get drafted by Dallas—you play for Dallas. If Ceelee will take you back," he patted his brother on the back, knowing full well how he was feeling, "you hold your arms out and welcome her home." With that sage bit of advice, he kissed his own wife—thoroughly.

* * *

Several days later, it was confirmed—she was pregnant. Cecile hugged herself close. She was pregnant with Bobby's baby. Picking up the phone, she did the only thing she could, she called Annalise on her cell phone. Bobby might answer the house phone, so Cecile never called it. She still wasn't ready to talk to Bobby. But, she had to talk to someone.

"Cecile? Is that you?"

"Hey, how are you?"

"I'm fine. How are you?" Was there something in her voice? Yes, she distinctly heard an underlying despair in Annalise's voice. "What's wrong? I can tell something is wrong." A dozen things ran through her mind. "Is it Scarlet?"

"No, the operation was successful and they're both doing well. In fact, they're on their way to Graceland on their honeymoon."

"That's a relief." Cecile was sincere. The whole

family was important to her.

"It's Bobby."

Cecile's heart jumped. Visions of a mammoth bull stomping Bobby into the ground had haunted Cecile's dreams. "Is he all right? He hasn't been hurt, has he?"

"No, nothing like that." There was that tone again.

"Tell me." She was insistent.

"He's just going through some stuff. I wish you'd talk to him. He misses you, so much," Annalise whispered. "I've never seen him like this."

"I can't," Cecile stated a little too fast. "Not yet." Dead silence. Cecile got the idea that they both knew the other was hiding something.

"What's up with you? Did you get my chapters I sent you, yesterday?"

She had, but she hadn't looked at them. Cecile had been too preoccupied with baby thoughts. "Yes, I got them and I wanted you to know that I'm sending you a cover mock-up. You let me know what you think. Okay?"

"We usually handle this by email, Cecile." Annalise sounded a little confused. "Are you sure that's why you called?"

Cecile let out a ragged sigh. "I'm pregnant."

"What?" Annalise roared. Cecile had to hold the phone away from her ear.

"It's Bobby's, of course." And then it hit Cecile what position she had put Annalise in. This was no longer just her best friend. This was the sister-in-law of the man she loved. "And you can't tell him, Annalise. I mean it."

"Oh, my God." Annalise sounded horrified.

"I'm not that unhappy about it, Annalise." Cecile wanted that known up front. This was her child and there would never be a moment when it thought it was ever unwanted. "You just can't tell Bobby. Understand?"

"Now, how am I supposed to keep a secret like that?" Cecile heard her huff in exasperation. "I'm with him every day. Are you feeling well? Have you been to the doctor?"

"I have, and I'm as healthy as a horse." The tension that Cecile had been living under made her dizzy, she felt lightheaded. "And you have to keep the secret. I'll tell him when I figure out how. This isn't easy for me, you know."

"I won't tell, but you're asking a lot. I don't know if I'm that good of an actress."

"Do it for me, Annalise." Cecile lowered her voice and begged. "And take care of Bobby for me, please. Our time together didn't mean the same thing to him that it did to me. But, he'll always have a place in my heart. He gave me a gift that no one else ever has. He made me realize that I am worthy of a man's love." It hadn't lasted, but at least she knew it was possible.

* * *

It had been the worst month of his life. Losing Ceelee was the worst, but having to wait on the DNA results for the paternity test wasn't a picnic, either. But, thank God, at long last it was over. Bobby opened his truck door and pulled himself in. Mary Alice Solice was pregnant with Prescott Ford's baby, not his. Prescott was a bull-dogger that she hooked up with occasionally. The only problem for Mary was that Prescott was married to a woman with oil. And there was no way he would leave his wife for the buckle bunny. More than likely, Prescott's wife would solve this problem with money. There were rampant rumors that she had done this before, several times.

He watched as Mary pulled her little foreign car out into the traffic. Maybe, they had both learned a lesson from this. He pulled out behind her, but his destination was the forty acres, so he made a left at the next light and headed back to campus. Today was the day. He had a meeting with a Dallas rep and before the day was over he would know if they were going to make an offer.

Thoughts of Cecile were never far from his mind. What was she doing? God, he hoped she hadn't seen the gossip rags and the news speculation about him. The coach had given him a hard time—told him to rein in his dick or they were going to make him wear a chastity belt. Bobby had said what he had to, he told the coach that he had learned his lesson and wouldn't fall into that trap again. And he wouldn't. He didn't want anybody, but Ceelee. And he was going to do whatever it took to win her back.

* * *

"Hey, boss. Did you hear the news on Bobby Stewart?" Cecile almost dropped her coffee cup. Her secretary didn't know about her fling with Bobby, but she did know of Cecile's association with the family. Just hearing his name made every nerve in her body jump.

"What news?"

"He's had a rough time. Some girl accused him of fathering his child." That was all she let the poor girl say. With one swoop, she tore the magazine from her hands and headed to her office and shut the door. She'd worry about explaining herself later.

Not waiting to sit down, Cecile devoured the article. Reading quickly, she let out a sigh of relief. It wasn't his. The woman had a paternity test and Bobby was off the hook. Weak in the knees, Cecile found her chair. And then she read words that were like a knife in her heart. Bobby was quoted as saying, "I would stand by any woman that was pregnant with my child. But I have to tell you the truth, with everything that's going on with me right now, being a father at this stage in my life is the last thing I want."

Cecile had kept the magazine. She took it home and every time her resolve started to weaken, she reread the article. Finally though, it became evident that nothing Bobby could ever do or ever say would stop her from loving him. Every time she felt her child move deep inside of her, she remembered his touch and his smile.

Day in and day out she went through the motions, trying to make a life for her and the baby. Only the thought of holding her son or daughter made her life worth living. She had decorated a nursery and bought baby clothes. And today she was hanging curtains. Looking out the window, she pictured a handsome, bull-riding, football playing cowboy pushing a little boy in a swing. So when the phone rang, she nearly jumped out of her skin. But the voice on the other end of the line was the last person she had expected to hear from.

"I want to see you."

Those words were more a surprise to her than any she could have heard. What could Carl possibly want? "Why?" Cecile wasn't in the mood to take any crap from him. She was nauseous, her feet were swelling and she felt a little on the mean side.

"I need to apologize to you about something. Please. This is important to me." Carl's voice wasn't whining, but it was close.

"All right," Cecile gave in. She had to admit, her curiosity was aroused. In all of the years they had been together, Carl had never apologized to her about anything. "Come on over tonight, I can spare you a few minutes."

She took the intervening time to finish her business at the office and pull herself together. The last few weeks had been hard. Bobby hadn't given up, and to tell you the truth, her resolve to keep him at a distance had begun to weaken. Annalise had really given her something to think about, she said that Bobby wrote her a letter every day, sealed it in an envelope and gave it to Annalise to either keep for her or forward to Cecile's address. All Bobby had asked was that Annalise do her best to get Cecile to read his letters. That news had really made her think. She had done the only thing her heart would allow, she had asked Annalise to send the letters to her.

The last conversation she had with Annalise still rang in her ears. "He's changed, Cecile. Bobby Stewart is no longer a playboy. He hasn't had a date with a woman since you left."

Cecile had tried to explain it. "That's probably because of the pregnancy scare with that rodeo queen." Jealous much?

"I'm sure that had something to do with it," Annalise admitted. "Mostly it's because of you. And I have a box of love letters all written to you to prove it."

"Letters?" Every girl loves a love letter.

"He writes one every day." Annalise's voice grew serious. "You need to talk to him, Cecile. Bobby really loves you."

"What about the baby?" She couldn't forget what he had said in the magazine article.

"He would be on top of the world about that baby, and you know it."

Her best friend was very convincing. But Cecile had lived in a vacuum of self-doubt for so long she had a hard time believing that someone could love her that much. Carl had done a job on her, and she might never fully recover. "Send me the letters. I'll email you my address."

Annalise had refused to find out where Cecile had

moved to, she was afraid that she would give in to Bobby's pleas. "All right!" Triumph was obvious in Annalise's tone. "Bobby and you are meant to be. You'll see."

Cecile didn't know about that, but the opportunity to read his thoughts was too big of a temptation to pass up.

The doorbell rang, breaking through her dream. She opened the door. "Come in." Carl had lost weight. Funny how time can change your perspective of a person. Where once there had been resentment and anger, now there was something akin to remorse. Remorse for time wasted and remorse for so many unkind things that had been said.

Carl moved into the room about six feet and stopped. He looked around at the home she had created for herself. She knew it looked completely different from the living space they had shared. Gone was the modern art and the sleek leather furniture, instead, there were warm colors, soft fabrics and a collection of original artwork by Texas artists. Anyone who knew her association with Bobby Stewart would know she collected the western prints and sculpture to draw his memory closer to her. "Nice place."

"Thank you. Would you like to sit down?" She couldn't imagine what they had to talk about.

He went into her living room and set on the edge of the blue sectional sofa. "I want you back, Cecile."

If he told her that he was giving her a million dollars, it wouldn't have shocked her more. "What? Why?" Cecile stammered and stuttered. "You didn't want me when you had me. Why would you want me back?" Not that she was tempted, at all.

"I lied to you, Cecile." Carl's face was haggard as if he had just been rescued from a castaway's prison.

"What about?" This couldn't be good.

"I lied to you about your appeal, your sexiness, your desirability—all of it." He looked at her with such wistfulness that Cecile backed away, afraid he was going to try and embrace her.

She was stunned. Surely, she hadn't heard him right. "You lied to me? Why? For what purpose?" Her whole reality was becoming hazy. *What could he mean?*

"You were never frigid. It was all my fault." He didn't reach for her, instead he slumped over and put his head in his hands. "The problems were mine, not yours. I was too proud to tell you that I couldn't get it up for anybody. I've always been attracted to you. I still am."

This was pitiful. She was actually feeling sorry for the jerk. "What do you mean? What kind of problem did you have that was so bad you couldn't be honest with me?"

"I have a prostate condition. It's genetic. The medication that I had to take renders me impotent. I was embarrassed."

His confession didn't do a thing to make Cecile feel better. "So you're telling me that to save yourself from embarrassment, you led me to believe that I was a failure as a woman—a dud in bed, so undesirable that my own husband couldn't bring himself to fuck me?" She was livid.

"I've changed medications. I can get hard now. And I want you back. I love you, Cecile."

He looked so sincere. Cecile was speechless. She stood up and walked across the room. At one time these words would have been music to her ears. Not anymore. Besides, everything had changed. And she might as well tell him, it wouldn't be a secret much longer.

"I'm not going to take you back, Carl. I've moved on. I'm pregnant with another man's child."

His face grew red, and for a moment Cecile was afraid he might become violent. She moved to the other side of the bar, putting as much distance between them as she could.

"You're pregnant?" He said the words slowly, his words frozen with disdain. "That was fast. Have you been having an affair on me all this time? I should have known. Any floozy who would go down on her knees, uninvited, and take a man's cock in her mouth is just showing her true colors."

"Get out." Cecile didn't mince words. "The father of my child has nothing to do with you. But for your information, I was faithful to you until the day that I filed for divorce. If you had been honest with me, we could have worked this out. I loved you at one time, and I did everything I could to make you love me." There was a lot more she could say, but she was tired. "But all of that is over. I have a new life to build for me and my baby, and you will not be a part of it."

After he was gone, Cecile locked the door and put that part of her life behind her. At least now she knew the truth, Bobby had been partially right. Carl was the one at fault, all she had been was the fool.

Chapter Eight

"Hold him steady." The bullfighter gave Bobby a little help before the chute opened. "This is a wicked animal. Chicken-on-a-chain is no easy ride. I'll be down there waiting on you."

Bobby tightened the rope around his hand. It was a new one, and he wasn't used to it. Hopefully, he wasn't making a mistake in using it today. This was it, if he won today, the bull riding championship was his.

In the intervening months since Ceelee left him, Bobby had thrown himself into rodeoing and football. And he had excelled in both. The energy he normally expended chasing women had gone into his sports and his studies. He had graduated cum laude from The University of Texas with a degree in architectural engineering. He had been drafted by the Dallas Cowboys and was to report to training camp in two days—in Dallas. Where Ceelee was. Somewhere.

The bull lurched under him. Focus, Bobby. He wanted to live to fulfill his dreams, he had so many of them. And the dearest one was to get Ceelee back. He could have called Roscoe, but this time he wanted to do it himself. She hadn't been happy about being tailed and he didn't really blame her. But God had to give him a break somewhere. After all, he had been being very good. For him.

The crowd was screaming and the stadium was full of TV cameras. He wondered if Ceelee was watching. News reporters had been hounding him for days. His life was becoming more complicated by the minute. The air horn sounded and Chicken-on-a-Chain exploded from the chute. Bobby threw his hand up in the air and vowed to stick like glue to this whirlwind of hide and horn. Eight seconds might sound like a short time, but when you're in a churning mixer of heart-stopping danger, eight seconds was an eternity. He let his body relax, and didn't fight the bull. He allowed his spirit to rise above the noise and flashes of light from the photographers and viewed this as what it was—his chance.

This was his chance to prove to himself that he could do anything, be anything, and obtain any dream of his choosing. And when the horn sounded again, and the crowd went wild, Bobby knew that anything was possible. He could have anything he wanted—and what he wanted was Ceelee.

* * *

"Chicken-on-a-chain? Is that like soap-on-a-rope?" Alex wasn't even trying to be serious.

He knew his brother knew exactly what he was talking about, but Bobby played along. "No, it's a bull. It's the bull that I rode to win Bullrider of the year." Bobby explained himself like he was talking to a third grader. Alex and Scarlet were building a house just about a quarter mile from the B&B and Scarlet's kidney function had improved to the point where she had been able to reduce her meds. Her body had accepted Alex's kidney just fine. Alex was in a good mood, to say the least. "You did good, Bobby. We're all proud of you."

Alex's praise pleased Bobby to no end. "I was lucky, brother. I was using a new rope. And that was risky. It's a Brazilian, has a different feel than what I'm used to."

"Waxed, I presume?" It took a moment for Bobby to get it. Waxed. A Brazilian.

"Funny." At one time he would have cracked some sex humor right back at Alex. But, these days that didn't come as second nature to him. Sex had gone from being a sport to the Stewart brothers to being something sacred and precious. Annalise and Scarlet satisfied their men in every way and Bobby had no desire to seek meaningless sex. He had lost his appetite for it.

"When are you leaving?" Alex grew serious.

"In the morning. I have a meeting with my agent at ten."

"An agent? Aren't you big stuff?" Alex joshed with his brother.

"All the players have them. And I'll tell you after this rodeo win, I'm dreading the hype. I've been invited to four store openings, five TV interviews, fourteen parties and I've got three marriage proposals. And I haven't even got there, yet."

"You're going to do fine. We'll let you get settled and then we'll all come up and see you." Alex pulled Bobby into his arms for a bear hug. "I'm gonna miss you, buddy."

For a moment, Bobby was taken back in time. He still had memories of the first days he had spent in the Stewart family. For months he had expected to be sent back, rejected once more, left to go hungry and to left alone with his dread of the dark. That fear of abandonment was deeply engrained in him, it made Ceelee's walking away from him even harder to bear. "Do you think I have a chance with her, Alex?" He didn't clarify his statement, he didn't have to.

Alex let out a long breath. "If you love her like I love Scarlet, you've got to try. I have a sneaky feeling that it's all going to work out. I saw Annalise heading to the post office with a big envelope addressed to Cecile, and it wasn't a manuscript."

"How do you know?" Bobby wondered if it could be his letters.

"I asked." Alex winked at him and Bobby felt hope

rise in his heart.

* * *

BOBBY DOES DALLAS. That was the headline that met Cecile's eyes when she opened the newspaper as she stirred her de-caf coffee. Soon, she could go back to drinking her sweet elixir of caffeinated brew. Breast-feeding was exhausting but when she held Jaidon close to her heart, it was worth all the sacrifice. It had been hard going through the final stages of pregnancy and delivery by herself. But, she had made it.

Putting her little bundle of joy up on her shoulder, she read the words that both thrilled her and scared her to death. Bobby was here. "Jaidon, my boy, your daddy is painting the town." She read with a rapidly beating heart all of the personal appearances he was making, and the women he was making them with. She knew enough about the business to realize that most of these dates and photo opportunities were prearranged by his agent. Still, she was so jealous that she bet her pee was green.

Bobby's letters that Annalise had sent put Cecile into a tailspin. She couldn't get them out of her mind. The last one she read was still lying on the table. Pulling it to her, she read it for the umpteenth time.

> *Ceelee, My Love*
> *I'm lying in the bed dreaming of you. I can't get you off my mind. I want you so badly. Please, I'm begging you. Tell me what I did wrong. I would move heaven and earth to make it right for you. I have been faithful to you. I have not touched another woman, and I have no desire to touch another woman. My body and my heart want only you.*

> *I feel so helpless. I want to reach out to you so badly, but I don't know how. You know where I am. I haven't moved. Please call me. Please write me. And if nothing else, dream about me, because I dream about you every night. I wake up with a cock so hard that I could pound nails with it and there's no relief in sight for me. Darling, I'm begging you, come back to me. Please. I love you, desperately.*
> *Bobby*

Could he mean it? He certainly sounded sincere. She kissed Jaidon on the top of the head and imagined telling Bobby about his baby. Would he be thrilled or furious? Well, there was only one way to find out. She had to pull her big girl britches on and make plans. She still had his cell phone number, and even though she hadn't tried it, she knew that it would still be the same. But first, she had to see him in his element. Today was Sunday and she had tickets. Today, she would see Bobby play his first game at Cowboys Stadium.

The day passed quickly. Finally, she was there. Cecile sat in the nosebleed section. It had been hard to leave Jaidon with the babysitter, but she was a good one. Thank God for Tricia. If Cecile hadn't been lucky enough to find the middle aged angel, her life would be impossible. Being a single mother was a hard, hard job. She was exhausted. As the players started to come on the field, the familiar strains of the song from the TV show Dallas began to play. It got Cecile's attention. And the words from the announcer's box got it even more. "Today, we welcome Bobby Stewart to Dallas. We expect him to do as much for this town as Bobby Ewing did. Ladies and Gentleman...welcome *The Bull* to Dallas!"

The crowd stood as one as Bobby ran onto the field. The strains from the famous song filled the air. It probably had a different effect on Cecile than it did on everyone else. Her nipples peaked, her clitoris swelled and her whole body readied itself for possession by one Bobby Stewart. The announcer's words sounded over the music. "He's a star, Cowboy fans, in every sense of the word. He's a National Championship Bullrider, the toast of the town, there's even talk that he's gonna start making movies. Let me tell you one thing, Dallas. If the boy can play football today like we expect him to, then he's gonna become a legend. The words are everywhere—BOBBY DOES DALLAS—and we expect Bobby to do good by Dallas today!"

Cecile stayed on her feet watching him until he blended in with the other players. She wondered how his teammates were responding to all the hype. It was unheard of for a player to get so much attention before he had even made his first play, but then this was Bobby Stewart. He was a different breed.

She sat back down and tried to breathe. This was much harder than she thought it would be. All she wanted to do was run to his side, throw her arms around him and beg him to take her back.

But, this Bobby was so different. This Bobby was fast becoming a star. What would he want with an over-thirty mother with stretch marks on her stomach and milk stains on her blouse? Damn! She should have used the breast pump before she left. Now, here she was leaking milk like a faucet. Digging in her bag, she took a few tissues out and discretely tried to repair the damage.

Great! When she looked up, it only got worse. The camera had focused in on Bobby and showed him in a hug with one of the infamous Cowboy cheerleaders. It didn't do any good for her to know that fraternization between the two groups was severely limited and supervised. It still hurt to see him in the arms of any woman. Maybe, she ought to leave.

Before she could decide anything, the game started. And soon, Cecile was as mesmerized as everyone else by Bobby Stewart on the field.

* * *

As Bobby waited between plays, his last meeting with his agent bore on his mind. "I hear you," Bobby had answered Andrea, although, he hadn't really been listening. The woman was a maniac. She had booked him on so many shows and at so many events that he was plum tuckered out. She had followed him all the way to the place where it was *employees only*. He had stopped and waited politely for her to finish her thought.

"Tonight after the game, I need for you to make an appearance at the Ritz Carlton." She spoke in the false haughty accent of hers. Who was she kidding? He could hear a Deep East Texas twang in every word. "Shay Monroe is in town and we want to get your picture with her. She asked specifically that you be there. We can't let this opportunity pass."

Bobby just wanted some peace and quiet, but that didn't look like it was going to happen anytime soon. "Sure. Whatever," he'd said. "Just let me get out there and win this game or there won't be anybody trying to book me anywhere."

The game had finally started and he was in his element. "Now, it was the fourth quarter and they were up by seven. Come on, come on." Bobby talked to the ball as it floated to him, clear and straight. So far, so good. He had made one touchdown and if God was willing and the creek didn't rise, he was about to make another one. Like poetry in motion, he stood and waited. Time slowed down. His blockers did their work and the ball sailed through the air with his name written all over it. Just at the right moment, he jumped in the air and caught it. The crowd went wild. He tuned it out—he had forty yards to sprint and neither hell nor high water was gonna keep him from crossing that goal line.

"Look at him, ladies and gentleman. *The Bull* is in the house! The Texas Longhorns did a good job on this one. Old Mack Brown is to be commended. Bobby Stewart is a Texas power house, a rodeo star and now he is all Cowboy. The winner of the Doak Walker Award, my friends, has brought a win to Dallas!" As Bobby crossed the goal line, the clock ticked its last second and the theme from Dallas started playing again. Bobby turned and looked back. His eyes went to the big screen and what he saw made his heart stop. Ceelee! The camera was focused right on her! She was here!

Not waiting to celebrate, or talk to any of the players, he fought his way to the sideline to talk to anyone with a phone. He grabbed one of the defensive coaches and started talking way too fast. "Get on the phone. Call anyone. You see that woman on the big screen? Do whatever it takes. I'll give them anything they want, but stop her. Stop that woman and detain her. I don't care if you have to tie her to a desk, do not let that woman exit this stadium." The startled coach started his quest.

Bobby turned and watched her until the camera man moved on. God, she was here. She was here. She was here. Winning the game was good, but God in heaven, this was better. She had cared enough to come to his game and that was one of the sweetest gifts he had ever received.

After the hullabaloo he had started, it seemed everyone got in on the act. Word was passed from security guard to security guard. They brought Bobby a radio and told him where to go. Now, all he had to do was get to the place where they said they would take her—if they could find her. It was worse than a salmon trying to swim upstream. Bobby needed to go in the exact opposite direction from where the crowd was going. And everybody wanted to talk to him. Everybody wanted to touch him. Four guards were trying to get him through the crowd and they weren't having a lot of luck. "Excuse us. Excuse us. Please, excuse us." Over and over again, the guards held the crowd back, so Bobby could get to Ceelee.

* * *

"Excuse me, miss. You're going to have to come with us." At first, Cecile didn't realize that the security guard was talking to her.

"Me? Did I do something wrong?" Cecile was a little frightened. What could this mean?

"You're not in any trouble, ma'am. I'm just supposed to take you to the office. That's all I know."

Cecile hesitated. "How do I know I can trust you? I don't know you."

"I figured that. Do you know Jerry Jones?"

"Well, yea. He's the owner of the Cowboys."

The guard held out a phone with a video feed. When Jerry Jones started talking to her, she almost fainted. "Miss Fairchild. Everything is fine. Just go with the guard. You are perfectly safe."

Cecile still didn't know what the hell was going on, but she went. This had better be good. Her little boy needed her and she was still leaking milk like a sieve. The excitement of the game and seeing Bobby still had her blood singing through her veins. But this? This was just weird. There was no way that Bobby could know she was here. Could he?

The door opened behind her, and she heard footsteps. And then one word.

"Ceelee?"

Warmth flooded through Cecile like the noonday sun breaking through the clouds. Slowly, she turned. Bobby.

She didn't move.

But, he did. He still had on his pads. He was sweaty and tired and he looked good enough to eat. In two strides he was across the room. Without another word, he cupped her face in both hands and covered her mouth with his own. This was no ordinary kiss. Somehow, Bobby managed to pour more longing and tenderness into the melding of their mouths than she could have ever dreamed. He worshiped her.

Initially, she tried to resist, but her traitorous body and heart would not allow it. Her hands wavered desperately in the air for a moment, before finally settling on his broad, broad shoulders made even bigger by the football pads and gear. But, even though all of the clothing and padding, she could feel him trembling. Her big, bad cowboy was shaking. With one hard tug, he hauled her closer to him and his kiss changed from tentative and hesitant to demanding and dominant. Bobby was reclaiming his territory.

She was back in his arms—but for how long? He let his lips drag from hers as he gasped for air. Trailing his kiss down her neck, he fit his face as tight against her neck as he could. "You're here! Thank God, you're here! When I looked up and saw your face on the big screen I thought I was dreaming."

So, that was how he knew. Cecile hadn't even noticed

she had been up there at all. Her eyes had never left him. And now she was holding on to him as tight as she had been longing to. "I couldn't stay away. I'm sorry how I treated you the last time we were together." From reading his letters, she knew that there had been some sort of misunderstanding. She still didn't know what it was, but she was willing to give him the benefit of the doubt and a chance to explain. That is—if he wanted it.

"You have nothing to be sorry about. I'm just grateful to have the chance to hold you again." His words were said next to her skin. It was as if he were determined to hold on to her forever. Cecile had never felt so wanted.

But, there was so much to say—so much to confess. And there was Jaidon. Her number one priority had to be Jaidon.

"I've got to go down for the post game meeting. Will you wait for me?" He pulled back and locked his gaze with hers. "Please, say you'll wait."

"I have to be somewhere…" she began, but his face was so sincere, so dear, so full of supplication that she could deny him nothing. "I'll have to make a phone call."

"Good." He took her by the hand and began to pull her along. "The crowd's cleared out by now. Before, it was a madhouse. I didn't think I was going to ever get to you."

"You played a wonderful game." How inane.

For the first time, he smiled. God, what a beautiful face the man had. "Thanks. It means more coming from your lips than anyone else in the world. Let's get out of here."

His legs were long and she had a hard time keeping up, he was in such a hurry. "Bobby, could you slow down, just a little?"

"Damn, baby. I'm sorry. Come here." Then to her

consternation, he swept her up in his arms and began to carry her.

"Bobby! I can walk. I'll run a little if I have to. You don't have to carry me. What will people think?" Grinning, he showed her what he thought about anyone else's opinion. He watched where he was going, but he also began to kiss her face. Over and over again, everywhere he could reach. How could she have ever doubted him?

When they got to the players area, Bobby waltzed right in with her and sat her down gently on the couch. "Don't move. I'll be back in two shakes of a sheep's tail."

She could do nothing but smile. Joyfully, she called the babysitter and told her that she was unavoidably detained and would be there shortly. She didn't know what Bobby wanted to do, but going to their son would be their ultimate destination.

"Who are you?" A sharp, harsh voice broke through her contented reverie.

Cecile looked up to see a stunning woman staring at her as if she were a piece of dog doodoo she had found on her shoe. Cecile actually looked around to see if there was anyone else who could possibly have offended this woman so completely. "Me?"

"Yes, didn't I see you being carried in here by Bobby Stewart? What did you do? Throw yourself at him? This is a private area and it's time for you to go."

Cecile tried to find the steel in her spine, but she had misplaced it somewhere along the way. Her voice didn't come out nearly as strong as she would have liked it to have. "I'm a friend of Bobby's. And he asked me to stay and wait on him."

"I don't care if you're Bobby's mother. I'm Mr. Stewart's agent and he has a date tonight with a Hollywood starlet. He doesn't have time to waste on you."

Cecile stood up and was just about to state her case, when the woman had the audacity to take her by the arm and begin to steer her out toward the elevator. Cecile tried to pull away. "Bobby and I have things to discuss. If he had a date, he would have told me."

"You can mail him a letter." The woman was incredibly strong. And she was pinching the tender flesh on the inside of Cecile's elbow.

"Listen lady, I'm aware that Bobby has to have an agent, but he and I have a relationship." At that the woman stopped so suddenly that Cecile almost fell.

"A relationship?" The agent's expression was actually laughable. But, Cecile wasn't laughing, in fact she was about to cry. And what the woman said next was just about the last straw.

"Relationship, my ass. You're practically as old as I am. You are certainly not the type of woman that Bobby needs to be seen with. As far as I'm concerned, you can consider your relationship over. I call the shots in Bobby's life now and he doesn't need to be spending time with some over-the-hill bimbo with stains on her shirt. Couldn't you have at least dressed properly?" With that final insult, Ms. Know-it-all pulled her by the arm again and started off. But, she met a barrier she wasn't anticipating.

"Andrea?" Bobby stood there looking more forbidding than Cecile had ever seen him. "Get your bony hands off Ceelee. She's with me."

Andrea had the good grace to look somewhat ashamed. "Bobby, you don't have time. We've got to be at the Ritz in an hour. And whatever you have to say to this woman can surely wait."

Once more, Andrea began to propel Cecile forward. Cecile instinctively moved toward Bobby who caught her to himself then slipped her in back of his intimidating form. Turning to give her a kiss, he took a brief second to brush a gentle finger down one cheek. "It's okay, precious. I'll handle this." Turning to Andrea he let her have it. "Let's get one thing straight, right now, at the onset of our association. If we can't come to terms on this, there will be no association. This woman belongs to me. She is more important to me than my position with the Cowboys. She is the most important thing in my life and I don't want to ever see you treat her with disrespect or say one unkind word to her again—or you are fired. Do you understand me? If you try to make me choose between football and Ceelee—you can see how far you get sticking a football up your skinny ass. Are we clear?"

Andrea seemed to be a hard-as-nails businesswoman, but Cecile could tell that even she knew when her britches had been ripped. "I'm sorry, Bobby. There are so many appearances you need to make—"

"I don't mind making appearances, Andrea. But never again will you refer to them as *dates*. I don't date other women. I'm in love with this one and there is no room in my life for anyone else—not even for the camera. Are we clear?"

Andrea stepped back and made her face a blank. "Crystal. If you'll call me tomorrow, we'll review your commitments and make appropriate changes."

Cecile was flabbergasted. If there had been any doubt in her mind how Bobby felt about her, it was gone. Uncaring who was watching she launched her whole body at him and he caught her to him and held her tight. "You do care about me," she whispered in wonder.

"I think I've told you that all along, baby." Bobby said in a teasing voice. "Let's get outta here. We've got a lot of lovemaking to do."

Chapter Nine

They walked to the parking garage and he kept his arm around her the whole way. In order to avoid the hassle of finding a parking place, she hadn't driven to the game. Now, she was thankful of that fact. Spotting his same pick-up, she instantly felt more at ease. "There's some things we need to talk about." She spoke hesitantly as he helped her in the truck. His hands on her body, his nearness, it was all so dearly familiar that she wanted to cry.

Tucking her into his side, he put one hand between her legs and curved it possessively around her thigh, that same familiar gesture that anchored her to him in no uncertain terms. "I know we do. We're gonna stop and get a pizza and then I'm taking you home with me. We'll talk all night long if we have to."

"Bobby, the pizza sounds great, but could we go to my house afterwards, instead of yours?"

He looked at her closely as if trying to read her expression, but he didn't argue. "As long as I'm with you, I don't care where we are." Cecile shuddered with emotion. Could he have said anything more perfect? Briefly, she told him where she lived and how to get there.

Calling on his cell, he ordered a large pizza with everything and swung by to pick it up. Waiting in the drive-through, he pulled her onto his lap. "Do you have any idea how much I've missed you?" Letting his forehead rest against hers, he caressed each side of her face with his hands. It was as if he couldn't get enough of touching her.

"Yes, I know. I've missed you, too. So much," she answered breathlessly.

"Will you tell me what happened? What did I do? Why did you leave?" His voice cracked a little under the strain. "I've got to know, baby. I don't want to make the same foolish mistake twice."

The pizza came, so she had a moment or two to get her answer ready. He needed to hear it and she needed to say it. Clearing the air might be painful, but it was necessary before they could move forward. He put the fragrant pie in the back, and then settled himself next to her, putting his hand back in the place he had made for himself between her thighs. Truthfully, Cecile was tingling all over. She was more than ready to open herself up and feel him take possession of her body as only Bobby could, but they had things to deal with first—namely, Jaidon. She was still on pins and needles about how Bobby would react to their son.

Refusing to let this perfect moment pass uncelebrated, she laid her head on his shoulder and clasped her own hands around his muscular arm—letting him know that he wasn't alone in the celebration of their reunion. It also gave her something to hold on to as she laid her doubts and fears at his feet. "The day of the wedding, you were out in the yard talking to your brothers. I came out to ask you if you knew where my pink lace panties were. They would have gone perfectly with the bridesmaid dress." She paused, but he squeezed her leg, encouraging her to continue. "As I was walking up to you, I heard you tell Ethan that I didn't have anything to do with it…whatever it was. And that you didn't intend to see me anymore after the weekend was over."

Bobby put on his blinker and pulled off to the side of the road. He just sat there for a moment and stared off into space and then he turned to her and pulled her onto his lap. It was fast turning into her favorite spot in the whole world. "Promise me something." His voice was gruff with emotion.

She didn't even wait to hear what he wanted promised. "I promise."

Her quick response earned her a kiss. "The next time you hear me say something stupid, will you please come to me and give me a chance to explain what I meant." He took both of her hands in his and tenderly kissed each finger. "You heard part of a conversation. I was talking about Mary Alice Solice *and* you."

Cecile gripped his hands as if holding on to the only line that had her tethered to earth. "I should have let you explain. I'm so sorry."

"Don't be, it's over. Let me finish." Bobby wiped a stray tear from the corner of her eye. "When I found you, anything that I had with Mary Alice became an unimportant part of my past, immediately—that's what I meant when I said it had nothing to do with you. And when I said *I don't intend to see her after the weekend was over*—I meant her, not you. She had just called and demanded to see me and I had agreed to meet her the next day after the time you had planned to leave."

Cecile sank against him, throwing her arms around his neck. "I'm so sorry. We've lost so much time, and so many things have happened. I acted so stupidly. If my self-confidence had been greater, I wouldn't have been so quick to believe the worst. And truthfully, I would have come to you, but things..." This was going to be harder than she thought. So much was at stake. She caressed his dear face, loving the rasp of his beard under her fingers. Where was her courage? Buying time, she shared her other news with him. "Carl came to see me the other day. He asked me to come back to him." At Bobby's harsh intake of breath, she instantly consoled him. "Shhh, I would never choose him over you. But, he did explain something to me. He was sick and on medicine all of these years. His cholesterol and prostate were off kilter and the medication he took for it rendered him impotent. Instead of being honest with me about it, he led me to believe it was my fault."

"I always knew it was something stupid like that," Bobby interjected. "I knew there was no way, in hell, that the problem was yours." They shared a soul-deep, tongue-tangling kiss that had them both panting with desire. "Let's go home."

"There's more for you to understand, Bobby." She tried to prepare him. "When we get to my house, there's someone I want you to meet."

* * *

Bobby wasn't in the mood to *meet* anybody. But, he was so happy to have his Ceelee back that if she asked him to stop and have tea with the Pope, he guessed he would try. The only problem was, his dick was so swollen and eager that every breath he took dug his zipper down into the engorged shaft. Pulling into her driveway, he noticed there was a car already there. "I'm not about to meet Carl, am I?" Bobby had a lot of self-control, but none so far as that idiot was concerned.

Cecile actually laughed. "No, you're not meeting Carl. I think you're going to like this fella pretty well. I do."

Bobby was thoroughly confused. There was a man in Cecile's house that she wanted him to meet. Hell, he wanted to take her to bed and push his cock so deep in her pussy that she fainted from rapture, that's what he wanted to do. Bad. "Baby, I don't know what's going on, but I trust you."

Taking her key out of her purse she led him up on the

porch of her small bungalow house. It was painted white and trimmed with light yellow. Big pots of mums sat everywhere proclaiming the glory of the season. She tried the lock and fumbled and had to try again. "Give it here, doll. It's time I started taking care of you." He held the door open for her and then nipped her on the neck as she passed by. "Now where's this fella I'm supposed to meet."

Bobby let his eyes take in Ceelee's home. It looked just like her, and surprisingly, him. There were touches that he would have chosen if he had been decorating. He liked it, he felt right at home. Furniture that was big and comfortable invited him to sit down and put his feet up. It was as if she had created a home with him in mind. He prayed that he was right. She walked through the front living room and headed for the bedrooms, he supposed.

"Teresa! We're home." In a few moments a smiling woman emerged. Bobby didn't know what to think.

"Hello, Ms. Fairchild."

"Teresa, this is Bobby Stewart. Bobby this is Teresa Sanchez. She helps me out."

Ah, the housekeeper. "Hello, Teresa."

Teresa bowed her head and smiled. "I recognize you. You look just like the little gentleman." As soon as she said the words, she covered her mouth.

"It's okay, Teresa. That's why he's here." She led the other woman to the garage and stood and watched her as she left.

When she returned, Bobby was ready for answers. "What did she mean? Who do I look like?

"Come with me," she took him by the hand. As they walked down the hall, Bobby could hear a cooing noise. He strained his ears. It sounded like a baby. No, it couldn't be. Could it?

Stopping in his tracks, he looked at Cecile with wide-eyed wonder. "A baby?"

"I realize this is the most important moment in my life so far. The two people that I love more than anything in the world are about to meet." She pushed open the door.

Bobby stepped inside an enchanted place filled with teddy bears and stuffed horses. The room was blue and a baby bed sat against the wall. The smell of powder and the euphoric scent of a baby filled the air. He could still feel Cecile's hand on his arm, she hadn't left him. God, he was scared to death. A series of ooohs and ahs and happy little noises floated across the room. A mobile turned playfully overhead and Bobby saw one small hand and foot rise up in the air. "Ceelee? Baby, is there something you're trying to tell me?"

"Robert Jaidon Sr., meet Robert Jaidon Jr.—she didn't use the last name, because they wouldn't take that privilege unless it was offered. She had tried to anticipate what Bobby would do and how he would react. But she hadn't been prepared for the reality.

Slowly, he walked up to the crib and looked at his son for the first time. Jaidon looked at him and tried to focus his little eyes. "God, my chest feels tight," he said softly. When his son held his hand up, as if reaching for him, Bobby took his little hand in his. He could cover the baby's whole hand with the tip of his thumb and first finger. "Hello, little man. Besides your mama, you're the most precious thing I've ever seen." Leaning over the crib, he kissed the tiny hand. "Can I pick him up?" He looked back at Ceelee, asking permission.

Ceelee was crying now. She wasn't even trying to hold it back. "Sure, you can pick him up. He's a sweet little boy." She wrapped her arms around herself and watched Bobby get to know his son. Oh, how different it could have been. He could have become angry, he could have expressed doubts, instead, it seemed to be love at first sight.

Bobby picked Jaidon up and brought him close to his face placing small kisses all over the baby's cheek. "Daddy's boy. Daddy's little boy." Meeting Ceelee's eyes, he smiled. "Let's go to the couch, I want to hold you both."

He said Daddy! That sounded so wonderful. Ceelee was totally entranced with both of her men. Bobby stopped to get a blanket and a pacifier, then led the way, making himself right at home. With a light heart, she followed and when he sat down in the corner of the sofa and patted the cushion beside him, she crowded in as close as she could. "Don't you think we need to talk about this? Are you sure you're not angry?"

Bobby laid Jaidon up on his shoulder and rubbed his back. "Do I look angry, baby?" He picked up her hand and kissed it. "Why didn't you tell me when you found out you were pregnant? Didn't you think I'd want to know?"

His voice held no trace of condemnation, still Cecile felt overwhelmed with guilt. She laid her head on his shoulder and waited a moment before answering. "Truthfully? I found out pretty quick after I came back. I discovered I had forgotten to take my pill during the great Carl debacle." She felt Bobby stiffen at the mention of her ex-husband's name. "The hurt from our misunderstanding was still fresh in my mind. I didn't think you'd want us."

"Baby, that hurts. Here I sit, holding one treasure and cuddled up with another and you still don't have a clue what you mean to me. The idea that you ever entertained the thought I wouldn't want the two of you kills my soul.

Not want you? Impossible. I would have dropped everything and come to you at any moment. I would have loved to have held you when you were tired, rubbed your feet when they hurt. Hell, I would have loved to bathe your face when you were sick. To think that you went through labor and delivery alone just makes my heart ache. What I wouldn't give to turn back the clock and share every moment with you."

His sincere outpouring of grief at their time apart touched her more than words could say. "I should have told you, and I almost did, but after you—" she stopped. There was no use bringing the magazine article up. Whatever he had said to the reporter had nothing to do with her and Jaidon.

"After what? Tell, me. Let's don't hold anything back, not now. We need to get everything ironed out."

"It doesn't matter," she protested.

"If it kept us apart, hell yes, it matters." Bobby was insistent.

"After you found out that Mary Alice's baby did not belong to you, you told a reporter that even though you'd never turn your back on your child, a baby at this stage of your life was the last thing you wanted." It felt good to get that off of her chest.

Bobby laid his head back on the couch and looked at Ceelee with sorrow and tenderness in his eyes. "Ceelee, I didn't love Mary Alice. I couldn't imagine what having a baby with her would be like. Jaidon and you? That's as different as night and day. A baby with you is the most welcome thing in the world, because I love you. And that makes all the difference."

"Thank you, Bobby. I regret that I ever doubted what we have." Cecile was so touched. Small snorty noises from the wee person in the room got their attention. "Somebody's hungry."

Bobby laughed at his son who was rooting on his shoulder like a little armadillo. "Is he on a bottle, or... God, this question turns me on. Are you breastfeeding him?"

Cecile opened her jacket and looked at him in dismay. "Breastfeeding. See what I was hiding? I'm a mess. When I saw you on the field, I got emotional. When I get emotional, or think about Jaidon, I leak. Isn't that embarrassing?"

Bobby stared at the little circlets of dampness which declared that she had milk for their baby.

"No, it's beautiful."

"I don't have a nursing bra on, I'll have to go in the other room and pull off my clothes." She got up to leave.

Bobby stopped her. "Don't go. I'd give anything to watch you feed our child. Do you mind? I want to be a part of everything you do. I've missed too much already."

Cecile flushed a little at the thought, but she pulled off the jacket, her blouse and then the shear bra that did nothing to hide her breasts. They were even bigger than before, and she knew they had been too big for her body-size to begin with. She almost crossed her arms to hide herself. "I've grown, I'm afraid."

Swallowing hard, Bobby licked his lips. "God in Heaven. Yes, you have. You are devastatingly beautiful and sexy. I'm almost jealous of my son. Honey, I can't wait to get my hands and mouth on you."

Arousal stormed through her, and she smiled at him. Taking the baby from his arms, she whispered, "I can't wait, either. I'm glad you still think I'm pretty." She arranged the baby at her breast and Jaidon showed his daddy that he knew just what to do.

Bobby pulled her back in the crook of his arm. "Sit next to me. I want to be up close and personal. I've never been privileged to watch a baby nurse, especially not my baby." Jaidon had this down pat. They were both enraptured to watch his little mouth working the nipple. Bobby chuckled when Jaidon put his hand on Ceelee's breast and patted and pushed on it. He laughed out loud when the baby smacked and snorted. "He's gonna be a big eater, isn't he? We'll spend all our time trying to put food on the table for this bruiser."

Ceelee nestled into Bobby's warm embrace. This was absolute paradise. She had her baby in her arms and they were both cradled by the one who had given him life, and given her love. "I love you, Bobby." She couldn't hold it back.

He kissed her temple. "I love you, too, Ceelee. How old is Jaidon? And yes, I have an ulterior motive for asking."

"He's a little over eight weeks old." She soothed the baby's soft black hair and stared into his dark eyes. "He looks just like you, doesn't he?" Bobby didn't say anything for a second, and Cecile had the worst thought. Did Bobby have any doubts that the baby was his? He hadn't acted like it, but she needed to put his mind to rest. "I haven't been with anyone else, Bobby. The baby is yours. Do you want me to have any tests?"

"Hell, no!" Bobby sounded taken aback. "Why would you say that? Have I given you any impression that I have doubts?" He stared at her face, as if trying to read her thoughts. "It's about Mary Alice, isn't it? Lord, that situation has caused me more problems than it has ever been worth." Cupping her cheek, he assured her. "Jaidon is my son. It's as plain as day to me. So, no, I don't need for you to take any damn tests."

Ceelee laughed at his consternation. Picking the baby up, she laid him on her shoulder and patted his small back. Bobby was looking at Jaidon eye to eye and when Jaidon smiled at him and let a huge burp go, they both laughed. "Here let me take him. I want to rock him to sleep. Is that okay?" Bobby looked at her and she nodded, giving him their bundle of joy. "You go get ready for bed. Can I make love to you, baby? Is it safe? I'll be so gentle, I'll treat you like you're made of glass."

Cecile pouted her lips a little. "I've gotten the release from my doctor, so yes, it's safe. But, I have no desire to be *handled with care*. I have missed you more than you could ever know and I want to be taken, ravished and possessed. I want all you've got, cowboy. My body is starving for you."

The big man just stood there holding the tiny baby. Then, he winked at her. "Oh, darlin'. You've just set off the launch sequence. Just give me a second to get our little man down for the count and I'll take you on a journey to paradise—Texas style."

Cecile was excited, but nervous. She took a quick shower and shaved everything that needed it. Since she had been with Bobby, she had visited a spa and got the full treatment, so her lady-parts were smooth and ready for him. Just the memory of how his cock felt as it filled her emptiness had her trembling and eager. Debating what to wear, if anything, she opted for a sheer white gown that covered everything but hid nothing. Since their first meeting, anything white and see-through reminded her of their hunger for one another. Realizing that she still had milk, she debated trying to pump it out and store it. Feeding Jaidon all he wanted wasn't a problem, she produced enough milk for two babies. But, she didn't know how Bobby would feel about the fact that when he suckled her, he would be getting more than a mouthful of nipple. And having his mouth on her breast was one thing she couldn't do without, she had been fantasizing about it the whole time they had been apart.

The decision was taken out of her hands when the door opened. "There you are. Sweet Boy is out like a light. I left him lying flat on the mattress with a light blanket. I don't know much about babies, but I didn't want him to smother." He was talking fast and happy. Apparently, fatherhood excited the hell out of Bobby. As he stepped further into the room, she walked out of the bathroom to meet him. The light from over the sink was the only light in the room so she was enveloped in a warm golden glow. "Holy Mother of God, angel. Look at you." Bobby was wearing a pair of jeans that he had already unbuckled and a white western shirt that he had already unsnapped, and in the most economical of moves Cecile had ever seen, he shed his clothes in about thirty seconds flat.

"I've missed you, Bobby."

"Missing you is a mild way to put it. I haven't breathed since we've been apart." He walked up to her slowly. His manhood got to her a couple of seconds before the rest of him did; she had never seen him so fully engorged. With a soft touch, she caressed the hard shaft, marveling that in a few moments it would be wholly contained within the aching depths of her body.

He lifted up her hair, cupping his hands behind her neck and captured her mouth in a deep, searing kiss that had her clit peeking out of its hood and begging for attention. "Hmmmm, baby. Your lips are so sweet." With hungry hands he soothed all over her body, from shoulder to hand, from neck to the cleavage that seemed to fascinate him so. In a move she wasn't expecting, he knelt at her feet and ran his hands up under her gown, caressing her legs from ankles to hip. "I've dreamed about touching you for months, Ceelee. It's been almost a year!" He laughed. "Jaidon's proof of that, a year since I touched you, a year since I sucked your nipples, a year since I pushed my cock into the haven of your body." He pressed his forehead into her abdomen and just inhaled her scent. "God, I want all of you. I'm overwhelmed. I've got to slow down. If I don't, I'm gonna explode just from touching your skin."

Cecile held out her hand. "Come with me. We've got all night. Let me give you some relief." She guided him to sit on the bed and lean back against the headboard. He watched with fire in his eyes as she skimmed the gown over her head leaving her nude. "I've never done this before, but I bet I can figure it out." Joining him on the bed, she backed up to him, straddling his legs and spreading her thighs, giving him full access to her womanhood. "Guide him in; I'm more than ready for you."

"I'm being selfish. I've done nothing to ready you or prepare you. But, hell, I've been celibate for almost nine months and my control is gone. I'll make it up to you, I promise."

As she sank down onto his iron-hard cock, the relief of his invasion was unspeakable. "Nothing to make up," she gasped. "I want this more than you do."

"Seriously doubting that." Bobby groaned at the tight, wet heaven that welcomed him. "Sinking into you is like being massaged by warm, whipped cream. Do you know what this position is called, Ceelee?" He held on to her hips while she proceeded to try and ride him into insanity.

"Wonderful?" She didn't have her full wits about her, all she wanted to do was grind her pussy down on his groin and whimper.

"It's a reverse cowgirl. Fittin' huh?" He pulled her back against his chest and angled her so he could drive her crazy with short hard jabs.

"It fits just fine," she let her head rest on his shoulder. "Touch my breasts, please?" She was beyond being embarrassed about begging, her whole body was about to go up in flames.

"Oh, yeah!" he breathed into her ear. "Two handfuls of delight." He lifted and molded them, massaging the pink areolas and pulling on the nipples.

Darts of ecstasy shot through her at his welcome attention to her breasts. But when milk started coating his fingers, she stiffened—not knowing how he was going to react. "Sorry," she whispered.

Bobby bit her on the neck and ground his cock up harder and deeper. "That's the sexiest damn thing I've ever seen." He licked the milk off of his fingers. "If that didn't belong to my baby boy, I'd give my eyeteeth to have a taste."

"There's plenty for both of you." She wanted to say more to him, she really did, but it felt so good. When he moved one hand down to rub on her clit she lost it, just flat lost it. "Bobby!" she screamed as her world exploded. He held her tight as she quaked and jerked in his arms.

"Lord, I missed this. Your little pussy is hugging my cock and fluttering around me, Sweet Jesus, baby, you are unbelievable!" Bobby didn't let up in his piston-like movements. With constant touches, he rubbed her body, fondled her breasts and led her from satisfaction back to full arousal. "I can't get enough of you."

Cecile laughed. "Don't get me wrong. I love it. But, you've never talked this much when we made love."

Bobby laughed too. And his answer brought tears to her eyes. "I can't help it, Ceelee. I'm just so happy to be here. I can't hush." With one strong movement of his body, he propelled them down in the bed so that they were lying flat. She was still impaled on his cock, but now she was lying back on his body, fully supine. "Hold on, honey. This is my grand finale." He lifted his legs so his knees were bent, giving him greater ability to move his hips. Grasping her breasts, he bucked his hips and carried her on a ride to the stars. "I love you. I love you. I love you," he chanted in her ear as their orgasms crashed in a simultaneous wave of rapture.

They cuddled and they whispered, but soon they lay still just enjoying holding one another again. Cecile lay on her side. She rubbed his chest in a movement of contemplation and contentment. His eyes were still closed and his breathing was just now settling down to something near normal. She wanted to ask him what the future held for them, but she bit her tongue. That would come, or it wouldn't. Placing one kiss in the center of his chest, she vowed not to pressure him. He talked like he wanted to be a part of her and Jaidon's life, but Bobby was young, handsome and had the world by the tail. It wouldn't be fair of her to make any demands.

To her right, the baby monitor let her know that somebody wasn't happy. "I bet he's wet. I'll be right back." She slipped from the bed, grabbed her robe, and headed to the nursery. Footsteps falling behind her let her know that Bobby was right behind her.

"Let me do it. I need to learn." He had hastily pulled on his pants, determined not to be left out. She helped him gather everything he needed and showed him how to lower the side of the crib so he could change his first diaper.

It was so sweet, Jaidon was so small and Bobby was so big. His hands dwarfed the baby's legs and Jaidon was in a kicking, squirming mood. "I'm gonna hog-tie you, boy," Bobby started playing with his son. "I've wrestled steers to the ground. I think I can handle a tiny mite like you."

Cecile wasn't so sure. When he took the diaper off and was met with a fountain of little-boy wee-wee spurting up at him, she thought she would die laughing.

"What in tarnation!" Bobby covered the erupting geyser with the diaper and looked at Cecile in horror. "Did you know they would do that?"

She couldn't answer for laughing. Every time he moved the diaper, Jaidon let loose with another spurt. If he wasn't so young, she would have thought that he was playing a joke on his pop. "Yes. When he takes a notion to go, you have to cover him up and get out of the way."

Bobby stood to one side and lifted the corner of the diaper warily. "You little bugger, you." He got rid of the dirty diaper in the pail and then set out to clean and change him. She had to help with the diaper alignment, but Bobby caught on quickly. And when he bent over and began blowing raspberries on Jaidon's stomach, Cecile lost her heart forever. She was so happy she could burst. It felt like nothing could come between them or take away this joy.

She was wrong.

* * *

Bobby had every intention of spending as much time with Ceelee and their son as possible, but things got crazy—fast. Practice, scheduled public appearances and out of town games forced him to split his time into too many fragmented segments to please him.

He moved a few changes of clothes to her house and intended to move more, but some nights it was so late when he got through with his obligations that he would crash in his apartment so as not to wake them up by his all-hours coming and going. Tonight, to hell with the world, he was going to sleep in his baby's arms if it harelipped Governor Perry.

It was ten-thirty and he had just finished with a moonlight photo shoot around the pool at Southfork Ranch. Since one reporter had called him *the next Bobby Ewing* that comparison just wouldn't die. Andrea was still being a bitch, but she was making him a helluva lot of money, so he put up with it.

Ceelee had given him his own key, so he used it to ease in the house. Warm, inviting smells hit him like a wave of nostalgia. She had left a light on for him, sweet thing, and there was a note propped up on the table.

> *"There is a plate of shrimp creole in the oven on warm and a fresh apple tart in the frig. Eat fast and come to bed—I'm hungry."*
> *Ceelee*

After he read the note, it wasn't his stomach that was screaming for attention. Before going to feed his craving, he stopped for some Jaidon loving. God, he loved that little morsel of humanity. If he had kissed that little boy once, he had kissed him a million times. He couldn't get enough of his sweet baby smell and how it felt to cuddle him close. Ceelee would never know what a treasure she had given him. Now, if he could just slow his life down enough to make them a permanent and legal part of his life. He had set the ball in motion and Alex and Ethan were going to help him. Even the Dallas Cowboy franchise was in on the act. When he proposed to Ceelee Fairchild the whole world was going to be a witness.

Tiptoeing up to the crib, he watched his sleeping boy-angel. Careful not to wake him, he got some baby-sugar. "Sleep tight, little man. I'll see you when you wake up."

Now, on to the main attraction. Bless her heart. She had lit candles and had on the sexiest little red baby doll jammies he had ever seen. But, he had kept her waiting too long and she had slipped into slumber. Lord, she was cuddly. Shedding his clothes, he joined her on the bed. Instantly, her body responded to his. She turned to him and curled herself around him, bringing his dick to full attention. "You're home." Were there ever sweeter words?

"Yea, baby. I'm home." Thinking she was too sleepy to play, he was pleased to feel her little hands rub down his stomach and follow his treasure trail south in search of big game. He didn't disappoint.

"Oh, you feel so good," she purred. The next thing he knew, he felt her hot, velvet mouth envelop the head of his cock and she began to swirl her tongue around and around, teasing the glans underneath until she had him moving his hips in the instinctive dance of desire. Taking his sac in one hand, she played with his balls as she sucked on his dick hard enough to make him bellow with enjoyment. "God! Ceelee!"

Cecile was awake now and ready to get down to business. With one hand she proceeded to jack him off—squeezing and rubbing, moving the skin up and down his granite-hard rod just enough to drive him mad. Her mouth was on to more exotic pursuits. Signaling him to spread his legs farther, she nuzzled his scrotal sac and surprised the hell out of him by taking one of his balls in her mouth and rolling it over her tongue. "Holy Shit!" At his exclamation, she released a little laugh letting him know that was the response she was after.

Bobby couldn't take anymore. He needed to come inside of her, deep inside. Workouts and lifting weights had paid off because Bobby's upper body strength was second to none. Lifting her like she weighed nothing,

Bobby stood and brought her up to sit on the bed. "That's a cute little outfit, and I'll appreciate it more later. But now, I need to feel your satin, smooth skin. He pulled the top off and tossed it behind him, freeing those gorgeous tits that were never far from his mind. "Pull down those wee panties and stand on the bed. I'm taking you for a ride."

Trembling with excitement, Cecile followed his guidelines. She had no idea what he had in mind, but she trusted him. That made him happy. "Wrap your legs around my waist." Only for a moment, did she hesitate. "Come on, I'm not gonna drop you. You're too precious to me."

Ceelee steadied herself on his shoulders and let him support her weight as she fitted herself to his body. Reaching between them with one hand, she fit the head of his penis to her opening and then held her breath as he pushed his way into her hot center. "Hmmm, that's so good." She moaned. After that, it was all Bobby. He was strong and rarin' to go, all she had to do was let him have his way. Soon, he had her riding his cock, moving her body in the most exquisite motions—the perfect drag and draw of his flesh against hers. "Do you like that baby?" Bobby had to ask. It felt wonderful to him, but his pleasure wasn't as important to him as hers was.

"Yes, yes, yes." Her answer was in cadence with his thrusts. Wanting to go even deeper, Bobby carried her to the smooth wall and secured her against it and began to pump in earnest. It must have felt good to her, because she gripped his shoulders with her fingers and dug her heels into his hips and added her own thrusts to the mix. "Harder, Bobby. Harder, please!" she begged.

Bobby didn't need to be asked twice, he wanted to ram into her with the force of a pile-driver but he was always conscious of being too rough. She was so little and he was so big. But Ceelee's hunger was a rival to his own, he had done good when he chose this sweet angel. She was a compliment to him in every way. He could always tell when she was really getting into it, her little body betrayed her.

He loved to watch the pink flush of excitement climb her chest, her nipples would grow larger and her feminine muscles would start clenching on his dick like a hot, little sex machine. Ceelee was so responsive. If he wasn't so damned excited, he could make his little doll cum three times, but it wasn't to be. When he felt the beginnings of her release, he couldn't hold back. He was so in love, so attracted to her, so happy with her that he exploded sending streams of his cum deep within her. "Sorry, baby. I couldn't hold back," he apologized.

Wiping a bead of sweat from his forehead, she crooned to him. "Hush! You're perfect. You please me every time. And even better, you let me know that I please you. I wouldn't change one moment of our time together. You make me the happiest woman in the world." With that declaration, she relaxed completely in his arms and he carried his sweet burden back to bed and held her as they slept.

* * *

"The last time I was on stage was a college performance of Steve Martin's Picasso at the Lapin Agile. I played Elvis." It was obvious that Andrea wasn't familiar with the comedian's controversial play. That surprised Bobby, he had thought she was in the know about such things.

"It doesn't matter, you're a natural," she waved a well-manicured hand in dismissal. "This is the address for the reading. Frankly, the movie producers aren't looking at anybody else. They say you're perfect for the role."

Bobby didn't know if he was perfect for any role. In fact, he wasn't even sure he wanted to act. Wasn't his life too full now? He wanted to have more time for Ceelee and Jaidon, not less. "What kind of movie is it? What would be my role?" He wouldn't dismiss it out of hand, he would listen.

Smiling, she gave what she thought was the piece de resistance. "It's about a bull rider who's trying to make it big. There's a romance and he gets hurt. It's sort of a tear-jerker movie."

Bobby had to admit, it did sound good. "All right, I'll go hear what they have to say."

He did go talk to the movie people, and it wasn't long before things started to get out of hand. Word got out fast. The morning headlines said it all. *Bobby Stewart, darling of Dallas, is up for a Hollywood movie role.* Bobby fumed. Andrea knew this would happen. All of a sudden his demand shot up from three appearances a week to six, some he had to turn down. He refused to work so much that he had no time for his family. Ceelee hadn't complained, but he could see the little flickers of doubt in her eyes. She never made demands and she never complained, but hurting her was the last thing he wanted to do.

When he met with the producers, he was surprised to meet his leading lady. She was a beautiful actress, but several years older than he was. When he got the script he saw why. The whole scenario of the story was a younger man/older woman romance. Only the movie didn't have a happy ending. The cowboy got injured and met this younger woman in rehab who nursed him back to health. At the end of the movie he had to choose between the young nurse and his older girlfriend and the cowboy chose youth over substance. Bobby didn't like it. It hit too close to home. If Ceelee got hurt by this shit, it wouldn't be worth it.

* * *

What was happening? Cecile didn't know which way to turn first. Her cell phone was ringing, her land line was buzzing, her computer was telling her that she had mail and her doorbell was pealing. She literally spun in a circle and then Jaidon started crying. Being the good mother that she was, she ignored everything and went to her baby. And it was a good thing she did. As she rocked Jaidon, she finally focused on the local news program that played on the set. Her eyes widened. It was about Bobby! Not that seeing Bobby on the local news, or national news for that matter, was unusual, it wasn't. Bobby Stewart was fast becoming a household name. It was obvious his name would go down in the annals of football with the likes of Tom Brady and Peyton Manning. He was just that good. But what she heard coming out of the reporter's mouth made the blood in her veins turn to ice water.

"Bobby Stewart has hit the big time. The Championship Bull Rider turned pro-football player is now going to be a movie star. And Dallas Digs For The Truth has learned that the movie Cowboy Heat is somewhat autobiographical. It seems that Bobby's love interest in the movie is an older woman and DDT has the scoop that our beautiful Bobby is involved with a woman nine years his senior. Nine years, folks! Does that make this Cougar Country? DDT has also found out that Bobby has a child with this woman of advanced years. Her name is Cecile Fairchild and she's an editor with Passion Publishing, the erotic romance house. Maybe that's the appeal for Bobby, she probably has sexual experience that puts the rest of us to shame. We're making every effort to contact her, she does deserve equal time. After all, a woman that is *doing* Bobby-Does-Dallas must have a little fire left in the furnace. We'll have more on this story, tomorrow, I promise."

Cecile sat there stunned, mortified, humiliated and crying like a baby. She clasped her own baby to her breast and let the tears flow. How in the world was she ever going to face her coworkers again? Her boss would probably let her go. This wasn't just publicity, this was bad publicity. And Bobby! Poor Bobby! How was he going to hold his head up long enough to catch a football? What was she going to do? She had to do something, but what?

* * *

Bobby was livid. This was Andrea's doing. When he got to Ceelee's there were reporters parked nine deep in the driveway. He fought through the mire of humanity without saying a word. Right now, they didn't want to hear what he had to say. Opening the door, he shut it fast behind him, almost taking off one reporter's hand. *Good!* Right now, they were a low form of humanity as far as he was concerned. "Ceelee! Ceelee! Honey, where are you?" He knew there was no chance she didn't know what was going on, it was everywhere. And he knew, also, that nothing could have happened that would hurt her more. This was her sensitive issue, and he would have cut off his right arm rather than have her experience one shred of doubt about how he felt about her. Hell! The people that were talking about her had never seen her, didn't know her, and hadn't taken the time to research their lives. They were just a pile of rabid dogs going after a story, uncaring of who they hurt in the process. "Ceelee!"

Rushing through the house, it fast became apparent

that she wasn't home. But, how had she got out without the school of piranhas in the front spotting her? The back! She had to have escaped through the back yard and through the neighbor's yard to the adjacent street. Looking hastily around, he searched for a note. Surely, she would have left him some hint at where she was going. Ah! He found it!

> *Bobby*
> *I love you. Don't think for one moment that I don't. This is so hard. I'm not running away this time because of a misunderstanding. This time I'm walking away because I understand only too well. I'll come back home when the feeding frenzy dies down, but until then, could you do something for me?*

> *Anything, baby*—until he read her impossible request.

> *Please explain to everyone that our situation is unusual. Yes, we do have a child together, and we are friends, but that you have no intention of tying yourself to 'the older woman.' Please assure them that I have always understood this and have made no demands. Perhaps, it would be better if we put some distance between us for a while. I would never, ever withhold Jaidon from you, so call me on my cell and I can arrange to meet you anywhere, anytime for you to take him for some 'Daddy time.' Again, I am so sorry for cluttering your world. You never understand how wrong something is until you see it through someone else's eyes.*

Ceelee

Damn! He wadded up the note and threw it across the room. Didn't she understand that she was everything to him? Looking out the window at what passed for Texas paparazzi, Bobby knew he could cheerfully wring every one of their necks and just tell God they died.

There was one thing for certain, he wasn't going to put up with this. He was going to get his family back if it was the last thing he ever did. After this, *Don't Mess With Texas* wouldn't be the battle cry, it would be *Don't Fuck with Bobby Stewart*.

As fast as a Texas tornado, Bobby set a plan in motion. He made statements. He insisted upon retractions. He told people to go fuck themselves and threatened Andrea within an inch of her life. The only reason he hadn't fired her was because he was making her clean up this mess. There would be no movie. He had paired down his public appearances to two a week and refused to be seen on the arm of another woman—for any reason. This was all his own fault, he should have made these changes immediately. But between the excitement of a winning season, the headiness of the media attention and the sponsorships he was still dealing with from the rodeo world, his life was mass havoc. But Ceelee and Jaidon had to be his priority. So, Bobby had been cleaning house.

Now, he had to get Ceelee to listen to him.

* * *

Cecile sat in the hotel room and rocked her crying baby. Jaidon knew something was wrong. He sensed her distress and he missed his daddy. She understood the sentiment. She missed him, too. Her cell phone continued to beep every few seconds and some of the calls had been from Bobby. She had let them go to voice-mail. It would hurt too much right at this moment to hear his voice.

Exhaustion made sitting up impossible, so she crawled under the covers and pulled Jaidon to her breast. Tonight, they would take comfort in one another.

The next day, she knew it was time to take his call. It was only right. He was Jaidon's dad and no matter what their relationship ended up being, that fact would not change. "Hello?"

"Oh, sugar. You're voice sounds so small. I just want to hold you tight and fight any bastard that threatens to come between us." Cecile hiccupped a muted sob. "Sweetheart? We've got to stop playing tag, baby. You've been crying, haven't you? Don't you know I can't sleep without you?"

"Yes, you can." She didn't say anything else, although she knew her silence would speak volumes.

"I don't want to live without you, Ceelee. You are my life, baby. I can't believe you and my baby wandered around the neighborhood in the dark. What if something had happened to you? How would I go on living?" Cecile knew he was pleading his case the best he knew how.

"Are the reporters gone?"

"Yes, they are. Haven't you been watching the news?"

Before she could hold it in, Cecile actually shuddered. "No, I haven't turned it on since I heard what Dallas Digs For The Truth had to say. They made me feel pretty worthless, Bobby."

"God, I could kill somebody. Listen to me, baby. I've taken care of everything. There will be no movie. I have made a lot of changes and all of them are geared to making you and Jaidon the center of my universe. Look, I've got to head to the stadium. I've got you tickets, season tickets by the way. Alex and Ethan are going to be there along with their blushing brides and there's a special family part of the game tonight. It wouldn't be the same if you and Jaidon weren't there for me. Please?"

"Can I be anonymous? I don't think I could stand it if I got singled out or anything." Ceelee wanted to see him, she wanted to be held, she was aching to be loved. She didn't know if that would ever happen again. But one thing was certain, she didn't want to be the brunt of jokes.

There was a long pause, as if he were thinking of just the right words. She almost asked him if something were wrong, but when he said, *Come on, baby. I'll take care of you*, that was all she needed to hear.

"All right. So, I'll be sitting with Annalise?" She felt safe with Annalise.

"Right in between Alex and Ethan if that will make you feel better. They'll beat the snot out of anyone that looks at you crooked."

"Okay. So you want me to bring Jaidon? Won't he get cold?"

"No, this time you'll be in one of the team family boxes. They have their own temperature controls."

"Okay, we'll be there. And Bobby?"

"Yes, sweetheart?"

"I love you. Despite everything, I love you. Everything will be all right, won't it?"

"Yes, baby. Everything is going to be just fine."

* * *

"I can't believe they're playing that song!" Annalise seemed tickled to death at how the massive, one hundred ten thousand strong crowd rose to their feet and cheered when Bobby ran on the field. Frankly, it made Ceelee nervous.

"Can I hold Jaidon?" Annalise looked at her with such hope, that Cecile knew she was thinking about her own inability to have children. As she handed him over, she knew she would have to make sure Jaidon spent many happy days with Bobby's family, it would benefit them all.

"Our boy has made something of himself, hasn't he?" Ethan spoke with pride. "Cecile, has Bobby ever talked to you about his childhood?"

She knew that Ethan was about to tell her something important. Cecile looked around to make sure no one else was listening. The last thing they needed was more family secrets being aired to the public. But there was no one near the Stewart family huddle. The men hovered protectively around them and their wives looked like poster girls for the well-loved woman's club. She was so glad to see Scarlet looking rosy cheeked and healthy and Annalise looked confident and content. If only she felt half as secure, she'd be happy.

"No, we've never gotten around to that topic of conversation," Cecile confessed.

"There's a reason for that," Alex pointed out. "Bobby was rescued from a terrible situation. He was abused and abandoned, beat up by his father and left to starve by his mother. When we got him, he lived in constant fear that we would decide we didn't want him. You've got to understand, that big man went through things that you and I can't even begin to imagine. We all have our deep-seated hidden fears and Bobby is no different. Even though he's as strong as an ox and would not hesitate to die for any one of us sitting here, he is a gentle soul and his one weakness is his fear that those he loves will turn their back on him and leave."

Cecile felt sick. She had done that. Oh, God forgive me, she thought.

Ethan stepped in, used to coming behind Alex and smoothing things over. "Cecile, we know you thought you overheard Bobby denying his love for you. So believe me, we don't blame you for what you did. But Bobby took it hard, harder than I've seen him take anything in years. And this mess with the press, that's just all foolishness."

Annalise put her hand on her brother in law's shoulder. "Cecile has been hurt, too. Her ex-husband abused her faith and her trust, almost crushed her sweet spirit. We've all been hurt." She put her arm around her sister. "Ethan, your ex-wife put you through hell, convinced you that you were lacking in the very qualities that make you a man." She put a hand to her own breast. "I was cruelly raped and scarred in such a way that I thought no one would ever love me again, and Scarlet suffered bullying and rejection, and spent years thinking her days were numbered." She looked from one to the other and then at Alex, and laughed. "Except you, bull-moose. You've always been cocky and confident."

Alex looked offended. "What are you talking about? I've suffered along with every one of you, and do you know why? Because I love you. I love you all. And I love Bobby, I don't ever want to see him or any of us hurt again."

Cecile knew it was her time to talk. "I love Bobby Stewart with every breath in my body." She took Jaidon from Annalise, he was beginning to get fussy and wanted some mommy time. "I can't be sure what the future holds for us, but I vow before all of you that I will never, ever willingly hurt him again." Her declaration seemed to ease Alex and Ethan's fears and when the kick-off started they were all glued to the action on the field.

Today, Dallas was playing the Eagles and the

Cowboys were favored to win, and Bobby Stewart was their go-to guy. He was fast and agile, yet big enough to plow through Philadelphia's defensive line like it was butter. During the first half, he scored two touch downs and Dallas was ahead by seven. Cecile and the whole family had yelled until they were hoarse. Half-time came and she was going to take an opportunity to sneak out and feed Jaidon. "Wait!" Alex grabbed her arm. "You can't leave."

"What?" She was confused. The baby wasn't fussing yet, but it wouldn't be long and she didn't want to risk missing any of the game. Besides, she had never been that into half-time shows. She knew Bobby wasn't tempted by the cheerleaders, but it didn't make her feel any better about watching them bump and grind.

About that time, she heard his voice. Turning, she looked down to see Bobby standing on the fifty yard line. He was looking up at the area where she was standing. The stadium was eerily quiet, everyone was watching him—and her. She looked up at the big screen and it was divided in half. One camera was centered on Bobby's sweet face and the other on her shocked one.

"Ceelee, sweetheart? I see you standing up there looking like a little angel." She blushed and she was afraid the cameras lens would be strong enough for everyone to see. "You can talk to me, baby. They've turned on a microphone up there."

Yee-gads, she thought. What was he up to? What the heck. "You're playing a good game, darling. I'm proud of you." He did say this was family time. Maybe everybody's loved ones were going to be introduced. She was just the unlucky one to go first.

Then, he got on one knee.

Oh, God.

"Ceelee Fairchild, you are the love of my life, the

most beautiful woman in the world, and the beloved mother of my precious son. Will you do me the honor of becoming my wife?" Someone handed him a ring box and he took a beautiful diamond out and held it up. The camera man zoomed in on it and the ring looked to be the size of a Volkswagen bus. "I think you're the most perfect woman in the whole world. I adore you. What do you say? Will you marry me?"

Oh, Lord. She had to go. "Here hold Jaidon, please. I have to go."

Ceelee left the family asking questions and appealing for her to come back and answer Bobby. But, accepting his proposal on camera was not the way she wanted to do it. She wanted to accept it face to face—in his arms, her lips on his—and she would do just that if she could find the right, damn exit. Running as hard as she could, Cecile made her way down from the private boxes to the stadium level floor.

* * *

Ethan, Alex, Scarlet and Annalise watched in disbelief as Cecile turned and ran out the door.

Bobby saw her leave.

The whole crowd saw her leave.

Millions of viewers at home saw her leave. All held their breath and suffered along with Bobby as they watched his face fall. The announcer stepped in and started, what he thought was talk to build the tension. "Ladies and gentleman—Bobby Stewart—in front of Dallas and the world has just asked his lady, Ceelee Fairchild, to be his wife. What has happened to her? Does anyone know where Ms. Fairchild has gone?"

Bobby's stomach sank. Maybe this wasn't such a good idea. She had told him she didn't want to be singled out, and here he had not only singled her out, but magnified their private business for the whole world to see. Everyone now knew how much he loved his woman. He just hoped she didn't kill him when he saw her again. Dejectedly, he bent his head and stared at the ground. How could he finish the game, now? He felt like he had been kicked in the stomach by an elephant.

"Wait, hold everything." The announcer's voice bellowed out of the loud speakers. "Nobody move. Everybody keep quiet. Bobby, this isn't over. I have reports that Miss Fairchild is about to give us an answer."

Yea, her answer will be no, Bobby thought. He had done some stupid things in his time, but this took the cake. Getting to his feet, he put the ring back in the box and started to walk away. Glancing up at the big screen he saw himself and knew that everyone there and on television could see the sorrow and devastation he was feeling. *Shit!* Then the screen cut to the player's field entrance. What was that he saw? He looked again. Everyone looked. Gasps of joy floated across the stadium. The announcer began to clap and one by one, all one hundred and ten thousand of the game attendees—Cowboy fans and Eagle fans, alike—all rose as one and began to clap and cheer. For what they saw was his little Ceelee, and she was running to him as hard as she could. Her arms were open wide and she was smiling. His angel was the most beautiful woman in the world.

He froze for just a second, watching her run to him. Then he wondered—*what in the hell am I doing standing here?* With a few long strides, he met her, swept her up in his arms and swung her around. She framed his face in her hands and kissed him, a hot, deep, sexy kiss that had the crowd going wild. He lifted her up, her feet weren't even touching the ground. She held up both arms and raised them to the heavens. "Yes, Bobby Stewart!" she shouted. "Yes, I'll marry you. I want to be your wife more than anything else in the whole wide world!"

* * *

Dallas won the game. Bobby made another touchdown and Ceelee sat on the sidelines with the players, except for the small break she took to feed her baby. Ethan had brought her Jaidon and a lot of the players took turns walking him around, far enough from the action so that he was safe and secure. As soon as the game whistle blew, Bobby came running to her, wrapped an arm around her neck and kissed her soundly. "I've been excused from the post-game meeting, let's go home. I want to make love to my fiancé."

Cecile wouldn't argue with that.

"I love you, Ceelee. You are my whole world." It seemed he couldn't say it enough.

"I love you, too." She looked at him, solemnly.

"Yea, how much?" He gave her his trade-mark, cocky grin.

"Biggern' Dallas." Ceelee grinned, knowing that those words would set his mind to rest. The age-old Texas saying, said it all. Ceelee loved him. She loved him *bigger than Dallas* and that was a whole helluva lot.

The bull-riding, Texas Cowboy was a happy man.

Enjoy a glimpse into some other Sable Hunter Books!

T-R-O-U-B-L-E

Trouble comes calling on Kyler Landon. He falls hard and fast for his beautiful, mysterious neighbor after she saves him from a rattlesnake attack. The sexual tension mounts between them with each sensual encounter, but he soon realizes that Cooper has been hurt and is leery of men. So he sets out to teach her that a real man can be gentle, loving, and sexy as hell.

Trouble seems to follow Cooper, and Ky makes it his mission to protect her from her past. Kyler would move heaven and earth to keep her in his bed and in his life.

Come With Me

Lacy spends her time planning events at a country club. Her latest and greatest project is the big Fourth of July celebration. Fireworks lighting up the sky – Red Hot and Boom! She loves the excitement and the spectacular display of sparkles and heat gives her a thrill. The only problem is... Lacy has never had any fireworks of her own. Despite having to listen to her friends tell of their sexual escapades, she has never experienced the big 'O'. According to the only man she's ever given herself to, Lacy is frigid. Is something wrong with her or has she just not met the right man for the job?

Jake is the manager of the golf course at the country club. He's designing and overseeing a building project and the sight of him shirtless and sweating and flexing...has given Lacy ideas. Jake has a certain reputation of being able to handle almost any task he's given. Rumors of his sexual prowess are legendary. Now, every time Lacy sees him working with his hands, doing some heavy lifting, his body gleaming with the sheen of exertion – she begins to hope that Jake can give her what no one else ever has.

Rogue

A loner by choice and a renegade by nature.

Rogue is living up to his name. He's lived life on his own terms, doing everything from team-roping in college, Texas Hold 'em champion to founding his own company, Lone Wolf Oil.

Everything he's accomplished has been in spite of Dusty Walker, a man who sired four sons by four women – none of them his wife. Rogue might be following in his father's footsteps, but he is nothing like his father.

And he never will be if he can help it.

When he flies to Kansas for the reading of Dusty's will, three brothers and a quarter interest in a half-billion dollar business aren't all he finds…Rogue feels like he's been hit by a tornado after he walks into a room and finds a woman in his bed. Not just any woman, either…

The last time he saw Kit Ross, she was racing off in her truck leaving him naked and hard by the side of the road. Of course, he deserved it; he'd hurt her. To say she wasn't happy to see him was an understatement. And when he wins her ranch with a good poker hand, the game is on.

It's not just poker that's being played. They can't keep their hands off one another. Rogue doesn't know if he has room in his life for family and love. He doesn't know if he can be trusted with people's hearts and happiness. What if he's more like Dusty Walker than he ever knew?

The Sons of Dusty Walker. Four brothers – one tainted legacy and a wild, wild ride.

A Breath of Heaven

Cade and Abby have a history. Years ago they were in love. Undeclared and unrequited, Cade waited until Abby was old enough for him to declare his love. Abby wanted nothing more than she wanted Cade. But something happened. Abby pushed Cade away and he never knew why. Since then, sparks fly when they're together. Antagonizing one another has become their favorite sport. The only problem is… it's all a front. They bicker because they both want the same thing – each other. A wedding brings them together and Cade is determined to learn Abby's secret. He'll do whatever it takes to win her love. Meet the King Family of El Camino Real – five brothers, one sister and a legacy as big as Texas.

Be My Love Song

Madeline needs a hero. She hires an architect, Weston, to save Windswept and an escort to convince her meddlesome sister she has a boyfriend. Unfortunately, she gets them confused. Weston, like most heroes, will save the day. What he's not expecting is to fall hopelessly in love.

True Love's Fire

While vacationing at a cabin in the Ozarks, Scott Walker - Austin neurobiologist, gets snowed-in and has to be rescued by local, Lia Houston. She brings him food, helps him fix his heat and tries to get his car on the road. A monster storm has paralyzed the mountain and as she's trying to chain his car to her truck, a huge ice-covered limb falls, crushing the front of her pick-up and almost flattening Scott. If she hadn't moved fast, he'd be a memory – but the brave action on her part comes with a price, she's injured and stuck with Mr. Know-It-All until the weather abates. Scott doesn't believe in love, much less love at First Sight. So when he meets Lia, he welcomes the attraction, but fights the tenderness with every breath in his body. Join Sable Hunter as she chronicles their journey from lust to love with a lot of fireworks in between. They meet at the dawn of the New Year, and by Valentine's Day the fires of True Love are burning bright.

**Content Warning: Contains explicit scenes, details and language. Intended for 18+ Audience

Texas Wildfire

'I Am My Brother's Keeper' are the words engraved on the plaque awarded to volunteer firefighter/rancher Titan Sloan. Daily he risks his life to save and protect friends and neighbors. When he finds out the person he loves the most is the one he's failed to protect, Titan is fit to be tied. Titan Sloan is a hero, but he's no angel. For years he's secretly been in love with his Captain's wife. When he finds out their marriage is a sham and Makenna is being abused, all hell breaks loose. A Texas Wildfire is the backdrop for a story so hot and a love so intense, no one will come through it unscathed.

Head Over Spurs

From the moment Tanner Barron laid eyes on Desiree Holt, he knew she was the only woman for him. His dream girl. The only problem – it was an impossible dream. Their paths crossed early on, before she became a country music star and before he had anything to offer her other than his adoration. One night, in a dark alley off 6th Street in Austin, Tanner rescues Desiree from two men who have her cornered, threatening her. She wants to thank him, but he disappears just before the police arrive. Desiree doesn't forget, even when she's offered a record deal and whisked off to Nashville, where she pens a song in his honor – White Knight.

A decade passes before they meet again. Fate brings them together just when they need one another the most. He's trying to find peace after a failed search and rescue mission and Desiree is seeking healing after another attack – this time by an over-zealous fan which has left her traumatized and unable to sleep.

Their time together begins at Christmas, but it doesn't end there. They find solace in one another, despite the things that could keep them apart. They're from two different worlds, she's famous, he's just a cowboy who would die for her. Tanner's not sure he's good enough, she's not sure she can satisfy him – after all he's a young, virile stud and she's almost a decade older than he is. Will distance, age, and fame keep them apart? Or will the fact that they're head over spurs in love with one another be enough?

Love Me, I Dare You!

Joshua Long, World Champion Cowboy, is known wide and far as the 'cowgirl whisperer'. His looks are fallen-angel handsome and his talents in the bedroom are legendary. Josh prides himself on being able to give a woman sheet-clawing, back-arching, toe-curling multiple orgasms. But at the peak of his career, Josh loses it all when his knee is shattered by a one-ton bull and his reputation is shredded by a scorned woman.

After investing blood, sweat, and years into the rodeo, he has lost his career and the lucrative sponsorships that went with it. Returning to his hometown of Kerrville, a place he hasn't always felt welcome, Josh is uncertain of the direction his life will take. But sometimes fate is kind and the lifeline that we need to hang onto our hopes and dreams appears just within our grasp. Josh has such a moment when he walks into Isaac McCoy's HARDBODIES bar. There, surrounded by old friends who offer him a second chance, Josh's gaze lands on a beautiful, blue-eyed redhead who draws him like a moth to a flame.

Emma Zachary has lived life on a dare. There is nothing she won't try, she grabs onto happiness with both hands, embracing every moment of joy she can find. Unwilling to accept the hand that life has dealt her, Emma refuses to let her blindness hold her back. She intends to make all of her dreams come true, especially the ones that include a certain cowboy who seems to always be there when she needs him. Emma longs to know what it's like to be loved, so she takes a dare and bids on a date with rodeo Romeo, Josh Long. What she discovers is that one night in Josh's arms will never be enough.

Josh is tired of his reputation. He wants to be more than his father's son; he wants to be more than just a buckle-bunnies fantasy man. Joshua wants a woman who sees him for who he really is, failures and all, and loves him anyway.

Emma is tired of being alone. She needs someone who will look beyond her faults and want her in spite of the challenge she faces.

Their journey together is filled with laughter, tears, danger, and sex hot enough to set the Hill Country of Texas on fire. Join Emma and Josh as they learn the true meaning of love.

I dare you.

Wolf Call

Rafe Kenyon is all man…and all wolf. He's a shifter and a Texas good ole boy. And who would have thought the two would mix? But, it works for him. The only problem is: Rafe is alone, he has no mate. He loves women, he loves sex, but he can never get too involved. No one can know his secret. Until...it is a secret no more.

Karoline Durand comes to town to study the wolf sightings in a place where no wolves are supposed to exist. She meets a sexy wolf of another sort when Rafe spots her in a club. Sparks fly as their sexual energy combusts like a volcanic explosion.

But soon Karoline is not the only one hunting the wolf. Rumors fly and the woods are full of hunters – all intent on bagging Rafe. His world is closing in on him and soon he learns who he can trust and the true meaning of love and home.

Love's Magic Spell

Tory has one magical night to learn what love is all about.

Night after lonely night, she tosses in her solitary bed, longing to touch and be touched, to experience desire and rapture. Her body aches to know fulfillment, to be taken and possessed by a man—but only one man will do.

Raylan West is the man of her dreams, and Tory Summers would give everything she owns for a chance with him. But it isn't going to happen—a man like him is not for her. Unless...Tory finds a way.

Deep in the bayous of South Louisiana there are secrets, magical secrets. Hoodoo. Witchcraft. Will-o'-the-wisp floating over dark waters, lit by unearthly light.

Desperate for a chance, Tory places her faith in the supernatural. She travels deep into the swamp to acquire a love potion promised to bring Raylan under her spell for one night, one perfect moonlit Halloween night where anything is possible. For a few precious hours, Tory will be beautiful, desirable, and sexy in Raylan's eyes.

The only problem is…Tory wants the magic to last forever.

MURDER, MAGIC, VOODOO, WITCHCRAFT, LOTS OF LOUISIANA ATMOSPHERE
And plenty of STEAMY, SENSUAL, SEXY LOVE!!

About the Author:

Sable Hunter is a New York Times, USA Today bestselling author of nearly 60 books in 9 series. She writes sexy contemporary stories full of emotion and suspense. Her focus is mainly cowboy and novels set in Louisiana with a hint of the supernatural. Sable writes what she likes to read and enjoys putting her fantasies on paper. Her books are emotional tales where the heroine is faced with challenges. Her aim is to write a story that will make you laugh, cry and swoon. If she can wring those emotions from a reader, she has done her job. Sable resides in Austin, Texas with her two dogs. Passionate about all animals, she has been known to charm creatures from a one ton bull to a family of raccoons. For fun, Sable haunts cemeteries and battlefields armed with night-vision cameras and digital recorders hunting proof that love survives beyond the grave. Welcome to her world of magic, alpha heroes, sexy cowboys and hot, steamy to-die-for sex. Step into the shoes of her heroines and escape to places where right prevails, love conquers all and holding out for a hero is not an impossible dream

.

Visit Sable:

SableHunter.com

Facebook

Amazon:

http://www.amazon.com/author/sablehunter

Pinterest

Twitter

Instagram

Sign up for Sable Hunter's newsletter

http://eepurl.com/qRvyn

SABLE'S BOOKS

Get hot and bothered!!!

Hell Yeah!

Cowboy Heat
Hot on Her Trail
Her Magic Touch
Brown Eyed Handsome Man
Badass
Burning Love
Forget Me Never
With Ryan O'Leary & Jess Hunter
I'll See You In My Dreams
With Ryan O'Leary
Finding Dandi
Skye Blue
I'll Remember You
True Love's Fire
Thunderbird
With Ryan O'Leary
Welcome To My World
How to Rope a McCoy
One Man's Treasure
With Ryan O'Leary
You Are Always on My Mind
If I Can Dream
Head over Spurs
The Key to Micah's Heart
With Ryan O'Leary
Love Me, I Dare you!
Because I Said So

(Crossover HELL YEAH!/Texas Heroes)
Ryder's Surrender
A Guide to the Hell Yeah! Kindle World
Love Found a Way: Hell Yeah!
Toro
With Ryan O'Leary
Texas Holdem
Dreamweaver
Lily's Mirage
Only Heaven Knows (Hell Yeah!)
Saxon's Conquest
A Helluva Man
Just a Love Story
Heaven's Loss

Hell Yeah! Heritage
Godsend

Hell Yeah! Sweeter Versions

Cowboy Heat
Hot on Her Trail
Her Magic Touch
Brown Eyed Handsome Man
Badass
Burning Love
Finding Dandi
Forget Me Never
I'll See You In My Dreams

Moon Magic Series
A Wishing Moon
Sweet Evangeline

Hill Country Heart Series
Unchained Melody
Scarlet Fever
Bobby Does Dallas

Dixie Dreaming
Come With Me
Pretty Face: A Red-Hot Cajun Nights Story

Texas Heat Series
T-R-O-U-B-L-E
My Aliyah
Spanish Eyes

El Camino Real Series
A Breath of Heaven
Loving Justice

Texas Heroes Series
Texas Wildfire
Texas CHAOS
Texas Lonestar
Texas Maverick
Because I Said So
(Crossover HELL YEAH!/Texas Heroes)

Cowboy Craze
She's Everything

Wild West Series
King's Fancy

The Sons of Dusty Walker

Rogue
Kit and Rogue

Other Titles from Sable Hunter:

For A Hero
Green With Envy (It's Just Sex Book 1)
with Ryan O'Leary
Hell Yeah! Box Set With Bonus Cookbook
Love's Magic Spell: A Red Hot Treats Story
Wolf Call
Cowboy 12 Pack: Twelve-Novel Boxed Set
Be My Love Song

Audio
Cowboy Heat - Sweeter Version: Hell Yeah! Sweeter Version
Hot on Her Trail - Sweeter Version: Hell Yeah! Sweeter Version, Book 2

Spanish Edition
Vaquero Ardiente (Cowboy Heat)

Su Rastro Caliente (Hot On Her Trail)